FURY

J. R. ANDREWS

For everyone who read *Famine*
and demanded to know what happens next

CHAPTER 1

A BEAD OF SWEAT SLID DOWN the small of Tom's back as he reached into the cooler beside his rocking chair. The slurry of ice and water shocked his hand, but he left it submerged for several seconds after grasping a bottle of beer. The Georgia weather in July seemed to have been made for lizards and scorpions. What else could possibly enjoy a sultry ninety-five degrees in the shade besides those things and maybe hell-born demons? Not that he believed in demons, but before the past year, he hadn't believed vampires were real either. Could be that the whole lot of folktale creatures were out there somewhere, demons and werewolves and witches too.

"Demons or not, Lady, it's still too hot around here for anyone to expect us to do anything useful."

The German shepherd lying beside his chair raised her head and eyed him for a few seconds as if expecting something more profound. When he added nothing, she went back to lying with her muzzle atop her crossed forepaws.

He chuckled as he wiped the water and ice off his newly acquired bottle of Budweiser, replaced the empty one in his "World's Greatest Lover" foam koozie, and twisted the cap. Before long, he would have to branch out from the King of Beers, which had been his preference for years. He'd already drunk just about every bottle he could find in a five-mile radius around the mansion property Emily was using as the Chalet, her home and base of operations. She liked to switch them up often—they were living in the fourth such house since he'd returned with her group from Cincinnati—but the current one had a special feature. The porch he sat on belonged to the servant's house, a small structure about a hundred and fifty yards from the main house, where Emily and her vampire Family lived.

That distance had distinct advantages, both for him and for Emily. Last fall, when he'd first started living among the vampires in Atlanta, there had been incidents. Emily, the oldest known vampire and the matriarch of her Family, had sworn to keep Tom safe after he'd helped deal with a challenge to her authority from a rival one. He was the last man alive after humanity had been decimated by Charon, the deadly plague, and hunger was an increasing problem for the vamps. Even Emily's stern methods of controlling her sworn followers weren't always effective when a hungry blood-eater happened to come across a warm-blooded human. The last such incident had prompted the move to the current location two days after, and there hadn't been any sign of another move since.

He took a long pull from his beer and rocked back as the sun finally disappeared fully behind the tree line in the distance. For the fourth or fifth time in the last week, he considered the field in front of the servant's house. It was plenty big enough to grow something. How much trouble could it be to grow some barley? The beers he'd been finding weren't going to get any fresher, regardless of the brand. He could probably figure out how to brew more, right?

"You on your fourth beer by now or fifth? Smells like maybe five. And with the sun just now setting. Sugar, you keep this up, you won't need protection from no one because your blood's gonna be too pickled for any of us to want to drink it."

He turned his head to scowl at Lindsey, who stood in the doorway to the house. She must have just risen from her daytime Rest. Some days she rose earlier, but more and more lately, she'd been rising only as the sun was setting or after it was little more than a glow on the horizon.

"That doesn't sound like too bad a plan, Linds, all things considered. Does that mean, if I keep getting drunk, you'll stop threatening to drain me every other day?"

She pulled her auburn hair back into a ponytail and grinned. "Oh, no. Not me. Any day now, I'm gonna get tired of putting up with you and have myself a nice meal, even if it is strongly laced with beechwood aging. I'm never giving up my claim to you."

Her claim was something he'd learned came with being a vampire in Emily's Family. He'd come to Atlanta from Cincinnati, looking for a way to stay alive when one of Emily's rivals, Colin, had planned to make a move on the territory to the north. It was controlled by a third vampire Family led by one named Alexander. Colin had sent one of his own, Ana, to find a living human to use as leverage among the other clans.

Without Tom, though, Colin couldn't leverage total

control over Alexander's land, so Colin sent someone south to get him back. Tom found Lindsey first, though, and she begrudgingly took him to meet Emily. Before all was said and done, the fight between Alexander and Colin had settled in a fragile peace, and Emily had offered Tom her protection.

He never was completely sure whether that vow of protection extended beyond Lindsey's claim, but the two had become, well, something more than friendly since Linds first surprised him in that Walmart. He must have grown on her a little. Being honest, he had to admit that whatever it was between them, it was pretty mutual. Hard to imagine she would really do anything to hurt him.

"Yeah, yeah. I'm sure you'll kill me tomorrow."

At the sarcastic threat, Lady popped up from the floor and stretched. She then padded over to Lindsey in the doorway, who raised an eyebrow. Lady sniffed the air around her then the palm of one hand before shaking herself out and trotting into the field. Apparently, she had some business to attend to and trusted that particular vampire enough to leave her alone with Tom. Lindsey was lucky to be one of only two who had been granted such an honor. The other, of course, was Ana.

"Coming with me tonight, Tommy, or planning to sit here until you burn out your liver?"

"I figured you probably have a good enough handle on Emily's business without me. At least this once. Anything interesting going on?"

"She's supposed to have gotten some scouting info about what's been going on up north with Alexander and Colin. Or hell, could be between Colin and that Lars guy.

I can't keep track. If any of it matters, or if she gets a notion that Colin is working up to grander schemes again, I might have to go north and check things out myself."

"As fun as your security briefing sounds, I'd hate to waste this perfectly good cooler full of ice and beer. Heading over to the house, then?"

Lindsey shook her head. "Not just yet. Emily has a few things to go over before she wants to meet with me. I've got some time to get ready."

Tom nodded. "You could have a beer with me while you wait."

"Maybe later, hon. I just rose, and I'm still wearing yesterday's clothes. Nobody wants to meet with Lady Emily in a pair of dirty pants. Save me one."

"I'll try, but I'm not making any promises. If your meeting goes too long, we might need to go on a beer run."

Lindsey chuckled. "You really are a worthless bag of meat. Why do I keep you around?"

He raised the bottle to her. "My quick wit and understated charm, obviously."

She smirked and looked out at Lady, who snapped at a firefly among a crop of weeds. "Would you do something with him, already, Lady? He's a mess."

The shepherd ignored her.

"See? She's on my side."

"There's no arguing that, Tommy Boy. Try not to pass out before I get back."

He gave her a thumbs-up and took another sip of beer as she disappeared inside to get ready.

In the distance, Lady jumped, snapping again at a

firefly but apparently missing it. She spent ten minutes or so just about every night trying to catch lightning bugs out of the air, never with any luck, but that didn't stop her from trying again. Hard not to admire her tenacity. And while it might be a pointless exercise, at least it was entertaining. Tom, on the other hand, had little to do but sleep, sit on the porch, and drink beer. He would have to find some kind of hobby soon, or he would turn into pudding in his rocking chair long before winter arrived. Maybe if he…

Something heavy slammed into his right side, and the world spun sideways. A blossom of color and light like a Fourth of July sky flower filled his vision as a stinging explosion of pain radiated from his left shoulder. Somewhere far away, a dog barked, clearing his head. He was laid out on the porch decking, having landed on his side. Something—no, someone—lay on top of his right side, pinning him down. He couldn't turn his head enough to get a good look, but he caught a glimpse of shaggy brown hair. The smell of raw meat filled his nose.

"Relax," the attacker whispered. "You don't want to fight me. Just let it happen. You'll feel so much better in a second."

Pain, like being stung by wasps, shot through the right side of his neck, and he cried out. It faded as quickly as it came, though, like getting a vaccine. It was wrong. Bad wrong. He had to get whoever it was off of him. But that seemed impossible.

And why did he even want that, really? A cozy warmth spread through him. Wouldn't it be better just to relax, like the guy said? A nap, honestly, was starting to sound great. Definitely, just let the sleep come.

Another sharp bark startled him, and Tom's eyes flashed open in time to see Lady leap from the ground onto the porch. The weight that had been on top of him shifted away, and he rolled forward, away from the attacker.

He staggered to his feet, bringing a hand to a dull ache on the side of his neck. It came away crimson. "What the hell?"

The vampire shoved Lady away, and she rolled a few feet across the porch to Tom's right.

The monster stood, teeth coated in slick blood. Ruby lips curled upward. "Oh no, we're not done yet. I'll drain you both."

The dog, growling, stepped between him and the attacker while Tom crouched low. "I've killed scarier things than you, asshole. Let's see what you've got."

The vampire shot forward and was met with Lady's flashing jaws. She clamped down on his forearm and pulled. He growled back at her but didn't stop. An anvil of cold fear filled Tom's stomach, but he reached out with his right hand. God, he'd almost forgotten how fast they were.

A frenzy of vampire and German shepherd entered his circle of reach, and he swung upward with gritted teeth. The beer bottle he'd picked up smashed into the vampire's jaw with a satisfying crunch. The assailant staggered backward then to the side as Lady yanked hard on the arm still held in her jaws.

Twisting to his right and stepping forward, Tom

swung the bottle again, slamming it into the vampire's temple. It was a miracle the thing didn't shatter. They must not really do that, despite what he'd seen in movies.

Lady released her grip, and the attacker teetered to Tom's left before collapsing on the floor. Tom took as many steps backward as he could before hitting the porch railing behind him.

In a blink, the vampire was back on its feet, feeling the spot at its temple where the bottle had landed. "I didn't figure you for such a fighter. Thought you'd be easy prey, seeing how you're Lindsey's little pet."

"I'm not Lindsey's anything, asshole."

"That's not how I see it, pet. But I'm impressed. You've got a little more steel in you than the lapdog I took you for."

"Come at me again, and I'll show you a lapdog."

The words weren't out of his mouth before the vampire flashed forward, faster than he could react. He tried to bring the bottle back around, but the vamp caught his arm then crashed into his chest. Lady sprang on the vampire again, but he kicked her away, hard.

"I don't care if you relax now or not, pet," he hissed. "Just hold still for a second."

With his right arm pinned to his side, Tom attempted to swing his left, but with so much pain in his shoulder, all he could muster was a weak wave. Panic buzzing in his ears, Tom reared his head back then squeezed his eyes shut, intending to headbutt the vampire as it leaned in to feed again. He missed and collapsed forward as the force holding him against the rail disappeared.

Tom groaned in response to the pain shooting

through his arm as he landed on all fours. He looked up to find Lindsey restraining the vampire in a choke hold from behind, her face a furnace of rage. Her captive, eyes wide in alarm, slapped her forearm and bucked against her.

"Stop fighting, or I'll end you right here," she growled.

He croaked in reply and slammed his head into her face. Her head whipped backward, but she held firm.

Lindsey's mouth twisted into a grimace, and for the first time in months, Tom saw her vampire teeth, and her eyes changed. She shifted her grip, taking his head in opposite hands. With a grunt and a sharp twist followed by a half dozen pops and cracks, Tom's attacker dropped to the floor in a heap, neck twisted in such a way that, had he still been alive, he'd have been looking almost backward.

Sagging against the railing, Tom groaned. The wound on the side of his neck was ragged, not quite gushing blood. He pressed his hand to it but couldn't apply the pressure he wanted. The world turned gray around the edges, and everything in his vision swung like a pendulum.

"I don't… think. Something's not…" He looked at Lindsey but couldn't be sure she was still there. "Not right." Strong hands lifted him, cradling him like a child. His head lolled to one side. A soft "Linds?" was the best he could muster.

"I've got you, sugar. Just hang in there."

Everything bounced several times, with each down ending in a jarring thud. Then he heard footsteps on something hard and a pair of loud bangs.

"Everyone, out!" someone shouted.

That had to be Lindsey again, right?

Before another odd thought could cross his mind, Tom was placed on something soft. The fabric was hot, a pleasant sensation compared to how cold everything had become. He shouldn't be cold, should he? Wasn't it just summer? Someone pressed something even softer to the place on his neck where everything felt wrong.

"What happened?" someone asked from somewhere to his left.

He knew that voice, too, but couldn't place it.

"Nelson told me to hurry to Emily's with med… oh God, Tom!"

"I think he's dying, Ana. Can you save him?"

"What the hell happened?"

"Later." A third voice. More firm. "What do you need?"

"O positive. What can you spare?"

"Precious little. You can have some from my personal supply."

"My lady!" the first person exclaimed.

"Be shocked later, Lindsey. If we try to spare it now, no amount is going to help." Something sharp pinched the skin on his arm, then a line of warmth traced up his shoulder. The voices went quiet.

CHAPTER 2

Tom's eyelids fluttered then squeezed tight before slowly opening. His eyes, unfocused, looked past Ana's shoulder before shifting to her face and sharpening to match her gaze. Ana exhaled, barely believing he was coming back around.

"Ana," he croaked, lying on his right side on the couch in Emily's office.

Emily and Lindsey stood behind her, both in front of the lady's ornate wooden desk.

"Hold still. I am nearly finished. How do you feel?" She pressed gauze against the side of his neck and secured it with tape.

Before he could answer, a wet nose pressed close to his face and gave his own a quick flick of the tongue. The man gave the dog half a smile, and Ana's panic melted away, replaced with a tenuous sense of relief.

"Good girl," he said. Then, "My neck hurts like a sonuvabitch, and I've got a worse headache than the last time I woke up looking at you. God, I'm thirsty too."

"Nelson," Emily called in a self-assured voice, "a taste of water, if you would."

To Ana's left, Emily's aide, Nelson, muttered to himself before stepping over to the bar cart at the side of the room. After a few shuffled steps, he handed Ana a tumbler.

"I'm finished for now," Ana said. "You're going to be weak, but can you sit up?"

He tried to lever himself upward, but a shock of pain twisted his face, and he forced air through his gritted teeth with a hiss. "My shoulder. I landed on it when I was attacked."

In half a breath, Lindsey stood next to them, helping raise him into a sitting position on the couch.

Ana lifted the water to his lips. "Don't gulp."

He took a conservative sip then a second before a third, more normal drink. "That's good." He glanced to Ana's right at the couch, frowning at a wide blood-tinted spot covering the cushion where he just lay. "I'm sorry, Emily. Looks like I ruined your, um, furniture thing here."

"If my couch is the only thing ruined from this episode, Thomas, I'll count us all lucky."

"What happened?" He lifted his fingers to the bandage she'd just placed and winced.

She knew that even with the dressing, it would still be raw to the touch.

"Mathias was a dumbass with no self-control," Lindsey huffed. "And now he's dead because of it."

"That was his name?" Tom asked. "Mathias?"

"Yes. He'd always been a bit of a rascal," Emily added, "but I never would have suspected this sort of thing from him. Not to defy me so openly."

Ana tried not to huff audibly. Tom had almost been killed, yet Emily was marveling at the idea that one of her

Family might be a bit defiant. No one at the Chalet truly valued him as anything more than a bargaining chip at best. Some only saw him as meat. The idiot needed to be more careful.

Lady nudged his left hand with her muzzle and hung her head, tail between her legs.

He slowly patted her on the head. "Don't be like that, girl. This was my fault."

Lindsey clucked her tongue. "I don't want to hear your bellyaching, Tommy Boy. This was Mathias's fault. Not yours."

"No, Linds, listen…"

"You should have been spending more time with me in the lab," Ana cut in. "No one ever bothers me there."

Behind him, Lindsey's face went to stone. "Oh, sweetheart, you had best not be saying I can't keep him safe."

Ana fixed her dark eyes on Lindsey like gun barrels. Glaring, she opened her mouth to reply, but Emily cut them both off.

"Enough. The fix we're in is bad enough without squabbling. How is he, really?"

"I'm, uh, fine," Tom muttered.

"He's not fine," Ana replied. "He lost quite a bit of blood and could use another transfusion. If that's not possible, he'll need fluids and time to recover before he can act independently around here again."

"I'm not sure I was ever indiscreet around here." Tom frowned. "No, wait. I mean independent. What you said."

Ana pushed the tumbler back to his mouth. "See? Confusion or altered mental state is a sign of significant blood loss. He will need to be watched." She turned to Emily behind her.

The elder vampire circled her desk and settled into an ornate leather wingback chair. She narrowed her eyes and picked up a capped fountain pen then began flipping it end over end, tapping the desktop with each cycle. "I am vexed that maybe his safety isn't as sure around here as I figured. How long will he need?"

"Until he is fully recovered, and assuming we have no more blood to give him? It could be as little as a few days or as many as, say, two weeks. Every individual is different. In my previous experience with him, though, he seems to heal quickly."

"Would you all stop talking about me? I'm right here."

Emily clucked, yet somehow, she even did that with her customary genteel Southern accent. "You may be with us, Thomas. But bless your heart, only a fool would fail to see that you owe your life to Lindsey's fast action with Mathias and Ana dropping everything to rush here the moment I sent for her. If either of them had not been so quick to act, the results here would have been very different. And I'm afraid that means things will need to change around here."

Touching the bandage on his neck again, Tom frowned. "Wait. Does that mean I'm going to become a... well, like you?"

Lindsey barked a laugh. "That's not how it works. You can become a werewolf from a single bite, but it's a heap more of a process for us, sugar."

He blinked hard. "A werewolf?"

Shaking her head, Ana sighed. "Werewolves do not exist, Tom. They're just legends. Don't be ridiculous."

"Yes, daughter, the man's been through the wringer today. Let's not fill his already dazed head with children's ideas about fantasy monsters."

"Not too long back, I thought we were fantasy monsters, and that's saying nothing of the Feral." Lindsey shrugged. "How would I know what is or isn't out there?"

"Yeah. What she said," Tom agreed.

Ana shook her head. Trying to keep everyone focused on the matter at hand, the things that were crucial right now made her want to pull out her hair. Being the youngest vampire among them, she assumed it was easier for her to limit her thinking to the short term because she only had a handful of years of experience at being immortal. Unlike Emily, who was rumored to be well over two hundred years old, and sometimes older, Ana didn't have the memories of a second life to stack up in a long road stretching back to easier days with an abundance of regular people to feed them. In fact, Ana had never been a vampire in a time when there were plenty of humans. Her Maker, Colin, had Turned her just as Charon was beginning to ravage its way across North America.

Of all the miserable parts of the second life she'd never wanted, at least there was that. She'd never fed on a human, hadn't really had much opportunity to do so in her short time as a vampire, and never wanted to if she could help it. Keeping that thought in mind every single day went a long way toward focusing her attention on the tasks immediately at hand.

For vampires like Lindsey and Emily, though, tomorrow was just as likely to become twenty years in the blink of an eye. Not that framing one's worldview into the long term was a bad thing by itself. But Emily might see a copse of trees on fire and wonder first about the effect it would have on the forest around it and how much effort would be needed to limit the damage the small fire might have on the whole. If Ana saw fire, on the other hand, all she would think about was how to put it out.

And their world was very much on fire.

"Can we possibly postpone the discussion about the existence of fairy-tale monsters for now?" Ana fumed. "Unless someone knows of a werewolf or a witch we need to be concerned about? Otherwise, our biggest concern at the moment would appear to be keeping our most valuable asset alive while surrounded by things that want to kill him."

"Who's a witch now?" Tom muttered.

Emily's tapping pen stopped. "I would hold my tongue if I were you, miss. You may be useful, but I have not lived through centuries of idiots just to allow myself to be snipped at by children with poor manners. Remember that I can return you to your Master at any time."

Before she was Made, Ana would have colored brightly at a rebuke like that, half in humiliation at being called out and half in anger, ready to challenge her accuser. She still felt those things in equal measure, but it was nice not to have that heat rush to her face, giving away her feelings.

In her case, it was hard to decide whether to show objection or deference to Emily. She needed time and space to work on solving the larger food problem for all their kind, and the last thing she wanted was to be sent back to Colin, her Master and Maker, who had begrudgingly agreed to let her stay with Emily after his failed attempt to take over Alexander's territory last fall. But that woman could test the patience of a saint, and Ana was surely not one of those.

Pissing off everyone in the room wouldn't be productive, though, and the thought of having to go back to Colin after everything he'd done made her want to throw up. Deference, then.

"I'm sorry, lady. I'm just very concerned. My worries make me speak out more strongly than I should sometimes."

"We all understand your worry, girl. Believe it or not, your human has grown on me since he boldly—perhaps even foolishly—walked into my territory with little more than hope. He has been of more use to me than he ever would have been as a meal, and I swore to protect him to return the favor. I have not and will not forget that promise. But I am beginning to wonder if keeping him here, close to the Family, is the best method of protecting him."

Ana frowned. If Emily was thinking of sending him away, it could cost Ana research time. She'd been a doctor once, and a researcher, and had been tasked first by Colin then Emily to find some way to reduce or prevent the vampire's reliance on live blood feeding to sustain them. In a world where Tom was the only human left, the opportunities he provided Ana for continued research outweighed his value as a food source ten times over. Which, of course, was half the reason Emily had been letting him stay among them, even with the incidents.

"Lady, what are you thinking?" Lindsey asked before

Ana could. Her face was puckered in disappointment like a child who'd been told she couldn't have candy until after dinner.

The pen tapping resumed. "You all very well know this is not the first time Tom has been attacked since he came here, though it is clearly the worst. As it came so long after the last one, I had hoped the Family had settled and his presence among us had become familiar. Clearly, that must not be the case. The temptation of warm blood waiting here for the taking must just be too great for some of them to control. If this continues, it will never be safe for him here."

"I agree, it won't ever be safe here," a man said from the doorway. "Colin has agents among you."

CHAPTER 3

E MILY STOOD BEHIND HER DESK and floated to the man in the doorway, greeting him with a quick embrace and alternate pecks on each of his cheeks. "Lars, dear, aren't you a sight for sore eyes!"

Lars, as rugged as ever with a collarless button-topped waffle-weave shirt, returned Emily's greeting. "Lady Emily, always good to see you."

"The feeling is entirely mutual, dear. Please, come sit. Nelson, did you offer him a refreshment? Why did you not tell me we had guests?" Her eyes floated to the crimson stain on the couch cushion, and she tsked. "We surely could have gotten the place a little more prepared for company."

"Don't go making a big deal, Emily," Lars replied before Nelson had a chance. "Here I show up unannounced and, by the looks of things"—he glanced at the couch then Tom's neck—"maybe not at the best time." Turning to Tom, he added, "Looks like you had a close one there, Meat. You still handling yourself all right?"

Lars had done Ana a huge favor last year by finding Tom with Emily at the Chalet before Colin's headhunter, Ash, caught up with him. For that, she would always be grateful. But she couldn't help wincing at his arrogance. From the corner of her eye, she saw Lindsey bristle as well, but before either she or Ana could reply, the confused glaze over Tom's eyes faded, and his face went stone-cold.

"Some bastard thought I'd be easy pickings. He tore the hell out of my neck and busted up my shoulder before I saw him coming. But he couldn't quite finish the job in one go, and you know I'm too dumb to go down without a fight. So I ruined his jaw with a beer bottle and smashed it against his forehead to teach him a lesson. I was thinking that even with one working arm, I could likely come to an understanding with the guy before too much longer. But Lindsey got there, and she just isn't quite as forgiving as I am, so she separated the idiot's head from his spine." Tom paused, took a breath, and flashed a wolfish grin, staring a challenge back at Lars. "Pity too. I still had half a beer bottle to put somewhere in that asshole."

For several moments, Lars returned the stare, features just as set and solid at Tom's. Ana tensed and inhaled sharply. No one moved.

Finally, a wide grin spread over Lars's face, and he laughed out loud. "Same old Meat, eh, boy? Good to see you in one piece. Well, kind of."

Sinking back against the cushions, Tom relaxed, his hand once again covering the bandage over his neck. "This day gets any better, and I'll start wanting to be in a coma again."

Taking the opportunity to change the subject, Emily returned to the chair behind her desk. "What brings you with such dire warnings about spies among us, son? Last I heard, you were still busy searching for Alexander."

"Not quite, lady." Lars sank into another wingback chair next to the bloodied couch. "That's the story we've let get out, but Alexander found me not long after the big fight you joined us for. We've been keeping it quiet, though, with Colin still making trouble."

"Well, sir"—Emily shot an uncertain glance at Lindsey—"you could knock me over with a feather. I would have thought I'd have heard some whisper of news like that here or there. Especially after this number of months."

"Believe me, lady, we'd have let it slip so one of you little birdies in the world might have figured it out, but doing that would have meant Colin would find out too. Seems Alexander has some scheme where it's crucial that no one knows what's happening. So, we've been guarding that secret like it's everything."

"What's Colin been up to, then, that has you so spooked?"

"He hasn't made any direct moves against us yet, but he's up to something. He wants our territory, and I'd bet he'll do just about anything to get it."

Ana rolled her eyes. They had no idea what Colin really wanted. Even she, who had lived with him in her head in varying degrees for years, didn't fully know what he wanted. Pressed to guess, she might suggest that his ambition had no real bounds.

"He wants more than just your territory," she said. "He wants control. Of everything."

Emily's eye rolling matched Ana's. "That's an awful big bite to take, girl. One too big for even your Maker to swallow, I'd reckon. And just how does he figure he's going to gain himself the whole kit n' caboodle?"

"You know I can't say much directly against him, lady. He Made me. But as you're already aware, my work was part of it. He believes that by finding a way to synthesize food, he might steal enough followers from all of you to challenge anyone."

Emily tapped the pen on the desk once more.

"I don't know about any of that, but I wouldn't put it past him," Lars said. "Especially with what we found recently. He's been operating in your territory, Emily, just across the Ohio River, in the northern parts of Kentucky. He stays there because Alexander isn't keen on crossing the river and forcing you to have to get involved."

"That's ballsy, dude, even for him." Lindsey crossed her arms. "But it don't exactly seem like something you found out recently."

"Never slipping one past you, am I, Lindsey? No, you're right. That's not the recent news. What we did just find out is that today's attack on Tom here wasn't just some hungry idiot who couldn't control himself anymore. Colin got him to do it."

"Bullshit," Lindsey spat.

At the same time, Emily muttered, "I declare."

Ana narrowed her eyes, watching Lars for any sign he was misleading them. He seemed plenty calm and self-assured.

"It's true," he countered, "as much as I'd like to say I just made it up. I headed south as soon as I heard the news, hoping to get here before the attack, as we didn't know exactly when it would happen." He shifted his focus to Tom. "I'm sorry, Meat. I tried to get here for you. Believe it or not, I do appreciate what you did for us last fall. You don't know how glad I was to find you still alive."

"I'm not sure I am." Tom closed his eyes, and his whole body went slack.

Ana might have been concerned, but she and everyone else in the room could hear Tom's heart thrumming in his chest. Beating too fast to be sure, but that was to be expected with such blood loss.

Emily once again stopped tapping. "If you're not actually pulling our legs, son, that puts us in quite a pickle, now, doesn't it? And I thought we had enough trouble brewing already."

"Yeah, we've got trouble, and it all starts with her." Lindsey stabbed a finger in Ana's direction.

Ana shook her head. Incredible. Did the woman ever stop to think about anything? Hard to believe she'd gotten so far in her second life when "hit first and ask questions later"—if at all—was her default mode of operation. "You have got to be kidding me. You think any of this is because of me?"

"I'm serious as a heart attack, baby girl. Only one person in the compound has a link to Colin, and I'm looking right at her."

"I sent Tom to you last year, when Colin had him in his grasp. That's not something anyone would have done if they wanted my psychopath of a Maker to be successful. You should consider using that head for something besides attracting eyes or starting fights. Some of us use ours to think from time to time."

Pushing away from the desk, Lindsey curled the hand

that had been pointing at Ana into a fist. "Say something else, nerd. And we'll see how good you can do your job without those beady black eyes of yours glaring at everyone."

Smirking, Lars shifted forward, likely to put himself between the two women. He needn't have bothered.

"That will quite do, Daughter," Emily hissed. "Too much blood has been spilled in here already today."

Lindsey froze, gave Ana one more accusing look, then settled back against the desk, recrossing her arms.

"Now, then, if we can all be grown-ups for a few minutes?" Emily continued. "Ana, I do not believe you have or would intentionally bring us trouble, but Lindsey is not wrong. You bear the burden of having a connection to Colin that will never go away, no matter how much you try to ignore it or push it to the back of your head. So, that will always be a spot to worry over."

"I've been careful. And he cannot hear what I hear, right?"

"No, but he can see what you see, or have seen. Can you promise me you haven't given away something by accident? Perhaps you were deep in your work and forgot to guard what you could see? Could he possibly know how close you've come?"

"I..." Ana scraped at the cuticle around her thumbnail. It would have been nice to be certain about what Colin knew or didn't know, to understand what he was really up to, but she had to admit Emily had a point. The lady herself didn't know how far Ana had progressed in her work. But then, she also didn't know that Ana spent most of her time working on something other than what

Emily believed. Ana was close to breakthroughs on both her science projects, but the blood solution was not the one that drove her to near exhaustion every day.

That aside, could her link to Colin possibly give him some advantage here? Hard to see how it might be, but she couldn't assume the answer was no. "I don't know. But what could he have learned from me that would make it worthwhile to attempt disrupting your Family? Surely that would force you to come for him."

The pen tapping resumed as Emily stared off into the distance. Whether she was lost in thought or communicating with one of her other Descended vampires, Ana couldn't guess. Ana flashed a glance at Lindsey, who shrugged in return.

That lost expression vanished. "I suppose that's the case, but we don't know what we don't know, and I'm about done playing guessing games. It's high time we start getting some answers."

Lindsey flashed her teeth in a hungry grin. "Let me go north for a few days. I'll shake some answers loose. I'm tired of feeling all cooped up anyway. Wait, but…Tom?"

He still lay back on the couch, half sitting, half reclining, relaxed. By all indications, sleeping.

"We've said nothing since Lars walked in that has changed my mind about the fact that he isn't safe here anymore. In fact, you've reinforced the notion. If Colin believes he can get to Tom or get to us using him, well, that's an open gate any old horse can trot through. It's got to be closed and latched. Can he travel, girl?"

"As I said earlier, lady, he needs rest and blood if possible. Both would be good. He will be weaker than normal for a few days at least, which could be a problem beyond the confines of your compound, where more of us will be looking to do him harm, let alone the plaguers. And I need to x-ray his shoulder. He likely won't be swinging that bat of his for weeks. It's not a great time for him to travel, no."

"He can come with me," Lindsey said. "I'll keep an eye on him while I'm snooping on Colin."

Emily's response was flat and certain. "No."

"But, my lady."

"No. You can't do two things at once, Daughter. Surely not while doing either of them well. And this will be complicated. Whatever Colin is up to, he won't want you in the middle of it. Do we even know how many of his own he has in the area by now? Last year, there were maybe two dozen."

"I'm sorry," Ana replied. "I have no way to tell."

Lars was more helpful. "We know he has brought in more since his arrival, but we don't know how many. My last guess would have been fifty additional, give or take, but it could be many more than that by now. And I hear rumors that he's rounding up Feral."

"See, daughter? You'll need to have your wits about you at all times. But it's just as well. Tom has no better caretaker than you, Ana. And while I hate to say it, I can't let you stay here anymore either way. You still have my protection, but you can't have it here. Take your work and Tom, and go with Lindsey. Help her in any way you can, but your first duty is keeping Tom safe and getting us a solution."

Pursing her lips, Ana wanted to argue, but she didn't

have a leg to stand on. It was a hard pill to swallow, knowing that being cast away was mostly due to her loyalty being questioned. At least she would still be with Tom. Well, assuming she and Lindsey didn't kill each other. "I understand, Lady Emily."

"Good. When will you be able to go? It's likely too late tonight because the sun would be peaking before you get to Cincinnati. But we can't dawdle. Is tomorrow possible?"

"Do we have blood to give him?"

"Nelson," Emily called toward the door.

"Yes, lady."

"Please fetch another unit of O positive."

Her assistant paused for half a second, so short as to just be perceptible but still long enough to register the subtlest disapproval. "Indeed, lady."

"Don't give me any of that, you old goat." Emily chuckled. "Lars will need a room also. Oh, and please make arrangements to have this couch replaced. And burned."

"I thought you'd never ask."

"Good. Now, let's get Tom somewhere comfortable and safe until nightfall."

As if answering to his name, Tom snuffled and woke, blinking as he took in everything around him. Eyes settling on Lars, he screwed up his face in confusion. "What is he doing here?"

CHAPTER 4

TOM SHUFFLED DOWN THE HALLWAY toward the front door with Lady padding alongside as the last golden gleam of sunlight slipped behind a line of trees he could see through a window. The dressing on his neck itched worse than the skin under the cast he'd gotten when he'd broken his wrist in sixth grade, and it was likely to get worse before it got better. Ana had given him some kind of cream to put on it, but unless someone had put it in his travel bag, he'd lost it already.

Each step was more work than it ought to be just to make his way down a hallway. It was like walking underwater in a swimming pool—not impossible but not super effective either. On the plus side, his shoulder felt better already. She'd given him a shot or two of something that had taken away the feeling that he was carrying around a dead limb and had him swallowing some pills every few hours that ground the edge off the pain. Every now and then, he slid the arm out of its sling and stretched it to see how far he could reach. He wouldn't be swinging his bat like a major leaguer in the next day or so, but he had some hope it might be back to normal in a week or so, maybe.

"How do you feel?" As if thinking of Ana had made

her appear, Tom found her and Lindsey sitting in the living room, to his left. And to his surprise, they weren't snarling at each other. Those two had gotten under each other's skin since the first moment they spent together. He dared to hope that they would figure out a way to get along, or he was going to lose his mind while they were on the road for however long their little adventure took. And based on what he'd gotten from them after leaving Emily's office, it might take some real time. Weeks if not months, and even after, they might not be allowed to return to the compound.

What he'd never wanted to admit to himself was that he didn't belong there in the first place. Didn't belong anywhere, really. He was the last man standing in a world where being man made a person prey.

"I feel like I'm getting evicted a day after some asshole chewed a hole in my neck."

"Tom, look, it's not that…" Lindsey began.

He waved off the comment. "I know. I know. Nobody wants this. It's just how things are with the way the world is today. I get it. At least I'll have a chance to screw with Colin and Alexander. The thought of messing up their plans never gets old." He paused, leaning against the doorframe separating the room from the hall. "Somebody packed my stuff?"

"We did," Ana replied. "We didn't take everything. A few days' worth of clothes, not much else. We can get more when we get to Cincinnati."

"You mean Covington, right?" He looked at Lindsey. "You said we'd be staying on the Kentucky side of the river."

"Don't be a pain in the ass, Tommy. You know what she meant."

"I'm not being a pain in the ass, Linds. At least not this time. I'm making sure the plan didn't change and I blanked on it. Still not feeling like the elevator's going all the way to the penthouse, if you know what I mean." Tom pointed to his temple.

Ana scowled. "Are you feeling woozy? Do you need to sit? I can get you some water before we go."

"No, no, I don't want to stop to pee any more than necessary. And if I sit down, I'm not getting back up. Let's just get this show on the road. How are we getting there, anyway? Are we driving or taking the train, what?"

"We're driving, Tommy. It's not often anyone rides the Dragon without Emily."

"We're taking my car, then."

Ana sighed. "How many times do we have to talk about that dumb Mustang, Tom? Absolutely nothing is practical about it."

"It's my end-of-the-world crisis car. I'm not leaving it here."

Lindsey laughed. "I knew you'd be bullheaded about it. Lars is picking up a second car for us now. You and I will go in the Mustang."

Tom started to tell her he would be driving, but she hushed him right away.

"And don't feed me any bullshit about you driving, Tommy. I'm driving, and that's the end of it. You'll be asleep before we're halfway there with the pain meds she's got you on."

"Fine," he grumbled. "But I don't like it." He scowled, but she wasn't wrong.

The sound of gravel crunching under tires drew their attention outside.

"Sounds like our other ride is here." He picked up a baseball bat that had been leaning in the corner beside the front door, its usual resting spot. Running his fingers over the grooves etched into the head that made up the phrase "Speak Softly," he smiled. "Okay, let's go."

He cracked the door enough to confirm what was happening outside, and Lady slipped through to do her own check.

Lars stepped down from a larger Lexus SUV and came around the passenger side. He opened the door and offered a hand to the occupant. Emily gracefully slid off the seat and touched down with a light step. Tom had to chuckle. He was not even forty and already shuffling around like an old coot, and she was centuries old and jumping around like, as she would say, a spring chicken.

"My lady," Lindsey said with surprise. "I didn't expect you to come see us off."

"Now what kind of mama would I be if I didn't come to see off my best daughter? And it would be rude not to be here to say goodbye to my favorite dinner guest and his guardian angel."

Lady woofed.

Tom patted the dog's side. "Girl, I think she meant Ana, but I'm sure she'll miss you too."

Emily smirked at the shepherd. "I honestly never believed I'd see a dog I thought was anything more than a dumb animal, but you've done yourself proud, girl. You're always welcome back to stay with us."

Tom struggled to suppress a wry smile at the pleasantry. He was pretty sure they would never be welcomed back, especially considering the baggage that came with him. Not for the first time, he wondered if maybe he ought to ask Lindsey to Turn him. Being a vampire was about the last thing he wanted, especially since none of them had anything to eat. But at least then he wouldn't be alone. Starving, probably, but not alone.

"Tell me now, do y'all have everything you need? Tom, are you up for this? You could maybe stay another night if you're not ready."

"I appreciate the offer, but I'll make do. Feeling a lot stronger than yesterday, and by tomorrow, I'm sure I'll be as good as new. After what they've told me"—he nodded in the direction of Lindsey and Ana, who'd come out on the porch to stand beside him—"seems like the faster we find out what Colin is up to, the better."

"I do admire that boldness, Thomas. Same as the day you told me you'd go back to Cincinnati and kill both Colin and Ash if you needed to."

Bringing his bat up to rest on his shoulder, Tom grinned. "We got half the job done last year. Maybe I'll get to finish it soon."

A stern look flashed over Emily's face. "Hold your horses, there, son. You are not going up there to stir up trouble, do you hear? You'll stay out of sight, is what you'll do. My daughter will see to finding out what Colin is up to, and she'll report back to me."

She fixed Lindsey with the same look. "That goes for

you, too, daughter. You are not to go up there and dive right in. Don't confront anyone until you speak to me. You find out what's going on, you fill me in, you get back here in one piece. Am I clear, child?"

"Yes, my lady."

"Good. And remember what I've said whenever we part ways. If anything happens to me, you're to take control here and lead the Family. Keep them together and safe."

Lindsey nodded then smirked. "I'll say yes, but we both know you'll outlive all of us. You'll still be here another hundred and fifty years, looking for a nicer place to move to and bossing us all around."

"And don't you forget it!"

While Emily was wagging a finger at Tom and Lindsey, Ana and Lars had gotten to work loading a few coolers and several hard-sided shipping containers into the back of the SUV. One day, he would have to ask Ana what the hell all that stuff was for, since no one really seemed to have any idea of what she was doing. But he'd given Ana his trust a long time ago, and while there had been some pitfalls, he wouldn't start questioning her now.

Unable to help load her stuff, he instead shuffled toward the Mustang parked in the wide circular drive that connected his quarters with the main house then out to the highway. He looked back at Lindsey, who still chatted with Emily. "You got the keys? Toss them here."

She dangled them from her left hand but shook her head. "Nice try, Tommy. What do you want?"

"Pop the trunk."

With a tap of the key fob, the trunk popped open, and

Tom took stock. His travel bag was stashed to the side, and his leather jacket was folded on top of it. If he weren't already sweating, he might have put it on just because it felt like the thing to do when leaving to go get the drop on Colin. The trunk held a handful of other items he was glad to see, the box of notes his wife had written to him while he was in his coma, the revolver he'd picked up last fall from the same bar where he'd found the baseball bat, and the shotgun he'd carried into battle when they'd faced off against Ash and Colin. They had plenty of boxes of ammunition for both as well as the shoulder holster he'd had Lindsey pick out for him a few months ago. Carrying a sidearm in the waist of his pants wasn't nearly as simple as he'd seen on TV as a kid.

He looked up and gave Lindsey an appreciative smile. She winked back at him.

After checking to make sure the revolver was loaded, he slipped the gun back into the holster, secured it, then slammed the trunk shut. He'd have put it on, but the sling would be in the way no matter how he looked at it. And with luck, he wouldn't need it anyway. But if he'd learned anything since coming back to the world, it was that Feral could be pretty much anywhere along the open road. Having some form of protection ready and at hand could be the difference between standing over a plaguer with a pair of holes in its head and lying beneath one, bleeding out.

"Remember that I'll be leaving for the Conclave in two weeks," Emily said as she and Lindsey approached him beside the car.

"I know," Lindsey replied. "I don't have much time to get this done."

"This is the one chance we have to fix this without an all-out war, Daughter. But we need evidence. Nobody will be convinced to put that dog down unless we can prove he's rabid."

"I know, lady. I won't let you down. You know I can't leave Nelson with anything to hold over me." She gave the older vampire a grin that lit up her whole face, and Emily rolled her eyes.

"All right then, y'all best get going." Emily reached for Tom, took him by both shoulders, and squeezed. It was a light touch—she could have crushed both shoulders to powder if she'd wanted—but it was still like being clamped down by cold steel.

She leaned in and pecked him on each cheek. "You mind yourself, Thomas, and you mind the ladies. They'll do their damnedest to keep you above ground, so you do what they say. That said, you know they're as like to bite each other's heads off as to see eye to eye, so you make sure you keep them working together."

"Thank you, ma'am, for everything. I wouldn't have made it this far without you."

"And my Family would be knee-deep in blood from fighting Ash and his like by now if not for you. We're not even yet, son, so remember that I'll be behind you all the way. Now, get on out of here."

"Everything's ready," Lars said. "We'll talk to you soon, lady."

"You tell your Master I'm fixing to see this wrapped up for good, one way or the other, son."

"I'm sure he feels the same. Take care of yourself."

The ancient vampire turned from Lars to favor Ana with an honest smile. "Child."

Ana stared at her feet for a moment before meeting Emily's eyes with an awkward grin. "I don't know… After what you've done for me, I can't… I just…" She stepped up into the SUV and closed the door. Her head popped back out through the open passenger window. "Thank you. I will tell Lindsey as soon as the project is done. It could be any day."

"Good luck, child. Good luck to all of you. I'll see you soon." With that, she turned and started making her way to the main house in the soft glow of twilight.

Tom pulled his door shut, and Lindsey triggered the engine.

"You ready?"

"I'm trusting you to treat my girl right, Linds."

"Don't you worry your pretty little head, Tommy. You know me."

"Let's see what you can get out of her, then. Hit it."

With a chuckle, a sly grin, and a not-too-delicate touch on the accelerator, Lindsey sent the Mustang leaping away from the house in a spray of gravel.

CHAPTER 5

SHE HADN'T BEEN WRONG WHEN Lindsey had guessed Tom would sleep for half the trip. He managed to stay awake through part of Tennessee, but somewhere in the dark mountains, the combination of weariness, darkness, and medication won out. When he woke, the bluish glow of the dashboard lights lit Lindsey's face, giving a ghostly shade to her determined look.

"I'll never get used to how you all drive with the headlights off."

"We're too close now for lights. They could give us away. You know that."

Hoping it would settle his stomach, he took a sip from the bottle of water she'd set in the cupholder for him. Driving on I-75 through the hills, with its seemingly never-ending series of twists, turns, ups, and downs while not being able to see two feet in front of his own face was maddening. Add to that whatever medicine Ana had him on, and he wasn't sure if his stomach wanted him to eat something or swear off food forever. "I also know I don't have night vision. Where are we?"

"That's why I'm driving and you're not. And we're

about five miles from the Ohio River. We'll be getting off the road soon. How was your nap?"

He yawned, wishing he could stretch out. "Drug induced, I think."

Lady reached her muzzle forward from the back seat and gave his ear two quick licks.

"Good morning to you, too, girl."

"Is the stuff Ana gave you wearing off?" Lindsey asked. "I have something here I'm supposed to make you take. You know, at some point."

"At some point?"

"She's not good with details."

Tom laughed. "Ana's not good with them?"

"No, she's terrible about them. Everything she says is a detail about something. Who can focus on all that? She needs to learn how to summarize."

"You just like to complain about her. You two will be the death of me."

Lindsey laughed at that. "Not the two of us, Tommy. I'll be the death of you. I'll probably get tired of all this messing around tomorrow and make a proper meal out of you."

"I'm sure." He took another sip of water and screwed the cap back on. "What's our plan?"

"We settle in, and while you're getting better and Ana does… whatever she does, Lars and I will find Colin and wreck his big plan."

"Just like that?"

"No need to complicate things, hon. Lars has a couple of leads about where they've been active, and I've got a few hints of my own to track down. This'll go down quicker than a lemonade in July."

Tom stared out the window as the dark homes and offices of the long-dead suburbs streamed by. And then what?

A few minutes later, they started down the long, curved hill approaching Cincinnati from the south. Before crossing the river into Ohio, though, Lindsey veered off the interstate at the next to last exit in the state. Rolling slowly down the ramp, she immediately turned into a parking lot and cruised around the back of a tall building. She parked in a slot facing its large brick foundation.

"Here? You want to settle here?"

Years ago, before Tom's coma, the place had been an entertainment complex. A building over a century old had been converted into a collection of restaurants and nightclubs. He didn't know if it had closed before or after Charon, but by the state of the building, it had sat empty for quite some time.

"Yes, here. You couldn't have found us a sweeter spot. Good proximity to both the city and the expressway will make coming and going easier, and if they do somehow figure us out, we can make a quick run for it and head back south. Plus, it's a huge place with lots of stairs, and Feral don't do steps unless they're chasing food. Even better, old buildings like this have plenty of nooks, corners, and cubbies for you to hide in if necessary."

"I've killed my fair share of both Feral and vampires, you know."

"Oh, sugar, did the big, bad killer man get his little feelings hurt? Poor baby."

Before he could reply with something matching her sarcasm, the SUV pulled in beside them. "Looks like you've been saved by the cavalry. But you can be sure I won't forget about that last comment." With that, he picked up his bat and opened the car door.

"Wait!" Lindsey barked. "I didn't check…"

Ignoring her, Tom allowed Lady to shoot out first onto the parking lot pavement. She circled both cars three times, each time in a wider arc, then she sat down, ears forward, staring off into the dark of the adjacent street.

"What?" Tom shrugged. "It's fine."

Ana stepped out of the other car. "He's exasperating, isn't he?"

Lindsey eyed Tom then Ana and finally shrugged and shut the door of the Mustang. "We need to clear the building. Lars and I will take care of it. You two stay here."

"Bullshit. No way I'm spending half an hour out here in the open, especially with one arm literally tied to my side. I feel naked enough already. I'm staying with you."

Ana nodded. "I agree. He's better off indoors."

"This is my side of the river, remember? Colin would have to be sporting an exceptionally large set of balls to be rolling Feral of his own around here. Emily would rip his fool head off before giving him a chance explain."

Ensuring the revolver was loaded again, Tom slapped the cylinder back into place. "He strikes you as being conservative and patient, does he, Linds? Careful not to step on toes? Yeah, that's what I think of when I recall what happened with Ash last year. Colin's deep and abiding regard for the rules."

"Meat's not wrong, Lindsey," Lars added. "I won't say

for sure that I think Colin has plaguers around, but if he's using this part of town to operate while he tees up his fight with Alexander, I don't see why they wouldn't be in the area. If that's what he's doing, he's already in the water. Might as well start swimming, too, right?"

"Fine. But Tom's near me. Lars, you've got our backs."

Tom whistled, and Lady left her guard and trotted to the group near a service entrance. Lindsey pulled the handle, and the door swung open, squealing with indignation at having been in one place for so long. Tom ground his teeth.

Lady padded through first, not waiting for an invitation. Lindsey's green eyes narrowed in irritation, but she sighed without saying anything. Tom forced himself not to grin. She would remember how Lady worked soon enough.

Lindsey entered the building then paused, focused on the darkness around them without breathing. Finally, she moved ahead with silent, deliberate movements. Ana caught the door behind Tom, leaving his free hand, his gun hand, available. He slipped over the threshold and into the enveloping blanket of empty blackness beyond the doorway. The other two followed with Lars letting the door creak shut behind them.

"Hold on," Tom whispered barely loud enough to hear himself.

The others must have heard fine, though, and they all held their places. Lady came to press her left shoulder against his right leg as if to say, "I'm right here." He tapped her once then scratched behind her ears, taking a few seconds to let his eyes adjust to the lack of light.

When he caught a shine coming off Lindsey's eyes and could make out the waves of her hair against her shoulders, he nodded. "I'm good."

They'd entered the building in a restaurant kitchen with three long rows of service stations separated by two open aisles. Pots and pans were still stacked on top of the work areas, likely to be ruined by dust and rust before seeing use again.

"Be careful," Lindsey hissed. "Don't knock anything off."

She slid forward with grace that Tom could never have managed, even at his best, and shifted to the right aisle between the workstations. Lady veered to the left, and Tom followed, tense but with his finger resting outside the trigger guard. Shitty trigger discipline led to accidental shots, which was the last thing he needed at the moment.

Following Lindsey, Ana sniffed the air and frowned but kept moving. Lars, somewhere behind Tom, might as well have not been there for how little noise he made.

Lady stepped farther to the left just as Tom's foot landed in something slick, and he slid forward half a step. Lars was on him before he could blink, holding him up by the left arm. Pain radiated through his shoulder, but he managed not to cry out. Somehow. Gritting his back teeth, he moved ahead, out of the puddle of whatever seeped from the low refrigerator.

"Do I even want to know what that was? It smells foul."

"Imagine what it smells like to us. Shut up and keep moving," Lars growled.

They made their way to the end of the rows and

turned to their right. Lindsey pointed to a pair of swinging doors a few feet away. Before Tom could take a breath, she crossed the room to stand next to them, peering through the foggy pane of plexiglass seated in the center of each door. She shrugged.

Tom cringed at the return of a familiar icy lump in his gut. It had been a constant companion last year when he and Ana then later, after Ana help him escape Alexander, he and Lady had to focus constantly on avoiding detection from sunset to sunrise. He hadn't allowed himself to believe he was rid of it for good while they'd been staying at the Chalet, but a small part of him had hoped against hope that the rest of his life would somehow be safe, that the cold ball of fear and anxiety would live only in his past.

The past always did seem to come back with a vengeance.

Lars took a position next to Lindsey and looked through the door himself. After he nodded to her, she then glanced back at Tom and Ana and pointed at the ground, giving them the unmistakable instruction to stay put.

Without waiting for them to acknowledge her, she placed a palm on the door in front of her and gave it a soft push, creating a narrow gap. Lady, not given to following anyone's orders but her own, slipped through into the next room. Tom could almost sense Lars rolling his eyes, but the vampire followed her into the darkness, pivoting to his left. Lindsey followed on his heels, keeping to the right.

Tom and Ana, side by side, moved up to the door.

Pressing his face close to the glass, he tried to make out anything in the void beyond, but he might as well have been looking at a matte-black painting. His breath, growing faster to match the pounding in his chest, fogged the glass once, and then again. He forced himself to stop, but holding in the air wasn't any better, especially with the burning in his lungs being at strange odds with the chill emptiness in his belly. He exhaled hard again, once more covering the black square with condensation.

Before he could step back to break the cycle of hard breathing, something on the other side hissed. Tom yelped in surprise and nearly tripped over his own feet as he stepped back from the doorway. Lady growled then launched into a series of vicious, earsplitting barks.

"Don't let it get away!" Lindsey shouted just as dim light flashed in the darkness beyond the doorway, a shadowy gray that barely brightened his view.

The room was filled with a dozen or so high tables and tall stools, many lying on the ground and others in several jagged pieces. A dining room, if he had to guess. The light disappeared as quickly as it had come. Another door on the far side of that room swung shut. Something dark and half hunched had slipped through before it closed. The barking stopped, but Lady continued growling. From the sound of it, she had stopped near that far door.

Another flash of the dim light followed as Lars's unmistakable frame shot through. Lindsey moved to follow him, hand holding the door partially open, just as Lady gave a sharp bark of warning.

Lindsey stopped, her focus drawn to the dog, who backed up.

Dismissing Lady, the vampire turned back to the door, but before she could leave, Lars crashed into her, running from whatever was on the other side. The pair tangled together, each keeping the other from falling over as Lars directed them away from the opening. The room went dark again, and Lady let loose another string of sharp barks.

"Get him out of here!" Lars shouted. "It's a trap!"

The far door burst open again, slamming against the wall behind it and slipping off its hinges. In the charcoal light, half a dozen growling Feral bore their fangs, each one fighting to be the first one through.

CHAPTER 6

A NA DIDN'T GIVE TOM A second to catch his breath before she grabbed him by the arm and yanked him away from the door. He grunted in pain as she half pulled, half shoved him through the kitchen stations toward the door where they'd entered. Lady bolted through the swinging doors they'd just left and was on their heels in moments, racing with them to the exit.

They both turned as Lindsey came through the double doors with Lars crashing after her. She made eye contact with Ana for a moment before turning her back to them.

"Go! We'll buy you time," Lindsey ordered over her shoulder.

"No!" Tom cried, but Ana gave him no time for debate.

She grabbed him again and threw them both backward against the door behind her. Half turning, she hit the release bar with her hip, and the exit flung open, letting them out into the night.

Lady barked again twice and flashed past them. The plaguer between her and their cars growled in surprise. The dog took another step toward it, and the monster seemed to snarl and shriek at the same time. The noises they made, especially when angry, made her wish for the sound of fingernails against a chalkboard.

Enraged, the Feral lurched at Lady, swinging with a hand ending in razor-like claws. She pranced out of its reach, bared her teeth, and launched into its side before it could recover. Ana, expecting the lunge and Lady's subsequent reaction, raced forward, closing the distance between her and the Feral. With a scream, she hammered it with a closed fist to the temple. The thing's skull sank inward with a satisfying crack. It slumped against the pavement, not moving.

Her knuckles hurt plenty after the punch, but they weren't broken. She opened and closed her hand several times to make sure while watching the limp plaguer. Its eyelids fluttered, giving proof to her suspicion that she hadn't killed it. It would be very nice if she could spin its head around the way Lindsey did.

A pair of booming cracks in quick succession made her jump in surprise. Two dark holes, one where the Feral's eye had been and a second right where she'd hit it in the temple, began leaking dark fluid in a puddle under its head.

"Is it dead yet?" Tom held the revolver, smoke streaming from the barrel, over the thing's head.

Ana tore herself away from the Feral and looked toward the street behind them. Lady stood guard at the back of the cars, focused on the same thing. Nothing else appeared to be moving out there. Closing her eyes, Ana stretched out her senses, searching for any hint that something was about to jump out at them.

She found nothing. "Doesn't matter." Wrapping an

arm around Tom's torso, she directed him to the passenger side of the Lexus. "Get in."

"But what about…?"

"They can take care of themselves." She opened his door and whistled.

Lady hopped into the SUV then slipped over the center console into the rear seat.

Thankfully doing as he was told, for once, Tom climbed into the passenger seat. Ana flashed to the other side and pressed the ignition button before he'd even closed his door. As soon as it clicked shut, she threw the car into reverse and backed away from the building in a sharp arc. Ahead of them, the street ran back to the interstate on the right and off into Covington on the left. Which way?

"Lindsey said to go south if anything went wrong. They picked this place because it has quick highway access, so we could hop on and go. Get away from here and deeper into Emily's territory."

It made sense. But still, something about it bothered her. The interstate wasn't much better than a train track. Once on it, the options were limited to forward and back. She wasn't committing to that without knowing exactly what they would run into between there and ten miles down the road.

She pressed the accelerator, and the Lexus jumped forward then sprang over the curb into the street. She twisted the wheel to the right, approaching the expressway on-ramp.

But that many Feral in a dark, empty building, just waiting for someone to find them? And one of them knew

Lars and Lindsey were in that room, but instead of attacking, it ran away. Before they even knew it was there. Plaguers didn't act like that. Ever. They came at their prey relentlessly with claws and fangs and hoped they were killing something they could eat.

They didn't think.

They couldn't plot.

They certainly didn't lay traps.

As much as Ana wanted to second-guess Lars, that was exactly what they'd walked into. A trap. Those Feral had been under someone's active control. She had almost no other way to explain it. She stopped the car at a four-way intersection, just before the on-ramp, to check the mirrors and every direction around them. Nothing moved.

Lady gave her a soft woof from the back seat.

The expressway was built above them, leaving her no way to see what they were driving into from their current vantage. At least if they stayed in the city, on surface roads, they could see problems coming.

Giving it gas once more, she spun the wheel to the right, away from the on-ramp. Coming to another intersection, she didn't even slow but steered into a hard right again, pointing them deeper into the maze of city buildings and away from I-75.

"What are you doing? I said we should take the expressway."

"I heard you." She kept her voice cooler than she felt. "And I also heard Lars say it was a trap, and he wasn't wrong. If they set a trap in the building, they probably have the highway covered too. We're going to have to do something else."

Ana checked around them again as they drove past the tall building where they'd nearly been caught. The Feral guarding the back door was still a lump on the parking lot pavement. Lindsey and Lars were likely still inside, fighting for their lives behind those swinging doors. But she couldn't help them. She had to focus on doing what she'd sworn to do—keep Tom alive.

"Put on your seat belt."

They followed the street a few blocks before it began to veer to the side at an angle. Why did none of the blasted streets in this part of the country run at right angles, like cities are supposed to? She took a left turn then another right, almost choosing at random, trying to keep them headed in a general direction without thinking about it too much. A few more turns, a few more blocks, and they came to an intersection with what looked like a main street. A left turn should have them moving south, away from the river. But is that what they really wanted? They just needed to find a place to lie low until she could find Lindsey or Lindsey could find them.

"Which way?" she asked.

"That way, I guess." Tom pointed to the left. "That probably would get us farther from Colin, right? And if it really was a trap back there, wouldn't he have been the one who set it up? We should go that way until we get lost or something then hang out for a few days."

Realization slammed into her like a cartoon anvil. If it really had been Colin, and it almost had to be, they couldn't get lost—not so long as she was with Tom. Not so long as she saw where they were going.

Unbuckling her seat belt, she opened the door and

popped out of the driver's seat. She flashed around to the other side of the car and opened Tom's door. "Can you drive?"

"Probably won't be doing any stunt driving, but yeah, I think so."

"Good. Can you do it without your sling?"

"What?"

"I need the sling. We'll find you another one if you still need it."

He loosened it and lifted it over his head then rotated his left shoulder in a small circle.

"How is it?"

"Still hurts like a mother, but I can move it without crying. I'll survive without that." He handed her the sling.

Taking it from him, she ripped it hard, tearing where the straps were woven into the cloth cradle. She shredded the cloth into three long pieces then tied them together, end to end. When she finished, she lifted her work to her face, covered her eyes, and tied it off at the back of her head. The knots dug into her skull at odd places, but it would have to do.

"What the hell are you doing?"

"Colin can see what I see, so either I have to let you go alone, or I go with you blindly. Now get over there and drive us somewhere. Wherever you want. Just don't tell me where." Ana nodded at the driver's seat. "And hurry up. I don't like being out in the open like this. We're running out of night too. Blasted summer nights just aren't long enough."

Tom's clothing whispered together, and the car's leather interior crackled as he slid out of the passenger seat. As he stood maybe a foot in front of her, she sensed the heat in his blood, almost like seeing a red aura in front of her. It faded in concert with his footfalls as he moved away from her, becoming smaller and paler, eventually just a pink dot then nothing. His shuffled steps still gave him away, though, as he approached the driver's-side door.

Putting a hand on the doorframe and another on the seat, she pulled herself into the SUV and closed the door. The sense of that pale-pink dot returned on her left and grew again into the bright red of his heartbeat when he got behind the wheel.

"Whichever way I want?" he asked.

"Wherever." She sighed. "But I can't know. And stay away from the interstate for now. Just to be sure."

She heard the muscles in his neck contract and release as she imagined him nodding.

"Okay." He snapped his seat belt closed. "Let's find someplace to hide. Preferably someplace with coffee."

With that, the car began moving, and she forced herself not to think about which way. She should have spun around five times before she got back in the car just to fool her sense of direction. Then again, it probably didn't matter. The only thing that mattered was the bright-red pulse to her left and making sure it stayed that way.

CHAPTER 7

TOM DROVE, MAKING LEFT AND right turns at random for twenty minutes or so before doubling back. He pulled up in front of a squat building with a row of garage doors only half a dozen blocks or so from where they'd run into the Feral. Ana would have told him he was being an idiot for picking a place so close to the trap, but she didn't need to know where they ended up. And if the other place had advantages when it came to figuring out what was going on, it stood to reason that someplace nearby would share those advantages. Garage space meant they could keep the cars out of sight too. That had to count for something.

He slipped the SUV into park. "I found a good place with some garages. I need to go open the door and make sure we won't have any surprises inside."

He picked up the revolver from the console between them and checked the cylinder for what had to be the hundredth time since they left Atlanta. You could never be too sure of how many rounds you had.

"I'll go with you," Ana replied.

"That'll take twice as long with you blindfolded. Lady

will make sure the immediate space is okay, then you can make sure it's all clear inside."

She grumbled but didn't argue. "Fine. I'll stand beside the car and listen for trouble. If you see anything, shout, and I'll be right there."

"We'll be okay, I'm sure. They probably used up all the Feral around here for the ambush. We're safe from here back to Lexington."

"Don't count on it," she warned. "Be careful."

"Yeah, yeah. Girl, you ready?"

Lady stood on the back seat and looked out the door on the driver's side, tail wagging.

"We'll be right back."

Ana popped the passenger door just as he opened his, and they both stepped out, leaving the car open and running. Tom watched her feel her way around the door and take up a position beside the front tire. He then opened the rear door for Lady, who hopped down from the car. He closed it after her so they'd have one less thing to worry about if they needed to make a quick exit.

With Lady padding at his side, they approached the segmented steel garage door. Like everywhere else he'd spent time since Ana had woken him from his coma, the place looked dingy at best. Abandonment had a way of doing that. Everything was grungy, and trees and bushes that had once been trimmed back were overgrown. Vegetation was taking the world back over. Just at the corner of the block, some kind of leafy shrub had already half consumed an old newspaper machine.

The garage door had windows, but they had long since been blackened. The sign in front of the building read "Jones Transmission and Auto Repair," so he imagined years of exhaust fumes had smoked them over. No point in bothering to peek inside. Tom did put an ear to the steel just to make sure nothing growled at them from inside, but he heard nothing.

He gave the handle a strong tug upward, but the door didn't budge.

"Shit."

"What?" Ana asked.

"Door must be locked. I'll check a different one."

"No, wait." She left her place beside the car, using the hood as a guide. Coming up beside him, she held out her hand. "Put my hand on the lock."

Tom took her cold, wiry hand and placed his over it, guiding her to the lock handle, a rotating bar in the center of the door.

Shifting it first clockwise then counter, she cocked her head to the side. Then, she flexed her wrist counterclockwise, and with a sharp snap followed by a metallic clang, the bar spun ninety degrees. She gave him a smirk. "There you go. Unlocked."

"Open sesame." Tom lifted the handle again. But just as before, the door didn't move. "What the hell?" he muttered. "Still won't move."

"What kind of place is this?" Ana asked.

"I'm not sure I should tell you."

"He can't hear what I've heard. Only see what I've seen."

"Oh, right. It's a garage. Some kind of auto repair place."

"Then the doors are likely automatic, which would

explain why you can't lift it. You're pushing against the motor."

"Oh. Yeah, that makes sense."

"Is there a handle?"

"Yes."

"Put my hand on it."

As before, he placed her hand as she asked.

Facing the door, she tightened her jaw and pulled upward. At first, nothing happened, but after a few seconds, the door responded and rose over her head. It screeched like a train engine as the motor fought against her, and metal rollers that hadn't moved in almost four years followed their path along an unoiled track.

Lady trotted inside the garage the moment the door was high enough to let her slip under.

When it reached its top position, with most of its segments parallel to the ground, Ana eased her hold while leaving the slightest touch, making sure the door would hold itself up. Seeming satisfied it would stay in place, she said, "All right, what are we working with?"

Tom turned his attention to the space inside. Like most everything else he'd found in the world post-coma, the place was dark and musty, and the air hung stagnant around him. On top of the usual odors, though, he smelled the heavy tang of oil and metal mixed with a hint of dank funk.

"Seems okay," Tom whispered.

Ana shook her head. "No. Something is rotten in there."

The building was made up of six garage bays, four with lifts on the ground, including the bay in front of them. The other two, at the far end to Tom's right, looked like they might have an open space in the ground where someone on the lower level could access the underbody of a car.

Lady had already made her way to the back left corner of the garage, where a door led to what looked like an office, working her way around the perimeter of the space, pausing to sniff here and there. She walked past them from left to right and approached the open-floor bays. When she got to the end of the front wall, she looked down into the sixth bay and sniffed for several moments. Then she sat down, looked back at Tom, and woofed.

"She says it's clear," he said to Ana. "But I think there's something she wants us to see."

"Get the car inside, and close the door. I'll go see what she found."

"Are you sure? How can you…?"

"I'll be fine. Just don't hit me." Without waiting for a response, she turned to the right and made her way along the wall of swing-up doors.

"Be careful near the end," he called after her. "The last two bays are—"

"Open to the level below," she finished. "I am aware. As if falling ten feet would hurt me."

Shaking his head, he went back to the Lexus, closed the passenger door, and climbed inside. He pulled it in at idle speed, careful as he rolled over the lift. Then he killed the engine, hopped out, and pressed the red Close button on the control panel next to the door. It rumbled down its tracks, the second time with a good deal less irritation.

"Lucky the power still works for these doors," Tom

said. "That probably also means Feral haven't been able to get inside, right?"

"Possibly," Ana replied, "but not everything about this place seems to be so lucky." She stood beside Lady, looking nowhere in particular but pointing at the space in the open bay below them.

"What is it?" He approached.

"I don't know. I don't want to see it in case it gives Colin a clue about our location, so you'll have to tell me. But whatever is down there, Lady definitely found the source of the rotting smell."

Reaching the space in the floor, Tom frowned at the scene below. "Oh my God."

"What is it?"

The rectangular underground bay was home to what looked to be five—no, six—skeletons. They were arranged almost if they'd been seated at a dining table. Two of them slumped together, with bones intermingled, which made it difficult to count them at first glance. An impressive collection of beer, wine, and liquor bottles were arrayed between them, most of them empty. A deck of playing cards sat in the center, mostly stacked into draw and discard piles. A few cards splayed around each skeleton as if dropped.

What looked like a nine-millimeter pistol lay on the ground beside one skeleton.

"Several bodies are down there—skeletons, that is. Looks like they decided to wait out the end of the world with a shitload of booze and a card game. There's a gun too."

Ana nodded. "I've seen similar scenes before. Once

the story of Charon took hold in the media, many places issued stay-at-home orders. Some people complied. Others not so much. Some, like these people, it seems, shut themselves in together in what came to be called 'Charon parties,' hoping that they could stay clear of it."

"Doesn't look like it worked."

"Some groups of infected self-quarantined, promising to end it before anyone got too bad. This could be that too."

"What? You mean like a suicide pact?"

"Technically not suicide. Euthanasia. But yes. That's probably why there's a handgun down there."

"Christ, that's morbid."

"It was morbid, Tom. People were scared and didn't know what to do. The hospitals were all running well over capacity, health-care workers were getting just as sick as their patients, and no one had supplies. Might as well stay where you were and make the best of it until the end came for you."

He tried to imagine the skeletons below with muscle and skin, faces and hair, but the image wouldn't come to him. All Tom could see were stacks of bones covered in dusty, stained clothing, like a Stephen King diorama of lunch hour at the transmission shop.

He cocked his head. "Wait. If they shot each other when it got too serious, there would be stains on the walls or something. Spray patterns and spatter, right?"

Ana shrugged. "They might have just expired as Charon came for them. No way to tell."

"Maybe." He paused. "I don't know, though. They

still look like they're in the middle of a game. Like when they died, it happened all at once."

"There is…" She trailed off as the fingers of her left hand started scraping at her thumb.

"There is what?"

She hesitated. "There is one alternative. They could have been survivors."

"Survivors?" Tom replied with more force than he'd intended. "What do you mean survivors? You said no one survived."

"I did not lie. When I told you that, there were no other survivors but you and two other patients."

"But?"

She exhaled. "Some, an unlucky few, did not succumb to the disease. I don't know if they were immune to the virus or carried it but did not get sick or just somehow managed to avoid contact with it altogether. Regardless, this is not the first scene I've come across like this."

He couldn't believe it. "Why didn't you tell me this before? Jesus, can you just tell me the whole goddamn story once—just one time!—and not withhold some piece of it from me? And you wonder why I spend more time with Lindsey, who's just as likely to drain me at a whim like everyone else, rather than with you."

Ana furrowed her brow. Her eyes were hidden behind the blindfold, but he sensed them narrowing into that blistering glare of hers. "I didn't mention it because it didn't matter. By the time I found you, what miniscule percentage of people that survived Charon, no matter for what reason, were all still just as dead."

"But that doesn't make any sense. How could we have six survivors all in one place?"

"Because." She paused again and looked down. "Because for the first six months after Charon, survivors found each other. With cell phones and apps they could still connect, and much of it continued to work for a few months. The few who survived used what they had to reconnect, hoping that by sticking together, they might find a way to start over. But then my kind started to panic, and what followed can only be called a grisly race to find and feed on as many survivors as possible before someone else got to them."

With Ana's chilling words, Tom finally succeeded in making the bodies below into real people in his mind. Old and young, black, white, or whatever, huddled together in an auto service repair bay, playing cards and getting loaded, hoping to live out the night. It was a feeling he knew all too well. Then he saw them come, one vampire or a small group, descending with a violent, blood-crazed fury on the poor souls below. His stomach lurched as the scene played out in his mind.

"My God, Ana. People survived the fucking apocalypse only to be hunted down in the following months? And for what? Why didn't someone like Colin or Emily put a stop to it and give us a chance to build something back up? Wouldn't that have been better for all of us in the long run?"

"They weren't leaders then like they are now. Apparently, groups of us, or leaders, had never existed before. Vampires had always been relatively solitary. We didn't start working together, and our Lords didn't emerge, until well after all the survivors were gone."

"Why didn't someone stop and think? All of this could have been prevented."

"I wish I could tell you that might have been possible. But panic isn't rational. Just as humans raced to buy stores out of toilet paper, sanitizer, milk, and eggs when news of Charon began to spread, when my kind realized they would run out of prey soon, they went on a feeding spree the likes of which the world had never seen. Only after it ended, when the hunger began to set it, did anyone start asking smarter questions."

"But then, how did I survive? How did no one find me during the rampage?"

Ana shrugged. "Most likely because you were in a coma, hidden on a medical ward. In the early days, the hunters generally wouldn't go into hospitals. You've seen what they look like now. Imagine what it would have been like then, when the dead littered the halls, still rotting. On top of that, it didn't take long to figure out that feeding on Charon-tainted blood would turn you Feral. Once that became common knowledge, no one was going risk drinking what blood they might have found in a coma ward."

Tom knelt and stroked Lady's fur. She responded by giving him a swipe of her tongue along his cheek. "Jesus, Ana, I didn't have to be the only one. There were others, and you killed them all? But if that's true, how can we be sure? Maybe we should start looking for others."

She rested a cold hand on his shoulder. "Tom," she whispered. "They're gone. Everyone is gone. It's been years since that furious hunt, and my kind are… they are very good hunters. They even found you, eventually. But thankfully not until some semblance of order had been formed. I promise you, Tom, there are no others. Do not torture yourself by holding out a foolish hope."

He curled his fingers into fists, frustration making his shoulders tighten. But what was the point? Rage wouldn't help, and the tension made the wound on his neck ache. He exhaled slowly, forcing himself to relax. "Sometimes, I think you want me to have no hope at all."

"I want us both to have hope," she snapped. "But right now, that hope starts and ends with living to see another night. Come on, we need to plan. Let's find a room with nothing to give it away so I can take this blindfold off and look at your shoulder."

CHAPTER 8

THICK DROPS OF COOL, DARK blood from Lindsey's right hand splattered onto the ground at her feet. She surveyed the kitchen and found what she needed, a deep sink to wash off that plaguer's insides. The stuff dried hard, like enamel, if it wasn't cleaned off quickly. Dry Feral blood almost required sandpaper to remove. She turned on the faucet and waited for the inevitable sputtering to resolve into a steady stream of warm water. Massaging her hands in the stream, she took a moment to enjoy the feeling of warmth spreading over them. It was getting hard to remember what it felt like to be warm for more than a few moments here and there. Living on blood rations was barely living at all.

"We need to get out of here." Lars eyed the six Feral bodies piled around the open doorway that separated the restaurant kitchen from the dining room beyond, where the plaguers had tried to ambush them. The swinging door that once hung in the doorway lay on the floor among the tangled heap of bodies. "Come on," he growled at the heap. "I dare one of you freaks to twitch under there so I can tear you apart."

Judging by the way the plaguers' heads were all twisted

at odd angles, it seemed unlikely any of them would move ever again.

Lindsey joined him by the far door and nudged one body off another with her foot. Hard to say exactly what she hoped to find. She wouldn't likely recognize them. Feral were Feral, after all. They all looked the same to her. Those would have been Colin's anyway, given the way they'd been controlled.

"You recognize any of them?"

Lars shook his head. "But who recognizes a plaguer unless it was yours to begin with?"

"Let's go. This is a shit show already, and Emily'll be fit to be tied if we don't find the other two before someone else does." Lindsey turned from the open doorway and toward the emergency exit at the back of the kitchen that had long since given up sounding any alarms. "Which way do you think they went?"

"You told them to go south."

With a smirk, Lindsey paused at the door to the parking lot. "Does that girl strike you as the kind to do as she's told?"

"Ana? No." Lars chuckled. "That's about the only thing you two seem to have in common." He shoved open the door and stepped outside into the night, where Lindsey heard his breath catch.

At the same time, a whoosh of air signaled the end for one of the Mustang's tires. A short, stocky vampire with a shaggy mop of salt-and-pepper hair gave her a wicked grin as he pulled his hand away from the devastated rear passenger-side wheel. He looked about as wide across the shoulders as a pickup truck.

Someone else, a plain-looking guy with a much less impressive build and toffee-colored hair, stood by the driver's-side wheel with a similar smile. The car sat level, meaning all four tires had been punctured. It wasn't going anywhere. Not that leaving looked like an easy option anyway. Eight Feral stood in an arc in front of the car and the pair of Colin's goons.

The stocky one with the stringy hair crossed his arms over his chest. "Good evening, kids," he said in a voice an octave higher than she would have expected from his bulky frame. "Fancy meeting you here, in my part of the world."

Rage filled her. It wasn't his part of the world. It was Emily's territory.

"Not sure who the fuck you are, greaseball, but you're gonna need a lot more plaguers than this to put us down."

"My name is Kallus, and unless I'm mistaken, you're Lindsey, right? No need to worry yourself. I'm not here to put anyone down. My orders are to bring you back to my lord. Just come with us, and everything will be easy-peasy."

She shot a look at Lars. "You remember the plan I told Ana?"

"I do."

"I'm headed that direction. You go the other. Meet me in the middle."

Lars nodded.

Kallus raised his hands. "Now, don't you think you're gonna go running, Ms. Lindsey. I've got orders, and it'll only be worse for all of us if you make this harder than it needs to be. Well, really, mostly you'll just make it harder on yourself."

"You're missing the point, gremlin." Lindsey sprang forward to her left, slamming into the surprised Feral closest to her.

Her right hand shot up, jamming into the monster's chin, throwing its head back. The bones at the back of its neck cracked together, and it crumpled to the ground without even a growl.

Lindsey dared a glance to her right just to confirm Lars had understood the assignment. The first Feral he'd run into was a heap on the asphalt, its head twisted nearly backward.

"Stop them," Kallus muttered.

Toffee, the other vampire, moved around the car, taking up a position just in front of his stockier counterpart. The group of Feral growled at once, and the remaining six shot toward either Lindsey or Lars, claws extended and fangs dripping.

The three plaguers bearing down forced Lindsey to focus on the attackers coming for her, though she really wanted to tear apart that squat, squeaky asshole's face. She smacked the claws of the first Feral to reach her with her left hand and slashed at its throat with her right. It pulled back, realizing the pain in its neck was an open wound. The one behind it shouldered past on its right. She shoved it backward hard, driving the new attacker into the one she'd already wounded. They both barked in surprise then stumbled away from her, tangled together, and fell to the ground.

The third, still growling as it charged her, swung with

an outstretched claw. Lindsey ducked beneath the swipe and returned the favor with an upward slice of her own. The monster didn't hesitate to grab for her.

If Kallus was in control of those Feral, he had a particularly strong hold on the one she faced. She let it get close enough to put arms around her, then she sprang upward, leading with the back of her head. The plaguer's jaw shattered against her skull then exploded in a shower of warm blood that gushed down her back.

She shoved its chest in disgust, and it fell back to the parking lot. Without missing a stride, she stormed up the length of its body and stomped hard on its temple. She grinned as the skull gave way beneath her boot with an easy crack.

The other two had disentangled themselves and growled threateningly once again. They lumbered ahead, trying to close the few feet of space between her and them, but she wouldn't give them a second chance. She charged at the nearest one, closing the gap before it could respond.

The Feral being under the command of only two vampires gave her and Lars a tactical advantage. Plaguers could fight well enough on their own when motivated by possibly killing something for food, but it was a difficult thing to control multiple in a fight when the controller didn't *want* them to kill who—or what—they were attacking. Kallus and his toffee-haired buddy might as well have been herding cats, trying to control multiple Feral in a coordinated attack faster than Lindsey could cut them down.

Reaching the first of the pair, she knocked its claws away just as it started to raise them, then she took it by both sides of the head. With a quick motion she'd had all too much practice with lately, Lindsey twisted hard, separating the bones at the back of the Feral's neck with a satisfying pop. She shoved it aside like a rag doll of meat and bones.

Only one plaguer remained for her, the one she'd swiped across the neck as the fight had started. It roared in anger and launched itself at her, blood streaming down its neck and behind it. She let it come but, at the last second, slid to her right and away from its grasp.

The Feral lurched past her. Turning toward its back, she flashed behind it and pushed, half shoving, half carrying it right at the building where Kallus had laid Colin's trap. It put its hands up to soften the collision, but Lindsey kept pushing it toward the brick wall ahead. Face-to-face, it might have been stronger than her, but from behind and being shoved forward, it didn't stand a chance. The monster went headfirst into the cinder block. Its skull left a red stain on the wall as it dropped to the ground, limp.

She spun, breathing hard out of habit, turning her attention to addressing Kallus and Toffee.

Lars had finished his own group of Feral and was advancing on Colin's pair of vampires.

"What do we do?" Toffee barked, looking over his shoulder at Kallus, his voice giving away his fear. "Don't you have more? Get some more."

"They couldn't possibly arrive in time, you idiot. Colin sent you to protect me, Garret. You take care of them!"

Toffee—Garret?—backpedaled from Lars's advance. He collided with Kallus. "To hell with that. I'm getting out of here!" He turned from Lindsey and raced off across the parking lot, then veered toward the expressway on-ramp.

Kallus, looking from Lars to Lindsey then back to Lars, must have decided Garret had an okay plan after all. He turned and raced off after the other vampire.

Lars stopped just as Lindsey caught up to him. His face, set hard, looked like iron, and his eyes blazed. Feral blood spatter covered him.

"What do we do? We should probably find Ana and Meat, right?"

Lindsey looked at the bodies lying all around them. "I think that chunky one, Kallus, was controlling all these Feral."

Lars glanced around as well. "No way. One controlling eight? No one like him has ever Made eight Children."

She shook her head. "I know it sounds batshit, but Kallus said that other one was just supposed to protect him. I'd bet that means he wasn't in control of any Feral himself. Either way, I want to know. And Emily said to come up here and get to the bottom of what's going on. I imagine the story will unfold a lot easier if we catch that greaser before he finds Colin. You agree?"

"I've always liked the way you think, Lindsey. Can we kill him?"

"Not sure about that." She narrowed her eyes. "Let's trap him first then see what Emily says."

"Sounds like a plan. What about Tom?"

"I don't love that girl all the time, but Ana will keep him safe and under wraps. Of that, I'm damn certain. Let's go before those two chickenshits get too much of a head start."

Putting out a hand, Lars laughed. "After you, then."

Lindsey winked at him then took off, flying across the parking lot. Lars raced after her, on the heels of Colin's henchmen.

CHAPTER 9

TRACKING A PAIR OF VAMPIRES who could move quickly enough to seem invisible might have been a challenge in a town even the size of the little place in Mississippi where she grew up, let alone a city as large and empty as Covington, Kentucky. Lindsey could only grin, then, at the realization that Kallus and Garret didn't seem to have the sense God gave a common dog.

She and Lars raced up the expressway on-ramp, coming immediately to the bottom level of the double-decked bridge that carried I-75 across the river into Ohio. She lowered her head and tensed, planning to race across the long deck of the bridge at top speed, but was jarred to a standstill by something clamping onto her arm.

She pulled up and shot Lars a furious glare over his wiry grip on her forearm. "What the hell?"

Lars shook his head. "I don't like this. Feels like another trap. We should be careful instead of charging headlong after them."

"Lars, they're gonna get away. We'll lose them on the other side."

"Take a good look here, Lindsey. We're about to rush

onto a straight corridor with no exit between here and the other side."

Lindsey took a breath to calm herself. "Damn." She whistled. Lars wasn't wrong. "That greaser would just need to slip some plaguers behind us, and he'd have us surrounded."

"Maybe we should let them go for now."

"Or if it's a trap, honey, maybe we just spring it."

"Is your first idea ever *not* the most reckless one?" Lars chuckled.

"Hasn't been yet." She winked at him again, pulling her arm away. "But we'll go slow."

The pair started forward at a careful pace with slow strides that made her itch. Lindsey stretched her keen senses, on alert for any sight, sound, or smell that might signal an unexpected presence. The bridge appeared empty and smelled only of steel and old oil.

A third of the way across, though, that changed. Thumps and shuffles filled her sensitive ears, then she smelled them—at first, just the hint of rot and the tang of sickness she remembered from when Momma and her sister got struck by the flu when she was little.

Lars stopped. "Lindsey, I think—"

"Yeah, hon, I can smell 'em. And the smell's getting stronger."

The first Feral stomped into view near the far end of the bridge, rising from the downward slope as the bridge emptied into Ohio. Others joined behind it, one after another, until a whole host of plaguers advanced on them, nearly shoulder to shoulder across the four lanes of expressway.

"Holy hell, how many is that?" The concern in Lars's voice was plain.

"Too damned many, that's for sure. I ain't never seen so many in one place before that weren't tearing each other up. These can't all be from that one grease bag."

As if she'd summoned Kallus, his shrill voice rang against the rafters. "You like my little welcoming committee, Ms. Lindsey? I think of them as *my* Family. Our lord Colin helped me put it together. We believe it's probably the biggest single gang of Feral ever made. I'm like the proudest parent at the talent show."

Lindsey frowned. The mob wasn't quite halfway across the bridge deck but was already close enough that she could see the saliva dripping from their fangs. And they were picking up speed.

Casting a glance beside her, she said, "What do you want to do?"

"Against that? Lindsey, that's more than we can take alone. We need reinforcements."

Narrowing her eyes, she caught sight of Kallus and Toffee behind the oncoming clan of monsters. "We don't need to take them all. We just need to kill him." She nodded in Kallus's direction.

"You think that's what Emily likely wants you to do?"

"Let's find out." She closed her eyes and stretched out with her mind.

Lady Emily—

"We don't have time for that. We have to go. We'll find them, but we're not crossing the bridge this way. There are other ways. Other bridges." He nodded to his right, toward the three others crossing the river. "We'll find them. You know I won't stop until we do. But first, we should pull back and regroup. Take a breath and consider our options."

Lindsey glared back at Lars. That greaser was too jumped-up for his own good, no matter how many plaguers he could muster, and she wanted to teach him a lesson. She balled her hands into fists and teetered on the edge of charging ahead, Lars be damned. But Emily trusted Lindsey to get to the bottom of whatever Colin had planned, and figuring it out would likely be a whole lot easier if she could beat it out of Kallus. The only real way they could take on all those stinking shamblers at once, though, was by killing Kallus first, and getting him to spill the beans would be a lot harder if he was dead..

She took another breath and relaxed her fists. "Fine," she muttered as she took a step backward. "We'll let him have this one. But if we don't come up with a better plan, I'm coming back to get him to tell me exactly what the hell is going on around here. Seems to me Colin's probably let that beast wrangler in on his plan, and I look forward to wringing every nugget of info out of him."

"That's the right idea." Lars nodded. "Take a rain check. I'll even hold him while you punch if you want. But right now, we need to go." He spun and dashed back the way they'd come, toward the expressway ramp.

Lindsey lingered a moment longer, glaring at the horde of Feral and the stocky vampire behind them. "This isn't over," she swore. "Not by a long shot, greaser." With that, she turned her back on them and chased after Lars.

She caught up to him at the base of the on-ramp,

where he stood watching her. She pulled up to meet him. "What?"

"I want to know if he sent them after us."

She looked back over her shoulder. "Surely, you don't think…" But the next words caught in her throat as the familiar reek of Feral smacked her in the face.

A second later, the herd of plaguers came into view from the ramp above them. They moved faster than she'd ever seen a plaguer—let alone a controlled group of them—move. They ran in a jerky, ungainly dance, one uneven, shambling step after another. If it weren't a vicious swarm of Feral, she would have laughed.

"What does he think he's doing?"

"I don't know," Lars replied, "but it looks like we'll have to lose them."

"Follow me." Lindsey raced away to the east.

They ran a few blocks, past a small collection of crumbling fast-food joints, before coming to a stop in front of a small building housing a liquor store with iron gates closed over its doors and windows and a replacement-glass showroom. She slowed to a stop and looked west. The Feral weren't yet visible, but they had to assume the monsters would follow as closely as they could lumber.

The sky on the horizon was taking on a soft yellow glow she didn't like.

"It'll be daylight soon."

"I have an idea," Lars said. "Let's go back."

"Go back where? Atlanta? No way."

"No, I mean to the building where they tried to trap us."

"Why?"

"It's got space. It was five or six floors, at least." He nodded in the direction of the Feral gang, who were just appearing as awkwardly shuffling specks two blocks to the west. "If we get trapped inside, we'll have plenty of room to separate them or maybe trick them into a trap of our own. I think it might hold a surprise or two for us as well."

"Okay. How far is it from here, seven or eight blocks? Maybe if we time it right, some part of Kallus's little herd will get barbecued."

Lars nodded. "Wouldn't hate to use the sun to our advantage for once."

"All right, beefcake." She smirked. "Lead the way."

The pair turned south and jogged along what the signs indicated was Main Street, past narrow, three-story storefronts, picking their way through the occasional jumble of parked cars until they reached an old corner diner. A sign hanging above the blue door inset into a facade of masonry named it the Anchor Grill, and an unlit neon sign in the window declared, "We may doze, but we never close." It seemed like the kind of dive where she might have enjoyed a plate of eggs and bacon after a boozy night out way back when, before Emily had found her.

They swung to the right around the corner and, in another few blocks, crossed the parking lot back to Tom's Mustang, still parked where they'd arrived beside the looming building with fading yellow paint. He would be so pissed about the tires, but not much she could do about that. Maybe she could make it up to him later by finding him a shiny new car with an unnecessarily large motor.

While Lars looked north, waiting for some sign of their pursuers, Lindsey looked west, trying to gauge how long before the sun would breach the horizon. The pale-yellow glow had become a golden aura.

"I'd guess ten minutes until daybreak, give or take," Lindsey said.

"Are we lucky enough for them to get caught outside?"

She turned her attention north as well and narrowed her eyes. "What if we helped them get caught?"

"Not sure how we'd do that," Lars replied. "Look around. There are old buildings everywhere plus an expressway underpass right there. There's probably enough shade there alone for them to survive daylight. Kallus wouldn't be comfortable, but he and his gang would be safe."

"Can't blame a girl for hoping, I guess. I still don't see them coming, though. Maybe we lost them?"

"Maybe." He didn't sound convinced.

"Either way, probably best not to sit here and wait for them to find us. Unless you changed your mind and do want to fight them."

"No. Especially not this close to sunrise. We need to get inside. Underground, if possible."

"Underground?" Lindsey asked, surprised. "You think there's some tunnels or something around here?"

"This building was one of the largest breweries on this side of the Ohio River. I have a hard time thinking that it doesn't have beer tunnels underneath just like Alexander's place."

"Well, beefcake, let's find out." With that, Lindsey slipped through the entrance they'd used earlier in the evening, back into the dark kitchen strewn with dead plaguers.

Nothing had changed since they'd left it a few hours ago, but both stopped and strained to hear or possibly smell if anything alive loomed in the dark. The air was as still as the dead and held nothing but the pungent perfume of decay and rot. They tiptoed forward through the room again, along the metal tables, toward the open doorway where a swinging door had hung a few hours ago.

Lindsey reached it first, and in such darkness, even with her accentuated eyesight, she could barely make anything out. A Feral-sized heap sat a few feet from the door, but it didn't move, growl, or even breathe. Not that breathing was necessary, but most plaguers usually did it anyway.

"I don't sense anything," she whispered. "No sounds, no heat, no heartbeats."

"Same. Do you feel that air movement, though?"

She frowned. She hadn't noticed anything before, but once she put her whole focus into searching for *anything* changing, she caught what he was talking about. Near the back of the room, directly opposite them, she could sense the slightest breath of air swirling, like some kind of draft. She should have noticed before, especially in a room so warm. The heating and cooling probably hadn't worked in years, so whatever it was, it was either another room, or a natural vent or passageway.

"Easy and quiet," Lars suggested in barely a whisper.

She slid forward with her usual grace but coiled like a spring, ready to pop at any time. She wouldn't get caught off guard in that room, or the building, again. Ever so slowly, they inched toward the back of the room, staying apace of each other, stepping over the dead Feral at the same time. Still, she sensed no other form of life.

At last, they reached the source of the swirling air, an ornate metal grate lying flush with the hard tile floor. Stale air filtered up through it, musty but without the telltale tang of fetid moisture Lindsey expected. It was cooler than the kitchen prep room, too, which had likely been closed for several years before the half dozen Feral were led inside to wait as a trap earlier in the night.

Lindsey cocked her head and smiled. A pair of hinges connected the grate to the floor, not quite flush with the back wall. At the corner of the opposite edge, an old, keyed padlock looped through a metal eye stuck up slightly from the ground.

"It's a gate." She bent to get a closer look.

Lars nodded. "Do you think—"

The squeal of wrenching metal drowned out whatever he said. Lindsey stood and handed him the broken padlock. "The gate is covering a set of old steps down to some underground space. It could be a way out of here those plaguers won't find. I reckon it's got to lead somewhere. What better way to slip across the river later tonight than to leave this place a different way than we came in?"

"Why not?" Lars bent and grasped a swirling flower in the wrought iron gate's pattern.

He gave a slight tug, and the front edge popped up from the floor. He swung it up and away from himself, squealing as it ground on hinges that likely hadn't seen lubrication in a decade or more. Lindsey froze as the grating of metal echoed throughout the room. She and Lars both forced themselves not to breathe and stretched out with their senses. Nothing changed in the deep darkness below except dancing motes of dust.

"Ladies first, then?"

"Of course. I'll need to make sure it's safe for y'all down here." Lindsey stepped onto the first stone stair and descended into the darkness beyond.

CHAPTER 10

Tom watched Lady sniff around the post of a stop sign while pressing himself against the building behind him, waiting to be sure she didn't come up with a reason to worry. Finally, she crouched slightly and let her bladder go, which was probably the clearest sign she could give him that they were alone on the sidewalk. He wasn't surprised, as he hadn't expected to find anyone—Feral or vampire—wandering the streets on a sunny summer morning at 10 a.m. Neither of those groups fared particularly well in open daylight. Still, seeing her at ease was contagious, and he tucked the revolver he'd been holding back into its shoulder holster.

After turning the corner, he proceeded up the block toward the convenience store. Ana had given him a small list of supplies she needed to change the dressing on his neck, and he and Lady both needed something to eat. As ridiculous as it seemed, he damn near had as much trouble keeping himself fed as the vampires did. At least, he did when they weren't at the Chalet. Emily had always taken care of that for him. His stomach rumbled to remind him it had been almost twelve hours since they'd left the mansion to head toward Cincinnati.

Lady padded up to the door of the little store that sat on a lot with six lonely looking fuel pumps. The glass door to the In-N-Out was closed but not fogged over, which was a stroke of luck. Hopefully, he could get a decent view inside. The dog sat and pressed her nose against the glass as Tom himself leaned in close and squinted. Nothing moved, and nothing looked out of place. Not finding piles of snacks or anything strewn about the floor was also a good sign. When Feral got inside a store, they generally tossed stuff all over the place in search of something worth eating, which he assumed meant a mouse or some other kind of critter, as he'd yet to find a plaguer who looked like they'd really enjoy a bag of nacho cheese tortilla chips.

"Looks okay to me, girl."

She stood back up and looked at him expectantly. He pulled the door with a light touch at first, just to see if it was locked. It wasn't. He opened a gap wide enough for Lady to slip through, and she darted inside without hesitation. He waited with the door still slightly open to give her a chance to slip back out if she ran into something unpleasant. After a quick lap of the store, she came back and sat down, looking at him with her head slightly cocked.

"All right, then, let's do this," Tom muttered.

He pulled the door all the way open and propped it with a gallon of windshield fluid. On the off chance they had to retreat to sunlight quickly, it would be better not to get slowed down at the door.

The air inside the store carried that familiar stale quality he had come to expect from every enclosed, long-abandoned space he explored. It made him think somehow of his poor grandmother's mothball-scented closet in the back den where he always had to play when he was little. How long before he forgot entirely what it was like to move through a world that actually felt lived in?

He looked at Lady, still sitting near the door, even as he made his way toward the snacks. "What do you think, girl? Jerky or Cheetos? Or should we live the dream and just get both? Maybe if we eat enough salty shit, the plaguers will lose interest altogether."

She got up and shook herself before padding over to him but didn't offer any opinions about breakfast. He rubbed her between the ears while considering the aging junk food in front of him. Jesus, the whole situation was depressing. On the run and hiding out again, standing in a convenience store, debating which packaged snack might possibly deliver a modicum of nutrition, all while having no freaking clue what horrors the next twenty-four hours would bring. It didn't help that his wounded shoulder ached every time he moved the wrong way.

Tom picked up a small bag of some kind of rolled corn chips dusted with red powder. He frowned. "What's even the point, girl? Somebody—no, make that pretty much everybody—is trying to kill us, and half the ones who aren't could be either dead or captured by now. Emily can't help, and let's be honest, she's about at the end of her rope trying to keep her Family from bleeding me dry. Ana means well, but Colin sure as hell doesn't, and she's one bad day away from having to once again do exactly what he says when he says."

Dropping the chips, he moved to the back of the aisle toward the coolers at the rear of the store. Finding what he wanted, he pulled open a door, and for half a second, he dared to hope he might get blasted with a bracing gust of cold. No luck. The cold room probably hadn't seen the lower side of sixty degrees in a couple of years. Still, he'd long ago gotten over the need for beer to be chilled. Frowning at the limited options—the case didn't hold a single can of suds, only bottles, which didn't preserved beer as well—he reached in and pulled out the first brown bottle his fingers hit, a Samuel Adams lager. He popped it open with a plain silver bottle opener he found hanging from a hook on an endcap.

"Prost, girl. Five o'clock somewhere, right?" He lifted the bottle in a toast to the German shepherd then took a long pull, swallowed, and tipped the bottle to pour a small bit onto the floor.

Lady cocked her head, sniffed the puddle of lager, and looked back at him, apparently uninterested in joining him in day drinking.

Shrugging, Tom muttered, "Suit yourself," and took another drink, paused, then took one more. He wiped his mouth with the back of his hand and belched. "And quit judging me. I work nights, so beer at 10 a.m. is perfectly reasonable."

The dog didn't move.

"I know, I know. I'm falling apart. But what are we going to do?" He drained the beer and chucked it over his shoulder. The bottle bounced several times, clanging hard on the cheap tile floor, but somehow didn't break.

Lady chuffed. He could feel her disapproval over the unnecessary noise. Sometimes, she was worse than Ana.

"We could just get out of here, you know." Tom

opened the cooler again and considered his other options before frowning a second time. More than half the shelves were completely empty with nothing larger than six-packs of craft bottles. Where the twelve-packs and cases should have been on the bottom, he found nothing but empty space. Not that a case of Bud was really what he wanted, but he was four hundred miles from the Chalet, where he'd spent the last few months purging the surrounding areas of Budweiser. Yet somehow, there wasn't any here either. He settled for another Sam.

Tom took a more measured drink from his second bottle as Lady looked on. Getting drunk wasn't the goal. After getting half lit in that hole-in-the-wall bar somewhere in Iowa last year, he'd attracted the attention of a roaming plaguer, and Ana had barely arrived in time to save his dumb ass. Jesus, she'd been mad. A day or so later, he'd learned just exactly why she'd been so mad at him for taking reckless chances. Chances he wouldn't have taken had he known the whole story. Of course, her not telling him the whole story was kind of the cornerstone of their relationship.

A soft woof shook him from his thoughts. He'd been staring idly at a carton of milk that had to have gone rock solid without seeing it. He had to pull himself together.

After another sip of the beer, he turned back to Lady. "Well, what do you say? Should we find another unreasonable car and put all this in the rearview mirror? I'm sure we can find someplace in the country far enough from anyone or anywhere else that they'd never find us, right? We could go find a cabin somewhere in the mountains. Let them kill each other or just starve while we learn to make whiskey or something." He drained the rest of the bottle.

Standing, Lady padded to him and nuzzled his hand until he scratched her behind the ears. Satisfied with the attention, she put her nose to the floor and began sniffing at something. Hard not to wonder what she "saw" with that nose when the best he could do was keep his attention on an empty beer bottle and the front door. She disappeared down one of the aisles.

"Hey, where are you going?"

Tom slipped the empty bottle back into the six-pack he'd taken it from and considered a third. Instead, good sense won out. A third would likely lead to a fourth then a fifth. Too much of that, and he'd be lucky to find his way back to the corner, let alone to the garage or somewhere else. He let the cooler door close and followed Lady's trail. She wasn't in the aisle she'd gone up, and Tom's heartbeat kicked up a notch.

"Lady, where'd you go, girl?" He kept his voice a few decibels lower than he had a few moments ago. He couldn't help but be on edge when she was out of sight. For probably the tenth time, he cursed himself for taking her tags off so she didn't jingle when she moved. Yes, it was still the smarter move so the dog didn't make noise that might tip off vampires or Feral if they needed to stay low, but every time they entered a dark, unfamiliar building, he had a hard time convincing himself.

Tom dashed to the aisle next over. Still nothing. Rising panic made his blood quicken, and his pulse thrummed fast in his own ears. He made his voice even quieter. "Lady?" Only one more aisle.

Peeking around the endcap, almost afraid of what he might find, he sighed a heavy gust of relief. Lady sat halfway to the front of the store, tongue lolling from her mouth.

"What are you doing over here? You almost gave me a heart attack." Not quite running to meet her, he dropped to one knee and rubbed the fuzzy sides of her neck.

She closed her eyes for a moment, reveling in the attention before standing again and shaking herself out. Then she sniffed at the shelf in front of them.

"What is it?" Then, after realizing he was looking at gauze and Band-Aids, he added, "Oh, right. First aid stuff." Saying it out loud reminded him of the wounded shoulder and how it was starting to ache more noticeably. Maybe he should grab some ibuprofen too.

He picked up a package of gauze, a long roll of bandage, and the few other items Ana had listed for him. He turned to find the painkillers, but Lady again caught his attention. She stood a few feet away, farther up the row in the opposite direction from the way he'd come, nose down to the tile, sniffing with keen interest at something Tom couldn't quite see. He stepped closer and knelt for a better look.

On the ground, three tiny drops of fluid shined an unmistakable shade of crimson. The shepherd leveled her gaze to meet his eyes and cocked her head.

He ran his fingers over the dressing covering his wound. They came away clean. If it was blood, as he suspected, it wasn't his. "It isn't you, is it?"

Lady offered no reply, so he ran his hands through her

fur then checked her face and each of her paws. All clean. No bleeding.

The droplets were barely the size of M&Ms. Tom put his finger on one deliberately, as if afraid some monster might grow out of it in a split second and devour them whole. When nothing materialized, he scrutinized the red stain at the end of his index finger. Still fluid and barely even tacky. It had to be pretty fresh, then. He scowled, and his heart picked up its pace. Something had been there not long before him, and that something had been bleeding. Or at least, it had been dripping blood from mouth or claws.

Lady moved farther up the aisle, muzzle once again to the floor, sniffing intently.

"Easy, girl," he muttered. "We don't know what it is." He tiptoed after her, attention laser focused, intent on catching the tiniest rustling of cloth or a hint of breath in the air that might be out of place. Inching forward, he found a swinging door to his right, undoubtedly leading to a stockroom. The dog stopped and sniffed at the floor again then turned to face it. Another cluster of dark splotches stained the tiled floor, larger than the last. Several looked to be the size of a dime, and one might have been as large as a quarter.

Stepping past Lady, Tom made slow progress toward the front door. Months ago, the temptation to find out what exactly was bleeding back there might have gotten the better of him. But at best, it was a hurt plaguer, and as much as putting half a cylinder of shells into it might sound like fun, it could give him away to someone controlling it. Hell, the sound of gunshots alone could do that. No, he'd had a couple of drinks and had picked up the supplies Ana wanted. No use pressing his luck. He could grab a few bags of beef jerky on the way out for later.

He walked to the end of the aisle then took a step toward the entrance, but Lady wasn't with him. Looking back, he found her standing as before, stock-still and at attention while facing the storeroom door.

He clucked his tongue softly. "Come on, girl. Let's go."

She glanced at him and then back at the door before pawing it lightly.

"No, Lady. We've got to get out of here."

Ignoring him, she pawed the swinging door one more time and then tapped it with her nose, moving it forward an inch.

"Son of a bitch. Are you kidding me?"

One more time she looked at him and then back.

With a sigh and a soft groan, Tom put the stuff he was carrying on the checkout counter and met her at the door. He pulled the revolver from the holster and checked its load purely out of habit.

"All right, girl, it's your call. But if you get me killed, I'm not giving you any more jerky." He put his left hand on the door, took a deep breath, and pushed.

CHAPTER 11

T HE DOOR INCHED OPEN UNDER the pressure of Tom's hand. As soon as the opening was wide enough for Lady to slink through, she entered the storage room. Tom nearly whistled to try and hold her back, but he thought better of alerting whatever was holed up back there to their presence. He popped his head through the gap and paused to let his eyes adjust to the darkness inside. Skids of soda and water stood to the left of the door, and in front of him, several rows of short shelves ran perpendicular to the door itself. Hundreds of dollars of forgotten backroom stock sat on them, likely to collect dust until the packaging withered to nothing.

Lady stood a few feet from him, sniffing another dark spot on the concrete floor, only one drop, unlike the others she'd found, but much larger and partially smeared like something had shuffled through it.

Great, it probably was a plaguer.

The dog showed no signs of giving up on whatever foolish crusade she was committed to, though, so Tom slipped the rest of his body through the doorway while making as little noise as possible. He held his gun at the ready but angled to the ground the way he'd been taught by his grandfather. He moved to Lady, who stared with intent to his right, but a tall stack of boxes kept him from seeing anything beyond it.

If she intended to keep an eye on that side of the room, he might as well make sure no surprises waited to their left. Moving carefully, he checked around each skid and glanced through the shelving aisles. Nothing but convenience store stock.

Satisfied, he sidled up next to Lady, looking toward the boxes obscuring that side of the room. The dog took a step forward.

Were they really going to do this? It was damn near madness. He could just let her go, of course, but that dog had been the only real friend he'd had since last October. If anything happened to her, he'd never forgive himself. Especially if he might have prevented it.

He took a slow step after her, forcing himself not to breathe but once every ten seconds or so. With each step, he stopped to focus on the room, searching for the kind of noise not even a mouse would make or an unnatural shift in the air giving away something's movement. One tense step followed the next as they grew closer to the ceiling-high column of cardboard Charmin boxes.

At last, just when the pulse racing in his ears neared deafening, they reached the boxes. Tom gave Lady the hand signal to stay. Her ears perked forward into stiff, furry triangles, but she stayed put.

Positioning himself with his back to the column and facing Lady, Tom closed his eyes and took another breath. Not nearly as deep and soothing as he would have liked, but stealth took precedence. Peering over his right shoulder, he tried to peek past the stockroom barricade to first get a look at whatever was in there with them, if anything. The angle was too sharp, though, preventing him from seeing more than a few feet. Nothing to do but go for it and hope for the best. Slipping his index finger into the trigger well, he started counting in his head.

One.

Two.

Three.

With that, he spun on his heel, coming to rest facing the opposite direction, toward the open space on the other side of the boxes. Tom's breath caught in his throat.

Six or so feet away, a younger woman—midtwenties, if he had to guess—sat on the dusty concrete floor, propped against the far wall. An ugly red splotch matted her chestnut bangs just above her left temple, and the white sock and tennis shoe on the matching foot was dyed crimson. She was trying to hold her head with her left hand and her ankle with the right, but neither seemed to be staunching much of the blood. She gave Tom a look that was half-challenge and half-misery before letting go of her head wound and slumping down farther.

"Just do it quick, Drac," she muttered. "At least you're probably better than one of those animals."

Lady padded up to the girl without any of her normal hesitation. Not so much as a hint of her hackles rising or even a soft, threatening rumble in her chest. Tom frowned then shook his head to make sure he wasn't seeing things. It couldn't be. It just… couldn't.

"Aren't you gonna kill me?" Her voice had a noticeable hitch. Then the girl gave the dog a confused glance before leveling her eyes back at Tom. "What kind of vampire has a dog?" she asked as if thinking out loud. "Or a gun?"

Tom finally forced enough air out of his chest to talk. "I kind of thought you might kill me. And what kind of vampire bleeds out on the floor of a convenience store storeroom?"

"I'm not a vampire, man. Are you?"

Lady snuggled up beside the girl and gave the girl's right cheek a swipe of her tongue.

"No, I'm not." He secured his revolver. "But until this moment, I thought I was the only person left, period. They told me everyone else was dead."

"Well, they haven't gotten me yet, but I don't know about anyone else."

Jesus. Tom's knees loosened, and his vision clouded. He had to crouch and put a hand on the floor to keep from collapsing entirely. "Goddammit, lady, how the fuck are you alive?" He paused, trying to get the hurricane swirling in his head under control. The best he could do was settle on the realization he shouldn't swear in front of someone he just met. "I'm sorry. I didn't mean to suggest—"

"It's fine, man. Sometimes I'm surprised I'm still around, too, you know?"

"Still, my first reaction to finding another living human shouldn't have been to drop the f-bomb and wonder how you aren't dead. I don't know how that was my first reaction. I'm sorry. And my name is Tom."

The girl half chuckled. "I'm fucking dying, Tom, so it's probably cool if we say a few bad words. But if it really bothers you, you can get a swear jar and put a dollar in it for me."

The room, the woman, Lady, everything snapped back into focus, and the buzzing in his mind stopped. "Jesus, what's wrong with me? Lady, stay here with her." The dog glanced back at him as if she'd forgotten he was there. Little need to worry that she would go anywhere.

Tom shot up and dashed back toward the main part of the store, slamming through the storeroom door with a loud bang. He probably should have been a little more careful, but he was pushing so much adrenalin, he probably could have lifted a car. Not much chance of going slow and steady. Besides, no telling how long the girl had left if he didn't tend to those wounds as soon as possible. He raced to the counter where he'd left the gauze and other supplies Ana had wanted then doubled back to the first aid aisle for a few more things. A minute or so later, he was back in the storeroom, at the young woman's side, fumbling to get a tan fabric wrap out of a plastic package.

"Is he always like this?" the girl asked Lady, scratching between her ears.

The dog woofed once in reply.

Tom first took a good look at the splotch on her head, thinking that head wounds should probably get attention. An ugly two-inch gash ran diagonally from her forehead toward her temple, but it seemed to have mostly stopped bleeding freely. He put a large piece of cotton wadding in her hand and set it against the wound. "Hold that there while I look at your leg. What do I call you?"

"I'm Shan. It's Shannon, actually, but nobody ever

called me that but my mom, and she's long gone. It's nice to meet you, Tom."

"It's nicer for me, Shan, I promise. For the last six months, I've thought I was the only real person left on the planet."

"Tell me about it. I'm going on three years now. I think. Wait, what year is it?"

Tom peeled back a damp sock and forced himself not to react. The ankle looked bad. Admittedly, he wasn't a doctor, but a jagged tear twice as long as the one on her head made a rough crescent around the bony bump in line with her heel. "Three and change sounds about right. I think it might be four this coming fall. How did this happen?"

Shan looked down. "I caught a glimpse of the sun coming up this morning, and he seemed so bright, and I'd spent the last few days hiding in some warehouse, so I thought it would be nice to get out for a walk. I went out early, hoping to maybe find some supplies. Things are getting hard to find over in the city, so I walked across the river, thinking I might have better luck here."

"Did you walk across the suspension bridge?"

"Yeah."

"I guess there aren't too many shadows for a plaguer to hide in on that one, huh?"

"That's what I thought. And you call them 'plaguers'? I've always thought of them as blood zombies."

"That's not bad. They're also called 'Feral.'"

"You mean, you call them that?"

"Uh, yeah," he muttered, nodding while focusing on the wounded foot.

Probably not the best time to fill her in on his living situation. She was the first human he'd spoken to in more than a decade, so the last thing he wanted to do was freak her out by explaining that he hung out with vampires.

He picked up a roll of wrapping and found the edge. "Okay, let's hope I make this better and not worse. Sorry, I'm not much of a medic."

"You look like you do okay. That dressing on your neck looks pretty tight." Shan gestured to his injury.

Tom forced himself not to wince at the mention of Ana's handiwork. "It's been a shitty apocalypse, right?"

That earned him a tight grin. "Damn right. Honestly, most days, I feel like I'm starting to get a little weird around the edges. You don't seem so bad off, though. Wait, you are real, right, Tom? And you're not crazy or nothing?"

"Jury's out on that, but I tend to think not yet. And I haven't been dealing with it alone as long as you have." He pressed tan flex wrap onto a big wad of padding and started rolling it around the damaged ankle.

"Anyway, I walked a couple of blocks in from the river but didn't really find a place I figured would be good for stuff until I saw this one. Not far away, I was walking on top of this brick half wall. Until I wasn't on top of it anymore. I tripped on something and fell off. Only a few feet, but I rolled the ankle, and I think I hit a stop sign with my head."

He started to say something like, "Ouch," but she barreled on without a pause.

"Yeah, I was really freaked and didn't know what to do. Like an idiot, my first thought was, 'What a dumbass way to go, bleeding out in the street. I'd be better off with a drainer or one of the stupid blood zombies.' But then I realized I wasn't dead just yet, so I got myself together and hop-limped in here, trying to keep from bleeding all over everything and leaving a big neon sign that there was a snack inside."

When she finished, Tom couldn't have said whether she'd taken a breath or not throughout the rambling. It was the most words in such a short amount of time anyone had said to him since he'd woken up. Did she always talk like that, or was she getting delirious?

"I've almost got you wrapped up here. Are you feeling okay? Head's not fuzzy or anything? You can see everything all right?"

"Who knows anymore, Tom. But I don't feel light-headed right now. You think I'm gonna be okay?"

"Oh, definitely," he lied smoothly. He wasn't one hundred percent sure, but she needed confidence, not concern. "Probably need to get moving soon, though. When the plaguers come out tonight, they'll be drawn here. Did you have someplace to stay over here, or were you planning on going back over before sundown?"

"I got a pretty secure place over the river, but I don't know if I can make it back on foot today."

"Well, you can probably stay with…" Tom trailed off as reality hit him like a bulldozer full of earth. No way could he take Shan back to Ana, half dead or not. Even ignoring that he didn't want to have to tell Shan his whole story just yet, the vampires took it as an objective fact that he was the last human left. They couldn't find out there were other survivors, even just one. And while he could probably get Ana to swear not to give up the secret, the danger of Colin somehow finding out through her was off the charts. He couldn't be responsible for them all coming after Shan like they did him.

He stammered. "What I, uh, mean, is, uh, actually I think I have a better idea."

"What do you mean?"

"Your safe place is somewhere in the city? Downtown area?"

"Something like that. You got a better way across than walking?"

Tom smirked. "There's always a better way. Stay here with Lady, and I'll be back."

The German shepherd pressed her muzzle against the woman's shoulder, making it pretty clear Shan was in good hands.

CHAPTER 12

TOM PEERED AT THE SKY and frowned as he stepped out of the small store. A shelf of menacing clouds was rolling in, being pulled across the sky like a blanket. He didn't quite smell the tang of summer rain, but a hot breeze blew across his face, threatening a good storm.

"A storm is all we need," he complained, expecting Lady to still be at his feet, having forgotten she'd stayed back with Shan. He sighed then whispered, "Shan," as if trying the name out to see how it felt. A tiny, thrilling tingle burst like a perfectly ripe cherry tomato at the nape of his neck, not from the sound but from the realization he was slowly accepting, as they were no longer face-to-face.

Another real, actual human being existed—someone else like him, another survivor, someone else, he assumed, who'd had to struggle through the past few years, living in a state of near-constant fear and dread. At least one more person in the world could understand his situation and the absurd choices he'd had to make to get by in what passed for a life.

If there was one, could there be more?

Tom shook his head. He didn't have time to be dumbstruck by the turn of events, no matter how miraculous it seemed. She needed help, and if he didn't get it, she might just decide she didn't need him in her life anyway. After all, Shan must have done well enough to get so far on her own. Time to prove he was worth sticking with.

He needed a car if he wanted to get her back to wherever she stayed at night, but going back to get the one in the garage with Ana wasn't a great option. He had no good way to explain to Ana why he needed to take the car all of the sudden, at least not without letting her in on the secret. He would probably have to tell her at some point—in fact, he probably should, as she was maybe the only vampire in the world he fully trusted to do the right thing where Shan was concerned—but too much was happening right then to toss that bomb onto the fire. Besides, it wasn't his secret to tell. At least not without Shan's consent.

With the auto center out of the question, his options were pretty slim. He turned away from the store and started making his way up the street alongside it. Cars lined the near side of the street but not as many as he would have liked. He started dodging from car to car, trying the driver's-side handles as he went.

"One," he muttered. Locked.

He only needed to find one car he could start.

"Two." Also locked.

Breaking a window was an option, maybe, if it was obvious from outside a car that he could start it. Maybe if keys were visible in the front seat or something. Judging by the clouds unfurling overhead, though, that was not the wisest option.

"Three." Locked again. No keys in sight.

He continued to count to himself, mostly to keep his rising irritation at bay. Shan depended on him. He had to prove he wasn't some useless idiot.

By the time he got to twelve, he was four blocks south of the In-N-Out and about ready to start cursing out loud. Tom sighed hard when one more handle came up with his hand but didn't unlatch. He moved on to the next.

"Thirteen," he muttered, taking the handle of a decrepit-looking Toyota while gritting his teeth. He forced himself not to clench the hand at his side.

Click.

The door swung open toward him, and he pumped a fist into the air. Tom dipped his head into the car then made a face and wrinkled his nose. "Jesus, how does it still smell like pot after all this time? I've smelled worse, for God's sake, but this is ripe. I guess the price could be right, though."

Out of habit, he checked the back seat to make sure it was clear of Feral, but there wasn't enough space for one to hide there. Especially not with a full assortment of old fast-food cups and bags filling both of the footwells and the seats. If he'd been forced to bet, he would have put money on the former owner being a college kid.

Sliding into the driver's seat, he frowned at the ignition. It was an old-school key mechanism rather than a Press to Start button like his Mustang. He checked both sun visors, hoping that he might get lucky. He didn't.

Tom leaned across the passenger seat and popped the glove box. A suspicious-looking bag of green herbs tumbled onto the floor.

"Of course," he said. "Well, maybe I can convince Ana to try it. She could stand to chill out a little."

Chuckling, Tom rustled though the remains of the box, sifting through a broken pair of sunglasses, a couple of parking tickets, several receipts for oil changes, and a forgotten air freshener that would have done much more good hanging from the rearview mirror. No keys, though.

A raindrop spattered the windshield, and his breath caught in his throat. "All I need is a damned key," he growled. "Come on."

Tom gave the back seat another suspicious look. Anything could be under all that trash. Anything at all. A key, rodents, or God only knew what else. He swore off going mini dumpster diving in the back seat as a last resort. Turning his attention to the console between the two seats, instead, he said a silent prayer, unlatched the storage bin, and swung the top upward. Not at all to his surprise, he found another food storage bag of green sitting at the top of the compartment, even bigger than the previous one.

"Who the hell owned this car? Pablo Escobar?"

Setting it aside on the passenger seat, Tom finally allowed himself a slight grin. Underneath was a half a pack of mint gum, a lighter, some CDs, and a single silver key with a Toyota insignia carved into the plastic base. He grabbed it, slid it into the ignition, closed his eyes to hope, and turned.

The car clicked twice, and the engine sputtered, but after half a second of uncertainty, it chugged to life. Tom threw his hands into the air.

The Corolla wasn't quite his Mustang, and it surely

wouldn't impress Shan, but at least it was running. The two engines couldn't have sounded more different either. For all the receipts proving oil changes had actually been done regularly, the thing sounded like it was damn near grinding metal under the hood. But with rain falling at a steady if not yet forceful pace, he would take whatever he could get. He'd be a lot happier when he got the 'Stang back in a day or so.

As he reached for the gearshift, he caught a flash of himself in the rearview mirror. Instead of putting the car into gear, he adjusted the mirror until he looked himself right in the eye. Tight lines surrounded his eyes. Puffy bags hung below them, and his appearance didn't quite strike him as nice enough to even be called haggard.

"What are you doing, Tom?" he asked the eyes glaring back at him. "You don't even know this woman, and you're already worried about whether or not she likes your ride? Jesus, get your shit together. Help the woman out, maybe talk about meeting again sometime—after you figure out how to tell her you live with fucking vampires—then get back to the garage before Ana starts wondering about you. Hell, for that matter, Shan might turn out to be just as big a nutcase as you've become, sitting here talking to yourself in a mirror. And wouldn't that be great? The loony pair of us wandering around, trying not to get eaten."

Tom turned his focus back to the gearshift, slid it to D, and gently pressed the accelerator. The motor lulled in reply, threatening to stall. It didn't, though, and quickly enough, it hit enough RPMs to slide forward a few inches. Tom allowed himself a tight grin and spun the wheel hard to the left, making a U-turn in the middle of the street. A few moments later, he pulled up next to the front door of the store, still propped open as he'd left it.

"Lady," he called, entering the store.

The dog popped out of the storeroom door, wagging her tail.

"Hop in the car. I'll get Shan."

The German shepherd trotted passed him toward the car without hesitating.

"All right, man, keep your shit together," he mumbled.

Tom swung into the storeroom, the door nearly crashing into a surprised younger woman.

"Oh!" she exclaimed, jumping backward before half leaning, half falling against one of the stock shelves. "Ow. Fuck that hurt." She bent forward, reaching for the foot, but then kept going, pitching toward the floor.

Tom grabbed her by the arm and levered her back upright, trying to ignore the searing pain in his shoulder. That didn't really work, though, and he hissed. "I'm sorry. Are you okay? I didn't expect you to be up."

She straightened and pushed back from him, reaffirming that she could still hold herself upright. "It's okay. I should have known better when I saw your dog go through the doors. I'll be fine. Just lost my balance there."

Tom pointed at the wound on her forehead. "Probably because of that. You've got a head wound, and you look like you've lost enough blood to make the… what did you call them? Drainers? Enough blood to make the drainers out there green with envy."

"Okay, yeah, right. You're probably on the money there. The ankle feels so shitty I keep forgetting that I smashed my head just as good. I need to get to my place.

I'll heal up quick enough when I get back to my own supplies. It's a damned good thing that…" She trailed off, as if catching herself.

"Good thing what?"

"Oh, never mind me. I run my mouth too much sometimes. Just shitting words because I don't know what else to do."

"I know what you mean." Tom smirked. "I'm sure Lady has had plenty of moments wishing I'd just shut up. Anyway, I got us a car. But I'll warn you, it's not fancy."

"It's not a beat-up white van, is it?" Shan laughed.

"No." He chuckled. "Instead, it's some college kid's beat-up old Corolla. Come on, I'll help you out."

Shan reached for him but then stopped. "Wait, where's your dog?"

"I told her to get in the car."

"And she just… did?"

"She's the smartest dog I've ever met. And she's saved my life more times than I can count at this point."

Shan put a hand on his good shoulder. "Okay, then. Lead on, Mr. Tom. But I'm warning you, if we get out there and it's a molester van or your dog is nowhere to be found, I'm going to beat the shit out of you."

"I already got the shit beaten out of me this week. Good thing all I have outside is a shitty Corolla that smells like weed and a German shepherd whose loyalty I probably don't deserve."

She gave him a small grin. "Smells like weed, huh? Did they leave us any?"

CHAPTER 13

TOM FIGURED IT MUST HAVE taken ten full minutes for Shan to hobble outside to the Corolla. Saying it was an awkward journey didn't begin to cover it. They got along well enough, but she seemed hesitant to lean into him and let him carry the weight she couldn't put on her foot. He couldn't fault her for that, of course. He had been vulnerable enough when Ana rescued him from that Feral in the high school where he'd recuperated from his coma and had probably played out dozens of times since how many ways that whole situation could have been worse for him. If he was being honest, he'd probably played it out hundreds of times. As a result, he said nothing as Shan did her best to make it to the storefront without putting herself fully at his mercy.

Plus, she had already threatened to beat his ass. It wasn't quite clear how she planned to do that with a head wound and a busted ankle, but he'd learned a lot about women and confidence in the past few months and was content to take her at her word.

The rain had transitioned from a drizzle to heavy, oddly timed drops, then all the way to a bona fide summer squall before settling into a soft, steady shower. Based on what he saw overhead, it wouldn't come as a surprise if the rain lasted the rest of day and well into the night, but his guess was about as scientific as making a wish when throwing a coin into a fountain. Tom missed a lot of things from his old life, but getting a reliable weather forecast at pretty much any time turned out to be much higher on that list than he would've thought.

They reached the car and shuffle-hopped outside toward it with Tom cussing to himself. He parked it with the driver's door facing the store and hadn't thought to turn it around so she could walk more directly to the passenger side. It wasn't much extra effort, but by the time they got around to the other side and she slipped into the car, both of them were soaked through. Lady eyed them while lying on the dry back seat, apparently having knocked all the trash off it before they got outside.

"I'm sorry," Tom groaned, dropping into the driver's seat. "I should've turned the car around."

"It's fine." Shan wrung water out of her ponytail. "A little shower never hurt anyone. I kind of like getting out into the rain every now and then anyway. It's been a while since I did it last. And real showers can be hard to get these days, but you don't need me to tell you that, do you?"

Tom said nothing, but he hadn't really thought about how fortunate he'd been to have access to running water and a hot shower at the Chalet pretty much whenever he wanted. Things had obviously been more difficult for her.

Seemed like a good chance to change the subject. "Where do you call home? Where are we headed?"

Shan leveled an appraising look at him. "Head north,

across the river, into Cincinnati. Doesn't matter which bridge you take. I'll tell you where to turn."

With a nod, he put the Corolla in gear and gave it some gas. The engine sputtered again, then they lurched ahead, and he directed them out into the street.

"You weren't kidding about the pot." Shan laughed, dangling the pair of bags from each hand. "Looks like it's your lucky day, Mr. Tom."

He winced. "Please, just call me Tom. And I don't know about that. I've gotten this far, I guess, but most days, that seems as much a curse as luck."

"Damn right on that." She paused, considered, then added, "Tom. Pretty much every day from when—"

She was cut off by a loud metallic pop followed by the earsplitting screech of metal banging against metal. It sounded like someone was throwing chunks of steel against the engine repeatedly and forcefully.

"Shit." Tom rolled the Corolla to a stop, and the grinding slowed to match the engine. He put it in neutral and pressed harder on the accelerator. The song of metal on metal quickened accordingly. "Shit, shit, shit."

"Fuck. Sounds like you threw the chain, man," Shan said. "Turn it off. Quick."

Tom cut the ignition. "What chain?"

"You don't know cars?"

"Not really. I mean, I can drive fine, but I don't know anything about engines."

"Sounds to me like you busted the timing chain. That pretty much means the engine is fucked. It might run for a little bit, but the thing is pretty much throwing shrapnel in there. And it's just going to get louder. We could probably still make it across the bridge, but we'll make a shit ton of noise doing it. And I don't know about you, but I don't want to let the damn blood zombies know that I'm coming home."

"Hard to argue with that. What were you saying about being lucky?"

"No shit. I don't know what our options are here, but they aren't great. You can try to find another car in the rain, I guess, or we can sit in here until it stops then try to find another car, but who knows how long this rain will last? It could be steady all the way to nightfall for all we know."

"Sitting in an exposed car after dark doesn't seem like a great idea."

She nodded. "True story. I'd normally be all for walking back across the bridge in the rain, but obviously, I'm not making that hike. It'd be dark before we got there, and I'd probably pass out from losing too much blood. Other suggestions? We really need another car."

Tom checked the rearview mirror. The garage was maybe two blocks down and another couple closer to the river. He could make it there on foot by himself in ten minutes or so then come back and get her. But that meant opening a whole different can of worms. Was it worth it? He could just try to find another car. Surely, that wouldn't be too hard.

Who was he kidding? He'd been lucky to find their current shit heap, and it had only sort of run for five blocks, give or take. It could take an hour to find another. Or more. Damned people dying of the plague could have been more considerate to the apocalypse survivors like him and Shan and left their keys in their cars.

"I don't know how much luck we'll have finding another car. I've been boosting them off car lots when I needed one, but I think we were lucky to find this un- locked and with a key inside. It's obvious the owner didn't care if anyone stole it."

She shook her head. "Even at the end of the world, there's that one guy hoping to get rescued by insurance. So, what then? Just sit here and hope the rain stops some- time soon? Maybe we could find somewhere to hide for a few days until I'm moving better? Could be something in the back we can use to smoke some of this while we wait." Shan gave the trash a curious glance.

"I don't like the idea of waiting," Tom began, "and I've never really gotten into that stuff. But what if…" He hesitated for a second. "What if I told you I had a place already? A pretty good one. And I have access to a good car. But it comes with…" He wasn't sure how best to put it. "Complications."

Narrowing her eyes, Shan grabbed the door handle. "Be real careful here, dude. I trust your dog, but you're on thin ice all the sudden."

"Look, just hear me out, okay? My story is going to sound crazy, but I swear I will give you the whole truth, no bullshit. And if you want to go after you hear it, I won't stop you."

Her grip on the handle tightened. He could see the fight between wanting to know and wanting to run away play out on her face. Finally, she said, "Okay, go on."

"I was in a coma when Charon happened, and I somehow stayed alive in that coma for years afterward. A group of vampires found me and must have spent a lot of time draining me slowly and doing some kind of experiments." He rubbed the round scars on his right arm. Both arms and legs were still covered with them, reminders of what Alexander had done before Ana had rescued Tom. "They gave me all these."

"What happened?"

"Another group, one from out west, were looking all over the country for survivors. One of them found me, rescued me, and brought me out of my coma. She saved my life."

"Okay, I'm definitely calling bullshit now, Tom, if that's even your name. Drainers don't save people. They drain them."

"I know. I know it sounds crazy. I told you it would. But Ana doesn't drain anyone. She doesn't drink human blood. She swears she never has, and I believe her. Trust me, she could have emptied me hundreds of times in the past six months. She was a doctor before everything, and she was Turned into one of *them* against her will."

Shan pulled the handle and threw the passenger-side door open. The rain thrummed down, blanketing her. Ignoring it, she twisted to get out of the car but slapped her foot against the sidewall of the footwell. She winced. "Fuck!"

"Wait!" Tom cut in. "I swear, I'm not bullshitting you. Lady, tell her."

Lady looked at him then cocked her head in Shan's direction. She gave the girl a soft woof then started panting contentedly.

The woman gave Tom a dubious glare and a softer one for Lady before settling her eyes sharply back on Tom. She shut the door. "I'll let you finish, but I'm not going nowhere with you. When you're done, you're getting out of the car and leaving with your dog, and we'll never see each other again. You got me?"

"If that's what you want."

"It will be. But go on. Let's wrap up your fairy tale about having met a drainer that don't drain nobody."

"Okay. This vampire—"

"What's her name again?"

"Ana." He raised his eyebrows.

"Well, at least you used the same name both times. Keep going."

"After Ana rescued me and woke me up, she told me about Charon and how everything was gone and everybody left was like her."

"Dracs?"

"Uh, yeah, exactly." A sharp twinge of guilt struck him in the gut for skipping over the part that Ana hadn't bothered to tell him that she and everyone else left were actually all starving vampires. But if his story worked, Shan would have a difficult enough time trusting Ana. No use giving her extra doubts.

"Anyway, we laid low until I was healthy enough to move, and she planned to take me west, back to her group."

"Wait, they got groups?"

"Yeah. Apparently, they divided the country into regions with a lord or lady or something in charge of each one. Here, in Kentucky, we're in the south one, but

Cincinnati over there is in one that's made up of most the Midwest. I think it runs north all the way to Michigan. The river is the border."

"Oh, you know what, that makes some sense now. I stay away from pretty much anything I see moving, and I've been seeing a lot more moving around lately. Used to just be blood zombies wandering dumbly, like they do. But lately, they've been moving like they have somewhere to be. Like someone is telling them what to do. And a lot of both kinds are going back and forth over the bridges at night."

"What you've been watching is a kind of turf war going on between some of the groups. It turns out that the guy in charge of the West, who I'd been told wanted to help me, really just wanted out of the sunniest place in America, and he saw me as a meal ticket when Ana found me. He Turned Ana specifically to try to find survivors so he could use them. I'm still not sure what his long-term plan is, though."

She narrowed her eyes again. "You're telling me that this vamp you want me to meet works for this guy? Maybe you're the idiot."

"Look." He sighed. "I know how it sounds. It's… complicated. But Ana won't give you away to Colin. I swear on my life—and Lady's too."

The shepherd woofed again from the back seat.

"And you and this lady vamp that saved your life have just been hanging, and that's not a problem for this Colin asshole who wants you dead?"

"I don't think he wants me dead. Not right away. Last year, I helped Emily, the lady who's in charge of the

South, bust up Colin's plan and keep it from turning into an all-out war. And Ana hates him for her own reasons."

"For someone walking around by himself with a body full of red vamp nectar, you're telling me you've spent an awful lot of time with vampires."

"Tell me about it."

"No, dude, you're telling me about it. Now give me the whole story."

Tom gave her a slight grin and started again. "After I woke up, Ana had a run-in with one of those Feral—the blood zombies, you call them—and after that, things got weird."

He spent the next half hour going over the ins and outs of everything that had happened the previous fall. Being captured by Alexander, saved, then turned on by Ash, his escape, meeting Lindsey and Emily, all culminating in a big vampire battle in an old brewery in Cincinnati. Right up to saving Ana's life and killing Ash.

"After that, Ana and I went to stay with Emily and Lindsey in the South, where believe it or not, the old lady has kept her word and kept me safe."

"Don't look much like she kept you totally safe, man." Shan nodded at the dressing on his neck.

"That wasn't Emily's fault. Colin somehow convinced one of the Chalet vamps to attack me. He's up to something. That's why we came up here, to find out what."

"You and Ana?"

"Yes, but not just us. She sent Lindsey and Lars to find out what's going on. She sent me to get me away from the Chalet. Her people have been getting less and less happy about me being there."

"I get it. They're junkies, man, and you're just sitting there like an asshole, reminding them they're not getting any of those sweet hits. You're lucky you haven't had more trouble, I'd say. Junkies'll do about anything when they're missing their juice. Believe me, I know."

He didn't reply, mostly because he knew she wasn't wrong. The arrangement that was supposed to be his ticket to relative safety was getting less safe by the day. But that was tomorrow's problem. For the moment, they had other issues.

"Anyway, that's my story. Yes, I'm here with a vampire. A few of them, actually, but I don't know what happened to Lars and Lindsey. Ana and I found a place to hide for the day, until she can go out again. We'll be safe there. Or I can get the car and take you back over the river to wherever you've been staying. Ana probably won't let me take the car until I explain you to her. And she's going to want to meet you. After that, if you want a ride back, I'll take you. Or you can get out and take your chances in the rain. I can't do much else to help you without letting Ana in on the secret."

Shan looked at him, back at Lady, then turned to face the rain pelting the windshield. She ran her fingers over the bandage on her head and stared into space. After what had to have been a full minute, she finally said, "Mothers, but I wish we still had weather forecasters. Okay, Tom, I'm going to trust you for now. I don't know why. Could be I'm just bored with spending all my time alone, talking to myself like a freak. Could be because my reading this morning said some weird shit was on the horizon, and I'd say this qualifies as weird shit."

She faced him again. "Could be 'cause I'm curious about this vampire you claim to know who don't drink blood from people, and that would top my list of shit I never expected to see. So, if you're serious, and you really want to go run five blocks in the rain to get a decent car just to help me out, I'll wait here until you get back. At least until it starts to get late and I have to do something else."

"Deal," Tom replied.

"One other thing, though."

"What's that?"

"The dog stays with me until you get back."

Tom looked at Lady in the back seat, eyes closed and seemingly asleep. As if feeling the attention, she opened one eye, focused it on him, rolled onto her side, and committed to continuing her nap.

"Looks like that's okay with her. I'll be back. No more than an hour."

With that, he threw open the driver's-side door and dashed out into the rain. All he had to do then was convince Ana.

CHAPTER 14

NA FELT ALONG THE WALL, making her way to the front of the main garage bay. She'd spent an hour or so Resting in the office, but there was only so much Rest one could get in an aging, squeaky wooden chair with her feet up on an even older steel desk. She wasn't used to needing comfort, but even she had limits.

For what seemed like the thousandth time, she adjusted the makeshift bandanna covering her eyes. The fear that it might slip and give Colin a peek into where they were gnawed at her. She was responsible for Tom, for making sure he survived long enough for her to finish her work. Well, at least that long—she didn't want to see harm come to him at any point, whether she'd solved their problem or not. And that underlying worry colored everything she did, affected every moment she survived. Concern about the bandanna was a raindrop compared to the downpour of worry when it came to Colin, his plans, and how Tom fit into them.

Reaching the front of the garage, she moved slightly to her left to where she expected the door for the first service bay to be. Placing the flat of her left palm against the door, she stretched out with her other senses, desperate for some sign of him outside. She'd heard him leave when she'd settled into the office for Rest and, for a moment, had considered racing to the door to tell him not to go, despite having given him a list of supplies. He needed to eat, though, and they needed those supplies to keep his wound in good condition, so racing blindly through a garage she didn't know to catch up to him just to find out he was doing exactly what they'd discussed had only three possible outcomes. Either she would alienate him further, end up running into a piece of mechanical equipment, or both. In that moment, she'd quelled her anxiety and let him go with one last check to make sure everything was as she'd expected. Hard not to wonder if that had been a mistake.

He'd been gone for far too long for just a trip to a convenience store—hours had passed. But as it was the middle of summer, they were still many hours away from dusk. Ana was trapped in the service center, unable to help Tom with whatever he'd gotten into.

With her right index finger, she scratched at the corners of her thumb while listening for some hint of him on the other side of the door, hoping to feel even the slightest vibration that might reveal his return.

Nothing.

Stepping away, she turned her attention two bays to her left, once again making certain the Lexus was where he'd left it. She couldn't see it, of course, but the way the air moved around it proved it was right where she expected it to be. He hadn't taken it when he'd left or returned to get it while she'd Rested.

Why wasn't he back yet?

With a frown, Ana turned away from the garage door and started toward the office. Better to be there, where the lingering scent of decay surrounding the bodies in the lower bay wasn't so noticeable.

Thinking of the bodies, though, struck a chord—maybe he was just done with her. She didn't want to admit it to herself, but the possibility that he'd finally had enough of trying to cope with being the only human surrounded by a family of predators, most of whom really wanted to drain him, was very real. And it seemed that at every turn, she did something to make him feel different and isolated.

She should have been the one closest to him. After all, she'd saved him from Alexander, woken him from his coma, fed him, protected him, and helped him regain his strength. As the only vampire she'd ever met that had sworn off human blood, she was literally the only one who didn't want to consume him. But no matter how much goodwill that might have earned her, it couldn't quite balance the scales against the moment when Colin forced her to give Tom Charon experimentally. Never mind that the test had proven he was immune to it, the image of that betrayal—the angry, confused, hurt look on his face—was etched into her memory like a stone carving.

They'd made up after, of course, and had remained friendly, but it was clear he seemed more comfortable around Lindsey than Ana. Having lost Lindsey last night then finding out that some of humanity had actually survived the initial wave of the disease might have been the straw that broke the proverbial camel's back. He very well might have picked out another unreasonable car and headed off in whatever direction seemed like a good idea. Honestly, she could hardly blame him.

She cursed the steady rain pounding the roof of the old building and the asphalt street outside. So much noise would make it difficult to hear him coming. At that moment, though, Ana caught the distinct sound of heavy footfalls splashing into puddles from somewhere outside. They came quickly too. It wasn't someone pretending to be a kid playing in the rain. They were running hard.

With cautious, silent steps, Ana retreated to the office doorway, fighting the urge to throw open the garage instead. As much as she wanted it to be Tom, whoever had set that trap earlier almost certainly had hunters out looking for them, especially if they knew Tom was likely still in the area. She very well might be about to receive unwelcome visitors.

Ana untied the wrap covering her eyes but kept them squeezed together. If it was an attack, she would need to see. Besides, with Tom not at the garage, it wouldn't matter what Colin found out through her. Especially if Tom never came back.

She pushed all her focus to her hearing, straining to pick up anything coming from outside. With her whole body tensed, she waited, ready to act, like a coiled spring.

The footsteps stopped just outside the door. Only one pair of them too. Whoever was out there was alone, without a German shepherd at their heels. Ana smashed her molars together and forced herself not to pick at the skin on her thumb.

A side door creaked open, and Tom's scent filled the room.

Ana sighed in relief and forced herself to keep her eyes shut as she wrapped the cloth around them once again. "I was getting worried."

"Why did you have your blindfold off?" Tom asked.

"If it wasn't you, it might have been a fight. I can't fight without my eyes."

"Who else would it be?" Tom asked. "It's the middle of the day. Even in the rain, you wouldn't get visitors from anyone you know."

Ana clucked her tongue. In all her speculating, that one simple fact had completely eluded her. She was worrying too much and not thinking enough.

"What's wrong?"

She could hear the confusion in his voice. "I am an idiot," Ana replied. "I didn't even think about that."

"We all have our moments."

"Did you get the supplies and something to eat?"

"Uh, I did get the first aid stuff, but the food was awful. And the service? Inexcusable. I'm never eating at that restaurant again."

She ignored the joke. "What else, then?"

"What do you mean?"

A slight tremor in his voice gave him away, and she could hear his heart rate elevate. Something had happened.

Ana frowned and chewed her bottom lip. "Out with it. And where is Lady?"

"Okay, I'll tell you everything, but you won't believe it. And I need you to keep an open mind."

"Tom…" Her voice was harder than she intended.

"I found someone."

That sentence, as plain and simple as three words could be, barreled through her with the force of a wrecking ball. Her mouth went dry, and her tongue stopped working.

Quickly, though, her faculties returned. "What do you mean, 'someone'? I want all the details, now."

"I found a woman, Ana, a human one, like me. She's hurt, so I left Lady with her until I could get the SUV and go back for her."

"That's impossible, Tom. There was no one left. I spent a considerable amount of time hunting for any clue. No one was here but you and the other survivors in that hospital."

"I don't know how she got through it. We didn't talk about that. She says she has a safe place somewhere over the river and basically just stays hidden, I guess. I planned to take her back there."

"That's out of the question."

"I had a feeling you'd say that. But I promised her—"

She knew a spike of anger flashed across her face, but it was too late to hide it. "It does not matter what you promised. You, out of all of us, are not going across that river into territory where both Alexander and Colin are up to who knows what kind of scheming. For all I know, this woman could be a dupe of some kind. A trap."

"Ana, she walked right out into the daylight. Admittedly, it was raining by then, but you know what I mean."

"Did you tell her? About us? About all of this?"

"Yes, because she's hurt. We need a car that works to get her someplace safe, and I didn't see how I could explain why I had one, and a relatively safe place as well, without being honest."

Ana shook her head. "What's this woman's name?"

"Shan, she said. Shannon, that is. But she goes by Shan."

"And you told her the entire story? Everything from the coma to the Chalet and coming back up here to figure out Colin?"

"Just about everything. I left out the times you lied to me," Tom said matter-of-factly.

There it was. With all the resentment in his voice, he might as well have punched her right in the stomach. "Tom, I know—"

He cut her off. "I'm sorry, that wasn't necessary. Both of us are still learning to put up with a life neither of us asked for. But I don't think you understand, Ana. I found another real live person! It's incredible, and I don't know what to do with myself. I thought I'd be the only one forever. Or until Colin or Alexander or someone got their hands on me again. Or Emily got tired of me being a pain in her ass. This whole summer has been nothing but bleak for me, and getting my neck and shoulder shredded didn't help. Let me be happy about this one lucky break, just for once. Please."

"Tom, I'm… sorry. You have every right to be upset about what happened between us. The fact that Colin compelled me and I couldn't stop myself is no excuse." He inhaled, preparing to offer some rebuttal, but she put a hand up to stop him. "Don't bother. This isn't the time. By my count, we both have saved the other's crappy life at least once, and that's all I need to remember. Take the

SUV and bring this woman back. We'll talk then decide what to do."

"I knew you'd see it my way."

Even without her sight, Ana could sense the smirk on his face.

"Just be quick. Get in the car." She made her way to the garage door controls and lifted her bandanna enough just to see the buttons for a second. She pressed the middle bright-green one labeled Open and waited as the door shuddered then lifted over her. The steady pounding of rain provided a decent cover for the noise, at least. With luck, reopening it wouldn't draw any attention.

After backing the SUV halfway out of the garage, Tom stopped with the driver's door next to her. "You can probably leave it open. I'll be back in ten minutes tops." Then he pulled the rest of the way out of the garage and sped up the street. A block or so away, she heard the Lexus turn left.

"I hope you do come back," Ana muttered, "but I would not blame you if you don't."

CHAPTER 15

THE SUV SLID BACK INTO the garage stall, and Ana pressed the close button she knew was red but only because she'd stared at it for five solid minutes while Tom was gone. True to his word, he left and was back in just over ten minutes. Ana tried not to hold an unnecessary breath before meeting the other person about to get out of the car.

As the garage door slid back into place, two car doors opened. Tom's heavy feet dropped out of the driver's side, and Lady landed right behind him. The dog padded over to Ana and sniffed her hand. Ana would never be Lady's favorite, but they got along well enough, considering dogs did not like vampires by nature. She gently scratched the shepherd's muzzle to return the greeting.

The door on the passenger side of the SUV slammed shut harder than Ana thought strictly necessary, but she figured the extra force stemmed from a case of nerves that made the woman overzealous. One ungainly-sounding footstep was followed by a lighter one, and Ana smelled dried blood even from where she stood by the garage door. Tom hadn't been kidding. The woman had been hurt and was obviously limping. It wasn't but a few seconds, though, before the awkward unmatched footsteps reached the back corner of the car.

"You really are one of them?" The woman sounded on the young side but carried more than a hint of challenge.

"Hi. I am Ana. Tom tells me your name is Shannon."

"Yeah. You can call me Shan." A pause. "Why is she blindfolded?"

"Because—" Tom began, but Ana cut him off.

"How much do you know about us?"

The woman didn't move. "Us? You mean you Dracula types? Not much. Enough to stay out of your way."

"Dracula was, apparently, just fiction, or so I've been told. I'm afraid the reality is far more troubling. But without boring you with too many details, the one who Made me can see through my eyes. We're telepathically linked. I do not want him to know where we are or that I'm with Tom. And I especially do not want him to find out about you."

"Shit, that's messed up."

"You don't know the half of it, Shan," Tom chimed in.

Ana ignored him. "Regardless, it is my pleasure—and of course, my great surprise—to meet you, Shannon."

"Shan," the younger woman corrected. "My mom called me Shannon, and she was a first-rate bitch. The only other person who called me that was my, um, mentor, who was amazing. At least, she was, right up until one of your blood zombies got to her. So just 'Shan,' thanks."

Ana swallowed the urge to groan. It was not going all that well. The woman's heart beat fast, and her breathing was quick and shallow. She was on edge, and Ana had not managed to do much to put her at ease.

"I will do my best to make sure that doesn't happen to either of you. How badly are you injured? I was a doctor once, and normally, I'd get right to work patching you up, but I'm afraid I can't do that without letting Colin know you're here. Do you mind if I touch your wounds? That would help me diag—"

"Yeah, lady, I do mind. I'd let *him* put his hands on me before I let you touch me."

Ana rolled her eyes behind the blindfold. Bringing her here had been a terrible idea. When she'd woken Tom, he'd had no idea the situation he was in, and she could control almost everything as she nursed him. He'd had no choice but to go along with it, but the girl knew exactly what had happened and clearly held some grudges.

Finding a way to make the arrangement work evaded Ana. She would have to let Tom play mediator between her and the other woman. She turned her head toward him and opened her mouth to say as much, but he must have finally reached the same conclusion.

"Hey, Shan, I know this is all kinds of weird, but I swear we're not messing with you. Ana's not going to suddenly go all fangs and black eyes on you. Like I said, she could have dried me out hundreds of times last year, and I wouldn't have known any better. You're safe here."

The other woman exhaled hard, and Ana sensed the coiled-iron tightness of her stress soften. "Okay, look, I'm sorry I'm being a jackass. This whole day has been nothing but a punch to the nuts. I hurt like hell. I have to figure out whether y'all are Jack and Jill or Chuckles and Hyde, and all I really want is some space to sit down and take care of myself then maybe take a nap."

Tom shuffled to Ana's left. "I get it. This is all a lot. I think we can probably find somewhere you can relax a little. And I can rewrap your ankle and touch up that spot on your head with the first aid stuff we brought back if you want. I feel like someone else always fixes me up better than I can do it myself. Ana, where's the best place for that, do you think?"

Before Ana could reply, Shan said, "No, thanks, dude, but I'm good. I'm pretty good at, uh, let's call it first aid. I'll do just fine with that stuff we got from the store and some of my own supplies." She patted something at her side. A bag of some kind, maybe? "I'm pretty good with, uh, natural medicine. Actually, T, if you want, I can take a look at your shoulder. I can probably get it fixed a little quicker."

Ana frowned before she could stop herself then made her face smooth again as quickly as she could. Hopefully, the girl hadn't noticed. What kind of nonsense was she peddling, though? Herbs or some other kind of idiocy? The last thing they needed was some superstitious faith healer trying to make Tom believe that everything would be fine if he ate the right granola and rubbed some dirt on his injuries. He had significant muscular damage in his neck and shoulder on top of the open wounds that had just started to seal.

She ground her back teeth again. It wasn't the time for that debate. This Shannon person needed to be made comfortable, not proven wrong. Not yet.

"The office is too cramped for much more than the desk and the uncomfortable chair that's already in there," Ana said instead, keeping her voice even. She pointed to the far back corner of the garage. "But I believe there's a stockroom back there that likely has more room. I haven't gone in there myself yet, but I checked the door. It seemed sturdy enough, so I didn't see the need to disturb it. We can move a couple of chairs from the garage back there, and I have some blankets in the SUV that we can set up so you can sleep. We might have some pallets too."

Ana heard Shan turn and shuffle-limp in the direction of the storeroom door. Tom slid past Ana to follow. Lady remained sitting at her left hand. After a few moments, the dog trod after the pair of humans. Ana started to join them then stopped. Should she follow or let them go? Shan had made it clear she had little use for Ana, so in all likelihood, following would only bring trouble. In the long run, it was probably better to let Tom make Shan more comfortable without a constant reminder of what had ruined her former life.

Hearing them make their way to the back through the large, empty garage, she couldn't help but wonder how much had just changed.

CHAPTER 16

T OM TURNED THE STEEL KNOB on the stockroom door. It clicked, but the door wouldn't budge when he pressed it forward. He frowned. Any other time, he would have just put his shoulder into it, but that was out of the question, wounded as he was. He held the knob open and shook the door in its frame but had no luck. "Looks like it's stuck. Maybe the hinges seized up? I'll see if I can get Ana to give it a shove."

"Why?" Shan clucked her tongue. "I'm sure we can get it open. Just give it a good kick. That's what I'd do if I could."

After taking a step back, Tom stroked his beard, considering. Couldn't hurt, right? "Can you turn the knob so I can get more leverage?"

"Pretty sure." Shan reached out and twisted the doorknob.

"On three, then. One—"

"Jesus, just hit it."

He shrugged then steadied himself before unfurling a front kick with as much force as he could muster. He twisted his upper body slightly to maintain his balance, and his foot connected with a satisfying clang. A wave of recoil rolled through him, starting from his foot then through his leg and into his chest. With a loud screech, the door shuddered and swung forward into the space beyond.

"See? You don't need her for everything."

Tom gave the younger woman an appraising look then a nod. "Maybe we're not a bad team. Shall we check out our new hidey-hole?"

Shan stepped forward, but before she could bring her wounded foot across the threshold, Lady darted into the darkness. The echoes of her padding forward stopped after she took a few steps ahead, and she sniffed. The dog sneezed twice before reappearing at the door.

"She always give things the once-over?" Shan asked.

He nodded. "Lady does that. She likes to check out rooms for me. And it sounds like it's dusty in there."

The woman reached forward and scratched Lady between the ears. The dog raised her head slightly in appreciation.

"That's a good doggo. And I've seen worse things than dust, man." Shan hobbled forward into the darkness.

Tom followed close behind, turning to his left as he entered the room.

The area was much as he'd expected. Running to the left of the door off into the darkness was a space not quite as long as the full width of the garage. An aisle wide enough for two people—or maybe three, if not too stout—to stand shoulder to shoulder split the room between two looming racks of what had to be replacement car parts, one each to his left and right. Somewhere in the shadowed distance, the shelving racks ended, giving way to more open space he could sense but not yet see. The ceiling wasn't quite two full stories above them but was higher than a standard room. If he'd had to guess, Tom would have said maybe twelve or fifteen feet tall. Dark lights hung from the ceiling on thick wire cords, each covered by an angled shade.

Standing in front of him, Shan reached to her left. A loud click echoed off the racks and walls, and the overhead lights snapped on. They were dim but still bright enough to force him to look away.

"Jesus, you could have warned me," he groaned, trying to blink back tears.

"Poor baby." Mirth tickled her voice. "I'm sure you'll survive."

A shower of dust mites flew all around them, like tiny flakes in a dingy snow globe.

"I wonder how long since anyone's been in here," he said.

"Three and a half years, I bet." She shuffled deeper into the storeroom.

The shelving racks only extended about two-thirds of the way into the room. Where they ended, rows of tires, each stacked eight high, lined the walls, leading back to a steel desk at the far back wall. A swivel chair with duct tape holding in what couldn't be more than half the stuffing the padded seat began with sat beside the desk, and a short three-rung stepladder was just in front of it. To the right of it stood a Coke machine that looked older than Tom by a good twenty years.

"C'mon, I'll set my stuff out on the desk and get us fixed up."

Tom raised an eyebrow. "What do you mean?"

She looked over her shoulder and grinned. "I need to tell you a secret, T. See, I'm kind of a witch."

He stopped and glared at the woman limping toward the desk at the end of the room. "You're messing with me, right?"

"Nope. I'll swear to the Earth or the Moon or the Mothers or whatever other God you think would best have your back. Don't get it all twisted, though. I don't mean like the pointy-hat, warty-nose, cackling-hag kind of thing with the boiling cauldron. Though, fuck, that'd probably be okay because I could for sure use a flying broomstick. But it's not like that."

She stopped and turned back to him, her face firm, without a shine of the humor he had begun to expect in her eyes. "Sometimes, I can feel energy around me, and I can mix up stuff that'll fix a wounded ankle—or shoulder." She nodded at his bandages. "Trust me."

"Bullshit."

"Come on, you baby. It won't hurt. And I won't bite or anything." She resumed limping to the desk.

He stared after her. There were, apparently, only two self-aware living beings on the planet who theoretically weren't interested in biting him. One of them was a vampire who refused to drink human blood, and the other just told him without a hint of irony that she was a witch of some sort. Then again, his life was defined by the vampires surrounding him. Was running into any sort of witch really that strange?

For that matter, he'd give her bonus points if she really did heal his shoulder. For the last hour, it had been aching like he'd carried an anvil on it all day. Stepping quickly, he moved to catch up with her.

Shan reached the desk and dropped the woven bag emblazoned with a regal woman holding a long sword straight up to the sky on top of it. The rest of it was covered in paperwork. Invoices, bills, purchase orders, receipts, work orders, and diagnostic reports littered the surface in a jumble.

"That's not gonna work," she announced, sweeping all the papers off it to the left, away from the Coke machine and into a heap on the floor.

Once again, the room became a freshly shaken dusty snow globe. Tom squeezed his eyes shut and tried not to inhale. Lady, sitting next to him, sneezed twice. With the desk clear, Shan began to unpack things from her bag. First came a stone bowl then something that looked like a small matching bludgeon.

"What's that?"

"You're kidding me, right, T?"

"No. I think I've seen something like that before but can't remember where."

"It's a mortar and pestle. You might have seen one in pictures of old drugstores. Pharmacists used to use them, I guess. Or at least, that's what Janine told me. She said it was used by people like us and pharmacists, mostly. Some people used them to make food, I guess. I don't know. I never paid a lot of attention to her history lessons."

"Who's Janine?"

"She was like my teacher. Or a mentor? She took me in when I was a junkie teen, living like shit on the streets. She taught me to do something useful with myself. I never got her to tell me why she bothered when there were always dozens of other dumbass kids doing stupid shit in the neighborhood. She just said she saw a light in me. Who knows what that means? Anyway, she's the one who taught me the witch stuff."

"Witchcraft? Like magic? Really?"

The younger woman shrugged. "Call it whatever you want. I really can sense weird energy sometimes, and I get, I don't know, vibes about people and places. But mostly it's doing readings. Like tarot? Then making, like, pastes and teas and stuff. I actually know a really good tea that'd help with the healing paste I'll put on me and your shoulder, but I don't have the right stuff here. We're in the middle of a city, and it's too late for a pair of walking wounded to be wandering around out there, looking for ginger and a particular kind of nettle."

He smirked. "Yeah, I don't know that this area is all that well known for its naturally occurring ginger."

She took out a small linen bag and shook a few herbs into the bowl. Then she added some kind of powder and grabbed a small stoppered bottle. She poured a short stream of some kind of oil from it into the mixture. "Do you have the first aid stuff?"

"Uh, yeah. Sorry." Tom pulled the plastic bag from his back pocket and handed it over.

After taking out a tube of antibiotic gel, Shan uncapped it and added a good dose of that to the bowl as well.

"So, what?" Tom laughed. "Eye of newt and Neosporin?"

"Hey, just because the old stuff works doesn't mean

you can't adjust recipes when modern ingredients add something useful."

He lost count of the various herbs and powders Shan added to the mortar before using the stone pestle to smash and mix it all into a pungent green paste. Then, after digging out a thin, colored piece of paper and a ninety-nine-cent cigarette lighter from her shoulder bag, she lit the paper and let the ashes fall into the bowl. She blew out the fire an instant before singeing her fingertips.

After another good stir, she leaned over her concoction and inhaled deeply. Nodding in apparent satisfaction, she took a container of gauze wrap from the first aid bag.

"Come over here, and take off your shirt."

Tom shot her an uncertain look but then pulled his left arm through the arm hole of his T-shirt. With it free, he lifted the shirt up over his head, bottom up, but grimaced hard when he tried to take it over his right arm. She shifted toward him and pulled it the rest of the way off.

He was suddenly very aware of the potbelly he'd grown by drinking beer on the porch all summer. The thought of trying to suck it in flashed through his mind, but he couldn't without it being embarrassingly obvious. And why did it matter to him anyway?

Shan stood from the desk chair and leaned over him, peering at the bandages covering his wounded neck and shoulder. Her fingers slid over the taped edges until she reached a corner at the end of the dressing and lifted it upward. She moved slowly, with a delicate ease that showed she'd done it before, but Tom didn't care. She could have ripped it off the way his mom had his Band-Aids when he was a kid, and he wouldn't have noticed.

With her face so close to his, her breath falling against the bare skin of his shoulder and her fingers working at the edges of his wound, the only thing he registered was warmth. Her warmth. Her fingers were warm, her breath was warm, and he could sense the heat of her body so near to his own.

His head swam, and his thoughts buzzed like he'd had one too many bourbons. For nearly a year, he'd been poked and prodded by Ana and had had plenty of physical contact with Lindsey, and over and over, he'd tried to convince himself that he was used to the steellike hardness and icy chill that defined their vampiric physique. But telling himself something was not the same as believing it.

He forced himself not to react, or hoped he did, anyway. The last thing he wanted was for the woman he'd just met to decide he was some kind of creep.

If she noticed anything, she didn't let on. With the old bandage removed, she grabbed the mortar and stuck three fingers into the mixture. Then she held it close to his shoulder. "Hold still. This might tingle."

Without waiting for a reply, she pressed the paste into his scab-covered neck. Fire exploded from the wound, racing both down his arm into his fingers and up to the crown of his head.

"Whua…" he grunted, gritting his molars. In his head, he sounded like some kind of wounded bear.

Shan spread the paste all over the injury, lighting new fires with every motion. Finally, with all of it coated, she wrapped it with heavy cotton gauze and taped that down. "All done."

"You could have warned a guy."

"I said it might tingle."

"Tingle? It felt like you set my arm on fire."

With a smirk, she winked at him. "That's how you know it's working."

Shan dropped back into the chair and unrolled the wrappings he'd dressed her ankle with back at the store then peeled away the gauze padding. The crescent-shaped cut around her ankle bone had stopped bleeding, but it had puffed up quite a bit.

Tom wasn't sure in the dim light, but he thought the edges might be discolored. "That doesn't look so great."

She shrugged then dipped into the bowl for another dose of paste. "I've seen worse. We'll see how it looks tomorrow." Then she wiped the mix on her ankle, hissing as she went. When she finished wrapping it, she said, "I'll need your help."

"Uh, okay. With what?"

"I need you to put the stuff on my head. I don't have a mirror, and I don't want to accidentally get some of it in my eye. You think it hurts to put it on an open wound…"

"Oh, yeah. I can see that. So, just scoop a couple of fingers' worth and wipe it over the cut?"

"Yep. And don't be stingy with it, T."

Tom stood from his seat on the stepladder and gingerly dipped his fingers into the mortar, half afraid he would get the same sensation as when she'd rubbed it into his shoulder. Thankfully, it only felt like pesto on his fingertips. In fact, the paste was cooler than he'd expected. He scooped out a generous dose and lifted it to her forehead. He tried to raise his right hand to push back the hair from her temple, but his shoulder burned disagreeably, making him wince.

"I got it." Shan pushed her hair out of the way.

Tom spread the salve across her cut while she hissed once more, then he wiped his hands on an old McDonald's napkin they found in one of the desk drawers. It only took him a minute or so to cover the cut with cotton gauze and secure it with tape.

"All done." He retook his seat on top of the ladder. "Seem okay?"

Brushing her fingers over the bandage, she smiled and nodded. "I'll make a mom out of you yet, T. I mean, a witch would be better, but we'll see what we're working with first."

"I wouldn't get your hopes up."

"Well, either way, don't piss me off, or I'll turn you into a toad."

She laughed and winked at him again, and he couldn't help but laugh with her despite having a pretty good notion that they were both just laughing at him.

"What do we do now, Tom?" she asked when the laughter subsided.

"What do you mean?"

"Like, what do you do? How do you keep yourself from going crazy? You all play cards or something?"

"Usually, I sit on my front porch and drink beer until sundown, but that's how this happened." He touched his bandaged neck. "Thinking back about it, probably not my best idea."

"Probably not. I could go for a drink, though. Not beer. Beer's fucking gross, man, but I could throw back something trashy and neon blue. Man, you never realize how much you're gonna miss shitty beach drinks until they're just fucking gone, yanno?"

The last time Tom had sipped a drink on a beach anywhere, he and Heather had been on a cruise somewhere in the Caribbean. It was their first-anniversary trip, and they were sunbathing on the beach of one of those islands the cruise company bought just to have something for tourists to do before the awkward Captain's Dinner with eight other strangers they ended up getting drunk with every night anyway. He might have had a piña colada, but that was so long ago, he couldn't exactly remember. Then again, it was probably the gigantic "collectible" thermos of overpriced fruit juice and cheap booze he was drinking at the time that helped him not recall exactly. Didn't matter anymore, anyway. Heather was gone. The cruise ships were all probably drifting somewhere, empty but for piles of skeletons, and as Shan said, overpriced vacation cocktails were a thing of the past.

The pair of them had involuntarily traded all that in for the chance to hide in dusty storerooms for the rest of their lives, secreting themselves away from the things that wanted to kill them. Hard not to wonder sometimes if carrying on was worth all the hassle. But at least he wasn't the only one anymore. He'd found someone like him, and that had to mean something.

CHAPTER 17

LINDSEY BLINKED BACK TO CONSCIOUSNESS, sitting upright with her back against a stone block wall. Lars's face, framed with a mix of gray-brown hair, came into focus. He dangled what appeared to be a moderately sized rat in front of him by its hairless tail.

"Do you want some? It isn't great, but it's better than nothing."

The thought turned her stomach, but she tried not to let it show on her face. Since Charon, they did what they had to do to get by. Thankfully, she hadn't been forced to resort to living on the blood of rodents yet. She had Emily, who made sure the Family was somehow still fed with moderate rations of human blood.

"Nah, thanks, hon. It's all yours. I fed before we left the Chalet. Where's the sun, you reckon?"

Lars looked toward the ceiling. "Feels like the day is about done to me."

She nodded. Even being underground, Lindsey marked the slight change in atmosphere, a nearly imperceptible drop in temperature that usually came with a summer sunset. The change wasn't as noticeable in the winter, but coping with very little winter was one perk of living in Georgia. Emily had spun some yarn once about some of their kind choosing to live in extreme north places, where they could see the northern lights and most parts of the year had very little daylight. The lack of daylight sounded nice, but she was a Southern girl, born and bred. She liked a chill about as much as she liked a rumbling belly.

"We should get ready, then." She took her own look up at the ceiling. "I reckon we're maybe a couple hundred yards away from where we found the gate down here. Which, if anything makes any kinda sense, that ought to put us on the far side of the building, where those plaguers won't be looking for us, if they're still around."

Lars's face twisted. "I'm about done with all these Feral. I've half a mind to go out there and see how many of them I can tear apart. It'd be like—what'd they call it?—therapy."

"Oh, hon, was therapy a new thing when you were Made? You gotta be older than my first-life grandmomma."

He shook his head. "Forget I said anything. Can we go kill some stuff now?"

"Believe me, I'd like that almost as much as a good drink of some tall, dumb, muscle-bound meathead that spent all day doing curls on the Gulf Shore beach. But I spoke to Emily last night, and she wants us to get answers, gramps, not make an incident. At least not yet."

Standing up, Lars clapped his hands, releasing a cloud of dust and rat hair. "Gramps? I thought you Southern girls were raised to be polite and respectful."

Lindsey also stood, meeting his eye. "Trust me, you

don't want me polite and respectful. That's when you really start to get the venom. Or would you rather I stick with 'beefcake'?"

The older vampire could only shake his head.

Lindsey looked back down the long tunnel from the direction they'd come. The stone steps they'd found covered by the iron gate in the floor of the restaurant above had led to a large room that must have been some kind of storage or cellar once. The foundation was old, a mix of uniform masonry blocks and even older, uneven stonework, as if the room had been built a very long time ago then added onto after its initial construction. But even the expanded section, if that was how the room had been built, could maybe be a century old.

The room led to an open tunnel that ran north under the street and building above. It was wide enough for three people to stand shoulder to shoulder but was just barely tall enough for Lars to stand at his full height. Both the room and the tunnel were empty except for piles of dirt and trash mostly consisting of beer bottles and cans, almost certainly the result of decades' worth of teens and young adults with nothing better to do with their time.

The morning prior, they'd made their way far enough into the tunnel that the piles of trash became less frequent, meaning they were probably deeper than most of the party kids were willing to venture.

"You think we're halfway?" Lars eyed the other direction.

Lindsey nodded in the dark, dusty air. "Give or take, based on the way the air is moving. It's not as stale toward the way out."

"What if there is no way out? What if we follow this to the end and that's it, dead end?"

She shrugged. "What sense would that make? Who makes a tunnel to nowhere? Especially underground. They probably built this when you were still in your first life and horses pulled carriages up on the street."

Lars started walking ahead, in the direction they expected to find the way out. "I'm not that old, girl. And you haven't spent much time in the underground parts of the area here, have you? Half the old ground in Cincinnati has some kind of tunnel or storage space from the eighteen hundreds. Over the years, though, modern technology made them unnecessary, and companies who owned buildings with underground spaces tended to worry about liability, especially with trespassers. Lots of the stuff below ground around here is sealed off, for one reason or another."

Lindsey fell into step beside him. "Not much like this in most places I've lived. Were these kinds of places still used when you were first alive?"

"No. I told you, I'm not quite *that* old. Alexander might be old enough, I guess. Never gave it much thought."

"How old *are* you, then? When did Alexander Turn you?"

"I don't belong to Alexander."

Lindsey looked at him sideways. "My bad, hon, I just assumed. Since you're his right hand and all."

He shook his head. "I'm not even sure I'm still his right hand. Ever since he came back to the Family, he's been acting… off. Nothing I can put a figure on, but he hasn't been as open with me. Half the time, I don't know what's going on in his head."

"Shoot, I wouldn't worry much about that kind of thing." She kicked a rock and watched it career off a nearby stone column. "Emily tightens up on me all the time. And even when she does tell me what's in her head, I ain't sure she's giving me the whole story."

"It's different for you, though, being her Daughter. You can feel her even when she isn't talking to you. I don't get any of that."

"Why do you belong to him, then? What happened to your Maker?"

"My Maker…" He stopped and stared down the tunnel. She got the feeling, though, that he wasn't actually seeing anything. "She was incredible, but I don't know what happened to her."

She stopped with him. "What do you mean?"

"Just that. I don't know what happened to her. When Charon came, she disappeared."

"Like, she died?"

"I don't know. Maybe. I'd always heard that when your Maker dies, you feel it. You *know*. But I never felt anything. I just realized one day that I couldn't feel her anymore. And when I reached out to her, nothing."

He started moving toward the end of the tunnel again, still staring straight ahead.

Lindsey cocked her head and watched him for a moment before starting after him. The thought of losing Emily was inconceivable. Emily wasn't just some being, a simple vampire. She was a given, a constant. An elemental force. She was older than anyone knew and had seen a world that had existed to most only as a weird idea in a history book or a Renaissance festival. She might as well have *always* been because Lindsey expected that Emily always would be. As a result, she'd never given much thought to what it might be like to lose one's Maker.

"What was her name? What was she like? Was she old like Alexander or even older?"

"You ask a lot of questions," Lars muttered.

She shrugged. "We're walking down a tunnel in the complete dark, and there ain't even the sound of mice in here. I'm filling the space, gramps. Besides, I'm pretty sure it won't kill you to talk about her."

"Her name was Genevieve. If she didn't kill you and you didn't annoy her, she might let you call her Vivi."

"There now, that's a start. Was that so hard?"

"Hard enough," he grumbled. "Let's just get out of here. I'm tired of being underground."

Lindsey smirked. "Somebody woke up on the wrong side of the coffin."

"Breakfast rats will do that."

"And now, hon, you know why I skipped it."

He grunted but added nothing. Instead, he started jogging. At the quickened pace, they reached an abrupt left turn a minute or two later. Following the change in direction, they hiked another fifty feet before coming to a narrow set of stone steps rising to a wrought iron gate matching the one that had led them there. The new one was flush with the ceiling and covered by a piece of plywood. A keyed padlock hung down from a clasp, sealing the gate from above.

Lindsey climbed a few steps and snapped the lock with

a simple twist of her wrist. She pushed the gate with one hand, but nothing happened. With a scowl, she climbed another step for better leverage and tried to military press the gate upward. It refused to budge. "Looks like I need an extra pair of hands here."

Lars climbed the steps to the one below her and set his palms against the gate. He nodded, and they both pressed up against the iron. It shifted but still refused to budge. Lindsey ground her teeth and pushed harder, trying to match the effort she could see on Lars's face. Finally, with the crack of shearing plywood, the opening gave way a few inches.

Once they'd freed it from whatever kept it in place, Lars prepared to shove the gate to open it, but Lindsey grabbed his arm and shook her head. She rose one more step and lifted the covering a few inches to take stock of the space above. It wasn't direct access to the street, as she had expected, but instead opened into another room. It wasn't restaurant space like the one at the far side but seemed like some kind of supply room or workroom for a brewery. A pair of wooden barrels stood to the right side, and crates of dusty bottles were stacked against the wall to her left. Otherwise, the room was empty save for decades' worth of dust.

"Looks clear." She walked up the remaining steps, swinging the gate open. "Good thing too. If anything had been in here, I'm betting the sound of that plank ripping open would've gotten a plaguer's attention."

"That would have been okay with me." Lars stepped up into the room. "I don't like sneaking around, and I definitely don't like hiding from dumb beasts."

"Look, I get it. You and I both know they're as dumb as a box of rocks, and I enjoy taking hacks at them as much as the next girl. Hell, you know I'm always ready to start swinging first. But that Kallus guy looks to be controlling a whole heap more Feral than I've ever seen somebody wrangle, and if even one of his slobbery pigs sees us, he'll know. Then we'll be right back where we started. So, I guess, for this one time, we probably ought to try not fighting and, heck, even avoid being seen if we can. At least until we figure out what Colin and his little pet trainer are up to."

Lars gave her half a smile. "Can't say I ever expected to see the day you were the one telling anyone to be careful. But I suppose you're right. What's next, then?"

"Well, keep in mind that it's what Emily told me to do." Lindsey smiled back. "And next, we tiptoe across the river. Then we find that greaser. I wouldn't mind taking a shot at him in a fair fight."

CHAPTER 18

TOM SNORTED AWAKE, SITTING UPRIGHT in the fraying desk chair, legs stretched out to the bottom rung of the stepladder like a makeshift ottoman. He was covered in a light weave blanket he couldn't remember pulling over himself. Several hours before the sun went down, he and Shan had independently come to the realization that a nap seemed like a good idea. They'd both had a long day—or in his case, a long night followed by a very eventful day—and between the steady rain falling on the garage roof and the tingling of his skin beneath the bandage, he was soon yawning uncontrollably. Every time he had, she'd followed suit, then he'd needed to yawn again a few moments later.

He'd fetched the blankets from the SUV and done his best to make a soft, or at least softer, spot on the floor for her to rest. She'd tried to tell him to sleep on the floor and she would stay in the chair, but of the two of them, she was in worse shape. Besides, he couldn't lie down properly with the shoulder still ragged from the attack, so sitting up had been fine by him. Of the many things he'd learned about himself in the past year, having the ability to fall asleep anywhere, at nearly any time, in pretty much any position, was almost as useful as knowing just how to hit a plaguer in the temple with a baseball bat if you wanted to drop it with one swing.

Shan snoozed on the collection of blankets a few feet away, covered in a patchwork quilt of college mascots someone's grandmother probably spent months putting together only for it to end up on the floor of an auto shop's storeroom. Lady was curled up beside her and peeked at Tom with one half-open eye. He nodded back at her, and she allowed that eyelid to drift closed.

The storeroom was dark. Shan must have turned the lights off after he'd drifted to sleep. A rustling sound caught his attention, and he glanced back toward the open steel door on the opposite side of the narrow room. A dark silhouette stood just inside, hands on her hips, motionless. He could probably recognize Ana's familiar frame in abject darkness after all the time they'd shared together in dark places.

Setting his blanket aside with care to avoid making unnecessary noise, Tom pulled his feet out from the step-ladder and stood, stifling a groan. Unfortunately, being able to fall asleep in any position wasn't nearly the same thing as that position being comfortable, and his back and neck would need some stretching if he didn't want to be sore all day.

Taking care not to disturb Shan, he shuffled past her makeshift bed, with Lady watching him. He thought the dog might get up and walk to meet Ana with him, but she apparently trusted the woman in the doorframe well enough not to feel the need.

When he reached the doorway, Ana began to speak,

but he stopped her with a light touch to the shoulder. "Out there. Let's not wake her."

She sniffed but nodded then stepped out of the storeroom. Tom followed through the doorway, closing it halfway behind him. He took a few more steps so they weren't right beside it.

"What time is it?"

"Shortly after midnight," Ana replied.

"What's up?"

"I need to check your wound and redo the wrap, then we should talk about what to do next."

"Do next?" He frowned. "Do you think they'll find us?"

"Who?" She slipped her blindfold up just enough to unwrap the bandage. "Colin, or Lindsey and Lars?"

"Anyone, I guess."

"I don't know. We need to keep you out of sight until…" Ana gasped instead of finishing the sentence.

"What's wrong?" Tom tried to crane his neck to look at the wound, but he couldn't see it without a mirror. For the first time since he'd woken up, though, he realized it no longer hurt, and the tingling he'd felt after Shan had applied that paste was barely noticeable.

"It's… better," Ana mumbled. "This is not possible."

Tom felt it, but instead of sticky, crusty gashes, he ran his fingers over bumpy, jagged scars covered in just the thinnest scabbing. He rolled his neck from side to side and windmilled his arm. The joints were stiff but didn't ache the way they had before, and his range of motion was no longer restricted.

He whistled. "Damn."

"How?" Ana demanded.

"What do you mean?"

"Again, this is impossible. A wound like this should take at least a week, if not more, to heal to this degree."

"I don't know. She made some kind of paste and put it on the wound. Then I fell asleep, and here we are."

Ana glowered. "What was in this *paste*? Did you see anything that looked like blood? Only my kind heal that quickly." It wasn't quite an accusation, but it was close.

"No." Tom shook his head. "None of it looked remotely like blood. I don't know what it was, but it had a lot of parts to it. But she said…"

"Said what?"

"She said she was a witch or something."

Ana cocked on eyebrow. "A… witch?"

"Yeah, I know what it sounds like, but you're a goddamn vampire, remember? How do I know what's real and what's actually only a bedtime story anymore? Besides, I guess you can't argue with the results." He ran his fingers along the newly scarred flesh that had been a mostly open wound a few hours ago.

"I don't like it," she replied, "and I'm not sure I like having her around. Keeping you alive is hard enough."

"Ana, I appreciate everything you've done for me, but you can't—"

"Can I not?"

"Why do you have to be like this? Look, I've been thinking. Maybe, well, maybe trying to keep me alive in the middle of a bunch of starving blood drinkers isn't the best idea anymore. Maybe I should… go. Maybe we should go."

Ana shook her head. "Tom, you know I can't."

"Yeah, I know *you* can't."

Her mouth snapped shut, and she glared back at him. Her dark eyes gave almost nothing away, but after a few moments, they softened, and she cocked her head, as if considering. Finally, she muttered, "I can't protect you if you're away from me."

"You won't always be able to protect me, Ana. And you're caught up in whatever Colin is doing. That's never going away for me. That is, not unless I go away from you. Would I be any worse off out there, one man in the vast wilderness, rather than here, where everyone knows who I am, what I mean, and generally where to find me? I don't belong here. I don't belong among you."

She sighed. "You don't understand, Tom. I'm so close, and I…" Ana's eyes went wide, and she turned to the garage doors behind them. "Someone's coming. And it's not Lindsey or Lars. Go! Hide in the storeroom and wake her up. I'll try to lead whoever it is away."

"But what if—"

"Go," she breathed, giving him a soft shove to the chest to get him moving.

He stumbled backward a few steps as she flashed toward the garage doors. Catching himself, he turned for the storeroom and charged through the door then pulled it closed as far as he could without it squealing against the doorframe.

"Shan, wake up. We might have company," he announced in an urgent whisper.

Lady was up in a second, trotting past him toward the door.

Whether it was Tom's urging or the dog's motion, Shan blinked as she leaned up on her elbows. "What?"

"Someone's coming."

Her face darkened. "Someone, who?"

"I don't know. I don't even know if they're coming here, but we need to be ready."

"Ready," she repeated. "Okay, yeah, that makes sense." She threw off the blanket covering her and popped up, showing little sign that hours ago she'd been hobbling like the Hunchback of Notre Dame. She flew to the desk and rummaged through her bag.

"Shan," he gasped. "Your ankle."

She took a quick look at it then resumed digging through the bag. "What, did you think I'm some kind of crackpot? Now come over here and help me look."

"Look for what?" Tom banged against the edge of the desk.

"Something to give us a bit of an edge against the Dracs."

CHAPTER 19

T HE GARAGE DOOR STOOD BETWEEN Ana and whoever was outside the building, a set of steel-hinged plates the only thing separating her from exposure that would almost certainly lead to catastrophe. She glared at the door while scratching at the skin of her thumb, mind racing with alternatives in case the door began to rise.

She could stay where she stood and hold her ground. Maybe she could take the offensive and start a fight to keep whoever was out there from realizing it was not only Tom hiding in the stockroom but another living, breathing human full of B negative blood. Or she could race to the office in the back, hoping to draw their new arrival farther away. Maybe she should pick up one of the large wrenches lying on the floor and start swinging at kneecaps as soon as the door opened halfway.

Ana had half a dozen choices, none of them good. She'd broken one of her own rules by allowing them to stay there, in an open space with no back door for retreat. They'd put themselves in a trap of their own making. The realization swirled like an electric eel in her belly, making the wait even worse. Could she possibly will them to go away?

As if spurred by the thought, the garage door's hinges groaned, and its wheels began to roll along their tracks. At that same moment, Ana was blasted with the overpowering scent of cigarette smoke, something she hadn't much appreciated back when she was human, with regular senses. She absolutely abhorred it now that she could, from ten feet away, smell the specific number of days it had been since Tom had last showered.

Oh no, it was worse than she thought.

The rising door reached its midpoint, and she raced to pick up the wrench. It probably wouldn't help much, but she needed whatever assistance she could find, no matter how little. She pulled the blindfold off her forehead and dropped it. As little as she wanted to help Colin, he would probably want to see what came next. Then she strode quickly over to the garage door just as it reached its apex.

Alexander's wrinkled face appeared before hers, a cigarette dangling from the corner of his mouth. He held the door steady with one hand over his head and exhaled directly into Ana's face. The acrid smoke burned her nostrils. She returned the gesture with a scowl.

"Now, before you start swinging that wrench, girl, and force me to defend myself, you should at least hear me out." Alexander smirked, dropped the cigarette on the pavement, and crushed it with the toe of his boot.

"How did you find me?" Ana demanded. Then, before letting him answer, she added, "You know I am under Emily's protection, so think very carefully before you do anything that might force her to react." She emphasized the last word for effect.

He ignored her and raised his eyes to the hand holding the door, then he cautiously let it go. Satisfied, he surveyed the service center behind her as he dug a pack of slightly flattened Camels out of his pant pocket. "These things are getting harder and harder to find. I wonder if I won't need to start looking in different parts of the country for them."

His deep voice seemed gravellier than the last time she'd seen him. The cigarettes might not kill him, but they did seem to be having some effect. How long, though, had he been smoking them? One hundred years or more?

"Answer the question. How did you find me?"

"Child, you do amuse me. I've come looking for someone."

Her hand holding the wrench twitched as he said it. He knew. Somehow, even though she couldn't sense them herself, he knew that Tom was somewhere behind her. Surely, he couldn't know about the woman, though. Unless Shan wasn't who she had told them she was.

He plucked a cigarette from the pack and lifted it to his mouth. "I heard tell that Lars was in the area, and I need him for something. I came down this way, where I'd been told he was seen, and wouldn't you know, I smelled car exhaust, which I must admit was a pleasant reminder of the old days."

The iron gripping Ana's chest relented somewhat, and she forced herself not to sigh in relief. It was almost too perfect. "He's not here. We separated, but I can show you where I saw him last. I can take you there now." She slid past him, stepping outside the garage, and turned toward the corner. Not that she had any inkling of where they were in relation to where those Feral had ambushed them, but she could pretend long enough to get her bearings if that would keep him away from Tom.

He grabbed her arm from behind and spun her to face him. "Now hold on, missy. Before we go anywhere, you're going to explain why you split up. And where have you got your little Pinocchio squirreled away that you're willing to go on a walk with me?"

Scowling again, she wrenched her arm from his grip. "I am not obligated to do anything for you or tell you anything, but if it will get you out of my hair, I'll help you. We came here—"

"I know why you came. To find out who convinced that idiot to attack your boy the other day. I heard he nearly got himself a full meal. And Emily sent Lindsey along to do a little digging for good measure." He lit the cigarette with a quick, practiced gesture.

She stepped back, in the direction of the stop sign and street corner behind her, both to put some space between them so she didn't have to smell the smoke as strongly and to lure him away from the garage. "If you know so much already, why are you here annoying me?"

"I want to know why you aren't together. Is he still alive?"

She sighed and tossed the wrench back into the garage. "We were ambushed when we arrived. Are you telling me you weren't part of that?"

"If I knew anything about that, would I be here looking for Lars?"

"Maybe it's just an excuse to see if you could find Tom."

"Last I checked, girl, he was still under Emily's protection. Didn't you tell me something about not wanting her to *react*?"

The old man was grating on her last shred of patience, but she had little choice but to cling to it. She was only a few well-chosen words away from leading the old man away from the garage, away from Tom. "Lars was alive the last time I saw him, when we were set upon by a group of Feral. I ran while he stayed back to fight them."

Ana paused and gave Alexander a cool look to match his own. "I can't imagine they put up much of a fight for him. Follow me, and I'll show you where." With that, she turned her back to him and strode up the street.

She forced herself not to grin when he fell in beside her, matching her pace.

Her relief was far too short-lived. They'd made it little more than a block and a half from the service center when the sound of a car engine filled the street between it and them. Ana and Alexander spun around to the squeal of tires just as the Lexus shot out of the garage in reverse. Its rear wheels popped up onto the sidewalk on the opposite side of the street and skidded to a stop. Then the front tires squealed again, and the SUV lurched forward, turning away from where she stood.

Alexander's cigarette hit the ground as he charged after them and was on the back of the car in a flash. Somehow, even with it accelerating away, he managed to leap up and grab the back bar of the storage rack on top with his left hand. He reared back with his right, then it shot forward, striking the rear windshield with a tremendous slap. The crackling as it broke reached her several blocks away. The safety glass spiderwebbed in front of him but didn't shatter.

The driver—Tom, she assumed—slammed on the brakes, and the Lexus spun thirty degrees clockwise, trying to shake their assailant loose. Alexander held tight, but his forehead bounced against the fracturing glass. He reflexively put his hand to his head just as the rear windshield finally gave up its tenuous effort to hold together with a thunderous *crack*. The glass shattered outward, shards exploding past him to fall in the street behind him.

Ana recognized the sound of another booming crack. It hadn't been from the windshield breaking but from the revolver Tom rarely went without. Alexander shuddered from the impact of what must have been a second shot but still somehow clung to the top of the Lexus.

Three more gunshots rang out in quick succession, though, finally driving him from his perch. He landed in the street with a dull thump as the car squealed away.

Finally spurred to action, Ana sprinted to where Alexander lay on the asphalt. She dared to hope the gunshots had been placed well enough that he would stay there forever. One less vampire Lord in the world wouldn't be such a bad thing.

Ana, though, had never had much luck, in either of her lives. As she reached him, Alexander sat up, examining the holes in his shirt. A pair of frosty eyes met hers. His face was stone, and he glared as he pulled another Camel out of what had become a crushed pack.

"*Two* people were in that car."

The words ran through her like ice water. She turned to watch the Lexus in the distance, already three or four blocks away. It raced forward a few more before making a sharp left turn.

Then it was gone.

CHAPTER 20

HUGGING THE TRUNK OF A large tree planted beside the road to the suspension bridge, Lindsey forced herself to be still. A block from where she stood, a pair of Feral shambled from one side of the street to the other, guarding the entrance to the bridge that crossed the Ohio River from Covington into Cincinnati. They made comical guards, a sad imitation of the kind of real security that marched with tight steps and sharp turns and looked far ahead for potential threats. They were there pretty much just to keep anyone like her and Lars from trying to cross, and only then if someone ran right into them.

Lars stood behind her, looking over her shoulder. If he were breathing, she would no doubt have been able to feel it against the nape of her neck. She wasn't used to having one of her own so close. It was a drastic change from being close to Tom. She would never admit it to him, but his humanity was intoxicating. The warmth of his body, the rhythmic beat of his heart, the scent of his soap and skin mixed with the natural pheromones, or whatever they were called, and a dozen other things reminded her of times before everything happened—before Charon hit then the frenzied hunt to find and feed on whoever happened to be left. Before she, Emily, and others like them realized they would have to work together to have any hope of surviving the long, thirsty years ahead of them.

Being close to Tom reminded her of the good times.

Lars, on the other hand, might as well have been a concrete pillar. No warmth, no heartbeat, hardly any scent but that of mild decay and freshly butchered beef.

She shook her head to clear her thoughts. They needed to get across the river, and she was daydreaming about the way a boy smelled. She hadn't even acted that way in high school. Still, Ana had better be taking good care of him. Lindsey wasn't done basking in his humanity yet.

Lars tapped her on the right shoulder and lifted his arm over it, pointing to the left of the bridge approach. She nodded in response.

The bridge itself was made up of three separate paths. A two-lane roadway in the center was made for cars, with separated walkways for foot traffic to either side. She figured that the central path had maybe been made for horse carriages when the bridge was built, but she didn't really know how old it was. Older than she was, younger than Emily. Probably older than Lars, though she didn't really know his ballpark age. He stayed pretty tight with his personal details. Maybe someday she would figure out why. Or maybe she would ask Emily, who seemed to know him well enough.

Lars had pointed at a set of steps to the left of the street, just ten or twenty feet away from the beginning of the bridge. The road approaching it was elevated at that point, built above what she believed was Second Street. If they worked their way around the tall building making up the block to her left, they could slip down to Second then come up the steps much closer to the bridge. That would get them within a stone's throw of it without the plaguers seeing them.

Lindsey pushed back against Lars with her shoulders, signaling she was ready to move. She felt him take a step back and to her left, using the trunk of the tree to hide from the plaguers' view, should they happen to put a little extra effort into their job and look up the street. It was about as likely as Emily appearing from the other side of the bridge right then, but props for being extra careful, Lindsey figured. She turned her body clockwise, rolling until her back was against the tree's trunk and she was face-to-face with him. Then, she gestured to her right, his left, at the corner of the building's foundation behind him. Her left hand pointed to the right and then down, signaling her plan to go around the building and approach from the steps. He nodded in agreement and backpedaled in that direction.

Following slowly, she didn't like being unable to see the Feral behind her, but Lars kept his eyes focused on them and showed no alarm. He reached the corner of the building a few steps before her and stopped, still watching the guards. She slid forward, next to him, and was surprised to find it wasn't the corner of a cross street. The road to her left, leading away from the bridge, curved to the right around the front of the building. A normal corner would have been better so she could see in straight lines to make sure nothing waited for them as they made their way around.

As it was, she found only moonlight and dark streetlights ahead of them, and Lindsey slipped around Lars. He spun after her, and they crept along the rounded front of the building. The structure itself was the kind of thing someone probably thought was pretty or clever, or both. Concrete embedded with streaks of tall windows that might have had a tint to them in daylight reached up to the sky in a kind of spiral that peaked on the river-facing side. The windows' design gave it a kind of striped curtain effect. It probably housed overpriced apartments for rich people. Humans loved to build that kind of thing to show off how much money they had, for all the good it had done them in the end. The tall, fancy-ass building with its clever architecture had likely become a foul-smelling crypt with no one to admire it but the plaguers and the crows.

The pair didn't quite tiptoe around the curved street but stole past it with more caution than she reckoned was necessary. They had not come across a single random, wandering Feral on their way from the brewery to the bridge, a trek of probably ten or more blocks. Lindsey might not know how it was done, but she had zero doubt Colin had engineered the concerted effort to harness all the beasts in the area. The idea that the whole mob of local plaguers had been rounded up and given something to do filled her with the kind of dread one got when they heard a tornado coming but couldn't see it yet.

Still, it was nice not to happen upon a Feral rambling aimlessly every four blocks, causing trouble. And the thought of them being collected by Kallus or whoever made her imagine them being lassoed like cattle for market. She grinned.

They reached the end of the curved street as it poured into a new one headed north toward the river. She stopped and raised a hand there, checking again to make sure nothing would wander into their path. Satisfied that the way was clear, they continued forward.

The road ended a block ahead of them at Second Street, and beyond that stood a reddish-pink plaza made up of a pair of uneven towers flanking some kind of small mall or marketplace. The one on the right stood probably ten or twelve stories tall and the other maybe fifteen. The small A-peaked storefront between them was only a couple of stories tall, with a sign over the doorway that read, "Rivercenter." Was it full of the dead too? Businesses weren't usually as bad as hospitals and apartments, so maybe it wouldn't be so bad.

They reached Second and crossed until they were right in front of the Rivercenter plaza. The sidewalk followed along the street, and trees, again, conveniently grew at regular intervals to provide cover if needed. They picked their way from tree to tree before stopping where the street ran beneath the beginning of the bridge, making a short tunnel. To her left, the bottom of the steps they expected rose from the street in two runs separated by a flat landing of eight or ten feet. Half squatting, they duckwalked to them, not sure how far the Feral above would be able to see.

Lindsey started climbing first, still trying to stay low. Lars followed closely, both hugging the railing on the left. When they topped the first set of steps, he tapped her on the shoulder and gestured that he would stay put. Lindsey kept climbing.

A third of the way up the second set, the first Feral rose into her view. She was hairless and had a round face centered with what reminded Lindsey of a bat's nose. Her clothes—a black Dave Matthews Band T-shirt and a pair of faded jeans—were ragged and torn in spots, but they weren't nearly as threadbare as others she'd seen.

Flattening onto her belly, Lindsey army-crawled up the remaining steps to get the full view. The second plaguer, wearing a polo shirt and shorts, looked younger than the woman, possibly Turned in his twenties. Hard to imagine becoming a vampire at such a young age, knowing that the process didn't just end that person's humanity, it stunted their maturity. Lindsey had a been an utter shit show in her early twenties and couldn't thank Emily enough for waiting until she'd been a little more grown-up before Making her.

The pair of Feral shamble-marched in opposite directions, each going from one side of the street to the other. She watched them move back and forth, over and over, studying the pattern they made together. After lying on her belly like a snake for who knew how long and tracking more of their repeated circuits than she could count, Lindsey was satisfied and slid back down to Lars.

"What the hell?" he whispered as she squatted in front of him. "I was beginning to worry you'd fallen asleep up there."

"Easy, beefcake. I had to figure out how to get past them."

He lifted his head over hers, looking up to the street above. "There are two walking in opposite directions. We knew that before we got here."

"Yes." Lindsey nodded. "But these aren't trained soldiers. Hell, most marching band kids match pace better than these two. It's a guy and a gal up there, and the guy's a little younger than she is. He also walks a step faster."

Lars cocked his head. "Okay, so?"

"So, they aren't in sync, and eventually, they'll end up walking together, both facing the same way."

He chuckled. "Never send a plaguer to do a real person's job."

"Right." She grinned. Looking down into the bed of decorative river rock in the landscaping beside them, she picked up a stone about half the size of her fist. "Now, how far can you throw a rock?"

After explaining her plan, she slithered back up the second set of steps on her belly and resumed eyeballing the sentries. The Feral still shuffled in opposite directions, so her long wait began. She tapped her fingers against the concrete below her in time with the frat boy's steps, squeezing out every ounce of patience she could muster. It felt like waiting for bedtime on Christmas night as a child. Sure, it would come eventually, but waiting it out was a killer.

Finally, just as she started to question her sanity, Polo picked up enough steps that at his next turn, he would be shoulder to shoulder with the Dave Matthews Band woman.

Lindsey gestured to Lars below, and he slithered up beside her. She nodded toward the Feral, both facing away from them.

With a grin, Lars jumped up and chucked the stone over their heads. It sailed across the road and down on embankment on the far side, cracking against what looked like a small two-story apartment building. The Feral both leapt toward the noise, growling and snorting while they charged after it.

Smirking, Lindsey stood beside Lars, and the pair dashed to the bridge entrance. He started to turn left to take the walkway on the nearest side, but she pulled on his arm.

"No, this way."

"Why?" He fell into step beside her as they started across.

"I'll show you in a minute."

They crossed the bridge at a steady pace, moving quietly and staying close to the steel girders marking the edge of the roadway at steady intervals. The bridge decking was steel gridwork that rang with careless footsteps, forcing Lindsey to move softer and slower than she would have liked. The care was necessary, though. If any Feral were crossing the bridge from the other side, she wanted to hear them before they reached her.

Luckily, they didn't come across anything—or anyone—until finally reaching the end of the bridge. With twenty or thirty feet left of their walk, Lindsey flattened herself next to one of the steel girders, Lars again pressing behind her. Just beyond the end of the decking, a pair of Feral marched back and forth across the concrete roadway in opposite directions, the same as on the other side.

"Looks like their paces match," Lars whispered.

Lindsey nodded in agreement. They wouldn't be able to use the same trick twice. Even worse, the bridge ended over a riverfront park, leaving them with either a two-story drop over the side or at least fifty feet of concrete road to cover before they would reach a cross street. Avoiding the plaguers as they came off the bridge into Ohio would be pretty much impossible.

"How fast can you kill one?" Lindsey challenged.

Lars smiled. "Faster than you. But I thought the idea was not to be noticed."

"That's why we're in the middle of the bridge. Once they pass each other in the street, they'll be facing away from us. We use that moment to slide behind them and…" She made a throat-cutting gesture.

"I like the way you think."

"Okay, here they come. I'll go for the one on the right since it's farther away and I'm faster."

"Oh, are you now?" He cracked his knuckles.

"Just go left, and don't screw up. Give him a couple of extra steps past you just to be sure."

"I got it."

Ahead, the pair of Feral shuffled by each other, each looking in opposite directions. Lindsey counted to five, giving the one on the right enough time to near the edge of the street. Then, willing herself to be as quick and silent as the wind, she rushed after it, sliding up behind it as it made the far side of the road. She pressed herself against it, bumping it slightly to put it off balance while grabbing its head by the front and back. She twisted her hands and was rewarded with a satisfying *crack*. The thing fell in a heap, lifeless.

God, she would never get tired of killing those things.

Spinning on her heel, she found Lars standing over his own dead plaguer, a smile in his eyes.

"Let's find somewhere to lie low and see what happens next," Lindsey said. "He'll likely send someone to check, assuming he knows they're dead."

Lars glanced forward, away from the bridge, pointing at a building with a wall of mirrored windows and glass doors. "That should do it."

"Yep." Lindsey nodded. "Let's hope he comes to check himself so we can give him a little surprise."

CHAPTER 21

FACE BLANK, ANA STARED SEVERAL blocks up the street where the Lexus SUV had turned to the left and disappeared. She fought the urge to start picking at the skin around her thumbnail. Alexander was picking himself up off the ground, and the last thing she wanted to show him was fear or weakness.

"Your boy ruined one of my favorite shirts," he growled, gesturing to the bullet holes in his chest.

"You didn't have to go after him," she replied. "I thought you were looking for Lars, not Tom."

"Girl, I am always looking for human blood. And you just let a pair of them get away. A pair!"

Ana twisted her face into a furious scowl. "I am not your *girl*," she hissed.

Alexander's hand moved before she could register it, and almost without warning, she reeled from the force of a closed-fisted blow to her chin that she hadn't seen coming. Her feet lifted an inch or so, and she fell backward, slamming the back of her head into the pavement.

Stepping closer, Alexander loomed over her, fists curled with menace. "I don't have time to deal with you properly. I'll have to assume your Maker will. But trust me, I will see you again soon, and you will pay for the mess you've made." With that, he disappeared, jogging away in the same direction as the SUV.

Ana stood and rubbed the knot on the back of her head. It would disappear soon enough, and the pain barely registered. She half wished that wasn't the case. She wanted to remember that feeling, the empty hatred percolating within. She hadn't thought she would ever hate anyone with the same fury that burned in her chest for Colin, but Alexander was close. Very close.

Being honest with herself, though, she was lucky Alexander had only incapacitated her. He easily could have killed her, assuming he'd had the time. He was, after all, more than a hundred years her senior. She would get him back, but it would take some delicate planning.

Turning west, where the sun had set a few hours ago and where both Tom and Alexander had gone, she chewed her bottom lip. Tom was gone, and somehow, she knew he wouldn't come back. Impossible to tell how long he'd considered going out on his own, but the string of events since his attack at the Chalet almost certainly had cemented his decision. Ana wasn't sure how to feel about it. She felt compelled to protect him like a little brother, but he could be just as annoying as one at times too. Regardless, he deserved better. Tom deserved a chance to make a life of his own instead of being a token on the game board of a few vampiric superegos.

But.

He was the only reason for her to exist as she was, and now he was gone. Did her purpose go with him?

Worse than losing Tom, though, nearly all her scientific work was in the back of that SUV. Everything that both Emily and Colin had commissioned her to work on had driven away from her, literally following the sunset.

What now? With Tom gone and her work gone with him, what should she do?

What could she do?

Her instincts screamed to follow the Lexus. She didn't know if Alexander had, but they'd had a solid head start. Odds were good that they'd gotten away and taken to the expressway. Was there any chance they might head back to Atlanta and Emily's protection? Not likely. Tom had a new friend, a real blood-carrying human like himself. Ana had a hard time believing that if they'd escaped Alexander's pursuit, he would take her to the Chalet and put them both in a situation that was, at best, unpredictably dangerous and, at worst, deadly.

If he wasn't taking them back to Atlanta, though, where would they go, and more importantly, could she track him? She'd hunted him down at that little bar in Iowa last year, but that had almost been easy. She'd laid out the road for him before sending him off and, even then, had put a few drops of an additive in the gas tank that had made the exhaust both linger and carry a distinctive odor.

In theory, she could track the scent of the Lexus's exhaust, especially considering it had not been long since they'd torn away toward I-75, but they were also going back the way they'd come a few hours earlier. Could she pick out the difference between them coming and going?

Did she have any choice but to try?

"No," she muttered at last. "My whole world is in that car."

Having decided, she jogged forward, following the path the Lexus had taken. As she reached her best pace, though, her body shuddered, forcing her to a jarring halt.

"Daughter."

Dread flooded through her. Colin hadn't reached out to her since giving her leave to stay with Emily last fall. She closed her eyes and ground her molars.

"Lord Colin," she thought, *"to what do I owe this honor?"*

"A modicum of honoring me is perhaps the place to begin, Daughter."

Ana shuddered, and her cold, undead skin prickled with goose bumps. The months since Colin had last contacted her that way had been a sweet reprieve from having her thoughts forcibly interrupted on occasion by someone else. The sensation still made her deeply uncomfortable.

Ana's jaw tightened further. *"Are we not past this, Lord? We have been fully plain with each other by now."*

"How is it that you alone, Ana, of all my Family, still refuse to see the wonder in my gift of your second life?"

It took every ounce of her self-control not to scream back through their telepathic link. *"You know why I do not, Colin, and I'm not doing this again. Why are you bothering me when I'm trying to fulfill the tasks you put before me?"*

"Oh? Are you still attempting to fulfill those tasks? It seems very much to me that your assignment has come to a disappointing end." The sensation of him chuckling in her mind sent a chill crawling up her spine.

"Admittedly, I've had a setback, but I'm confident I can

make things right for the benefit of both you and Lady Emily."

"*I am no longer interested in Emily's concerns or affairs.*" Colin's tone was full of steel and simmering with anger.

A cold lump even icier than her skin sank in Ana's belly.

"*I released you to her service some months ago, and at this moment, I rescind that gesture. I will inform her of this change at the next opportunity she and I have to discuss our… arrangement.*"

"*Colin, please—*"

"*I am your Maker, Daughter. I am your lord, and despite your vain pride, you will henceforth address me as such. You will show me the deference and honor expected of all my Descended. If you find that too difficult, I have amassed quite a large collection of Feral who would be willing to demonstrate my disapproval. Is that transparent enough for you?*"

Ana swallowed hard. God, but she hated the man, had hated him since the day he'd Made her, but her hatred did nothing to counter the fact that he *had* Made her. She was his, and for as long as she continued to live her second life, she was beholden to both his whims and his machinations. Still, every atom in her being longed to spit his venom back through her mind, but she wasn't done with her life just yet. She had work yet to complete, work that could change *everything*. That would fix everything.

With so much at stake, was pretending to be an obedient Daughter impossible? She was not an animal, after all, nor one of those mindless, slobbering Feral. She could control herself if it mattered that much. Nearly anything could be tolerated to achieve her goals. After all, nothing she would need to do at that point could possibly be worse than what she'd already survived.

"My lord, forgive me and my… entitlement. You know I easily become passionate and can be fiercely affixed to my goals. How can I serve you?" It didn't quite make her sick to send that thought through their connection, but it came close.

Colin let the thought linger there without reply, scratching, digging, aching in her mind. Irritation, reminiscent of the itchy wool sweater her mom had forced her to wear when she was little, festered deep within, despite lacking any actual form. Ana tried not to roll her eyes at the games he seemed determined play and forced herself to weather the silence.

Finally, he returned, *"Emily's pet bloodhound seems quite strong-minded about digging where her nose does not belong. I want you to find them and relay to me where they are and what they know."*

"Lindsey? Should I let her know you have… modified my priorities?"

"Absolutely not. Emily can provide her whelps with information, should it please her. That is not my responsibility."

Ana cringed. He would force her to act as a spy if not an outright manipulator.

"Your hesitation should surprise me, Daughter, but it sadly doesn't. Though I would expect better from someone dedicated to our success and, by extension, our survival. Keep in mind that they asked for your assistance. They put you in this position. But the time has come to focus on our own goals, and if Emily interferes, I will be forced to answer it."

"If you say so, Lord. But is our conflict not more with

Alexander than Emily? I thought it was his land that you wanted."

"Leave him to me, Daughter. My plans for him and his land will become clear soon enough."

"I saw him moments ago, for what it's worth. He said he came here looking for Lars, but when Tom and..." Ana trailed off, nearly forgetting that Shan's existence was known only to her and Alexander. Colin could not yet know, and Ana had promised to protect that secret. She would preserve that promise for as long as she could, until Colin forced it from her. *"When Tom fled, I thought Alexander might be trying to pursue him. I think Alexander still wants to simply bleed him."*

"Did he, now? Well, I hope your human pet has the strength to survive a Master of middling ability. Regardless, it is not the most pressing matter at hand. For now, let the other Family be, and find Lindsey and see what she has uncovered. My plans depend upon it."

"I understand, Lord."

She didn't understand, not in the least. Tom was running free out in the world, and Colin knew Alexander was probably following him. How could that not be the most pressing issue? Then to order her to abandon helping Emily and instead track down Lindsey? He was worried she might find something. Ana didn't know what it was, but she needed to figure it out. Because Colin was planning something, something more sinister than just taking over Alexander's territory. And Ana feared it had more to do with Emily than the others.

Emily was the only hope of defense that Tom had in a world filled with hungry, increasingly angry vampires. If

Colin intended to make a move on Emily, Ana needed to find some way to stop it without letting her Master know she was still quite intent on betraying him.

CHAPTER 22

THREE FERAL HAD COME FROM somewhere north in the city, bob-stepping side by side until they reached the start of the bridge where the two others lay dead. They shambled back and forth over the ground for several minutes before one of them turned away from the bridge and headed back the way it had come. The other two remained and began marching back and forth across the street. They'd come to replace the dead.

"I'd really hoped he'd come himself." Lars stood beside Lindsey, watching from behind the museum's glass doors. "Even if he'd brought those three with him, I think we could've taken them all."

Lindsey shrugged. "Not much use whining, hon. The good news is he sent us a present."

"Did he?"

She nodded in the direction of the plaguer leaving alone as it shambled across the sidewalk and turned north toward downtown. "He sent us a tour guide. Want to play a little follow-the-leader?"

Lindsey had been holding the museum door with her toes, and she pushed it open just enough for her slim form to slip outside. Lars followed, slowing the door as it closed so it didn't bang against its frame. The Feral at the far end of the road still marched like windup toys, paying no attention to what was happening at the far end of the street.

Lindsey slipped to the corner of the building and peered around it. Their guide was a block up the street already, its back to them. She watched it for a full minute, waiting for it to turn and check behind it. It lumbered ahead without hesitation.

"Move fast," Lars whispered behind her, "from cover to cover, just in case."

"Agreed." Without hesitating, she flashed away, crossing the block and the next cross street before coming to a stop, crouching behind a half wall built to protect the sunken expressway below the block. Lars arrived a half second after her. They waited as the Feral progressed up another block, beginning to climb the short slope toward downtown.

They continued their stop-and-go progress, block by block, ducking behind buildings and trash cans as they followed it. Several blocks later, the thing shambled to a partially open square featuring the statue of a woman with outstretched hands standing over several pedestals and a large basin.

The Feral crossed the square and stepped inside the open doorway of a small glass structure. They waited half a minute to make sure it wouldn't come back out then crossed the street to the square. Lindsey strode to the doorway and stole a look inside, where she found a parking ticket machine, an elevator, and a dark set of steps leading below street level.

"Why is it always underground?" she complained.

"Because there are more eyes above," Lars replied. "That and you can get more things done when you keep your work out of the daylight."

"What kind of work are y'all doing, anyway? All we need is to do a little hunting and make sure the Family is safe."

"That's a lot harder around here than it is with in Atlanta," he countered. "Follow my lead, and make sure nothing is at our back."

He walked through the doorway and over to the steps—barely wide enough for two and built of plain concrete and steel, without any apparent thought to making them look nicer than simply functional.

Lars peered down and turned his head, listening. Lindsey paused her breath, not wanting to distract him. Apparently hearing nothing suspicious, he started down.

Reaching the bottom of the first level, Lars stopped and listened again before shaking his head and continuing. Lindsey glanced back up the way they'd come before following, one careful step at a time. At least the concrete was solid, not prone to sound vibrations that could give them away.

At the second level, he strained to listen again before turning to her and crooking a finger. She stepped close and cocked her head to listen with her eyes closed.

Thump-shuffle.

Thump-shuffle.

Thump-shuffle.

It was distant but unmistakable. Their Feral was out there somewhere, though why it had decided to walk down to the second floor of a parking garage made about as much sense as a bucket with wings. A lot about what the plaguers were up to didn't make any sense, but Lindsey looked forward to having Kallus explain it to them. All they had to do was find him and get him away from his pets. She wouldn't need long to get him chatting.

They entered the parking area together. She didn't sense any other Feral in the open space, and usually they weren't exactly sneaky, but she wasn't taking anything for granted.

They didn't have to go very far before coming to what should have been a solid wall. Instead, a large steel panel, like a door with no handles, stood partially ajar, the gap large enough for a sizeable person—or brainless monster—to slip into the opening behind it.

She took a deep breath of the air on the other side and wrinkled her nose. Damp and slightly acrid, it reminded her of the old crypts she and her friends would break into when she was much younger. Strangely, though, it didn't carry the tang of decay that most closed spaces did after Charon.

"What?" she whispered to Lars.

"Subway," he replied. "It's access to an old subway tunnel. We can probably follow it back to wherever they're going for Rest."

"If that's so, we best mind ourselves in there. We could find 'em coming *and* going."

Lars nodded and disappeared through the gap. Lindsey trailed behind him.

The opening led to a hallway lined with crumbling tilework. Maybe thirty feet long, air movement told her that another opening stood at the far side, a bigger one. The hall had no side doors or other diversion, just a straight shot from where they stood to the far opening. It felt like a place for an ambush. She imagined a gang of Feral filing in behind them as they moved forward, only to run into another group when they got to the other end.

"I don't like it." Lars echoed her thoughts.

"I'll go ahead. You stay here." Lindsey started forward, but he caught her by the arm.

"No, I'll go," he hissed. "This is my place, and I know a lot more about these subway tunnels than you do. If you hear anything coming behind, you whistle then take off back to street level. I'll run them through the subway until they get tired or bored."

"Fine, but don't go having all the fun without me."

"Dealing with these things is suddenly a lot less fun than it used to be." With that, Lars entered the hallway and slid forward, his back against the opposite wall.

Halfway to the opening, the squeal of metal sliding on metal echoed off the tiled walls. A few seconds later came a dull, wooden thud. Lindsey froze, eyes fixed on Lars. He shot her a confused glance and shrugged. She didn't know what the thud was, but she'd heard that scraping-metal sound before. It was the unmistakable squeal of a railroad cart—not the big cars pulled by engines, but a small flat-bed that rode the rails with a hand crank, usually operated by two people. She'd seen them used by the Family that drove Emily's Dragon. Something had just arrived.

Desperate to know what was happening, she pointed to the end of the hall and nodded, signaling him to move fast. With a second shrug, he flashed to the end of the wall and peered around the corner. He waved his fingers at her, silently calling to her. She took one last quick glance over her shoulder then jogged to him.

Beyond the opening was a platform, the kind where people would wait for subway trains to come and go. Across the way, separated by a trench lined with metal tracks, was a nearly identical one, right down to the matching tiles. At each end of the platform opening, the tunnels narrowed, running off to the east and west. On the west side, as expected, a hand-cranked rail cart sat on the rails. A pair of Feral, one short and stout, the other average sized but dressed in the rags of a once-well-tailored suit, stood on the cart, as if waiting for instructions. A wooden shipping crate with no discernible markings was loaded on the back of the cart.

Lindsey didn't give a damn about the rail cart. Kallus stood in the train well along with four of what she'd started thinking of as his trained monsters. A pair stared up and down the tracks, one looking east and the other west, while the other two carried a second crate to the cart. Several dozen of those boxes had been stacked along one of the walls in the trench between the platforms.

Garret, the toffee-haired vampire who had been with Kallus and the gang of Feral outside the original ambush, circled into view from behind the cart.

"Take these two back to the terminal, get it unloaded, and come back. I need to check something above. I'll meet you back here."

"Are you sure, Kal? He said we should stay together."

"He also gave me about six things that all need to be

done right for this plan of his to work. Don't be a baby, Garret."

"Okay," the other replied before Lindsey stepped back and pulled Lars with her.

"He's going up top," she whispered. "We can trap him in the stairs and be done with him. Even if he's not alone, he'll likely only have a pair of Feral with him."

Lars cocked his head. "What makes you say that?"

"He's leaving guards everywhere that seems to matter to them, so I'm betting the pair watching the tracks stays put. I'll go on ahead and wait for him at the steps of the first-floor parking. If he's got more than the pair, we'll call it off."

"Fine," Lars replied just as the shriek of the wheels against the rails filled the platform. He turned and craned his neck around the corner for another look as the shrill song of the railway cart played off into the distance. "He's starting this way. Let's go."

Lindsey didn't hesitate. She raced back to the open gap into the parking garage then across the second level of parking until she reached the steps. She paused at the bottom and waited for any sign that something might be waiting for her above. Sensing nothing, she sped up the stairway, turning to her left at the landing halfway between the two levels then again when she reached the first level of parking. There, she stepped into darkness a few feet away and crouched, waiting, forcing herself to seem like a hole in the air around her. She once again stretched out with her senses, focused on the steps below—the steps where, with any luck, Kallus would walk right into their trap.

The waiting again made her want to pull out the fine, light hairs on the back of her arms one by one. Emily constantly preached for Lindsey to be more patient, and had done so for decades, for all the good it had accomplished. Lindsey was in luck, though. Kallus didn't make her wait long. Not even five minutes after she'd hunkered down, she heard footfalls echoing up the stairwell. She allowed herself a small grin. They weren't the thumps and drags that bob-stepping Feral had made when climbing steps, and there weren't many of them. She heard one distinct pair making the sounds of a regular gait, stepping up stairs one at a time.

Lindsey stood, unfurling herself. This guy, this asshole, had been a thorn in her side since they came north. Whatever they were doing, whatever *he* was doing, it was a direct challenge to her, and that made it a challenge to Emily. He had no right, and she would put an end to it.

She would put an end to *him*.

Curling her fists, she let her rage swell, her blood warming and her fangs extending fully, pressing lightly against her bottom lip. It was one of her favorite sensations. Her vision sharpened, pulling the landing on the steps below into almost magnified focus. Lindsey strode forward to the top step and growled softly, for once keenly aware of her fury, and her hunger.

Kallus stepped up onto the landing and turned to face her. "Well, looks like you have me at—"

With a shout, Lindsey launched herself from the top step, soaring downward through the air. Her knee smashed into his face, which exploded in a mist of dark, bloody spray. He fell backward, smashing his head against the wall behind him before sinking to the floor. Lindsey landed, straddling his chest, and rained fists down on his already-ruined face. He tried to bring his arms up to protect his head, but they were pinned beneath her. The best he could do was a few feeble flails against her calves and hips.

"Lindsey, we want answers!" a voice shouted from somewhere below, one she barely registered. Nothing mattered but punishing the vile piece of trash trapped beneath her.

She knew that voice, of course—it was Lars, and he was right. She should stop beating Kallus and drag him off someplace his pets couldn't find them so they could talk. But she'd waited and longed for the moment when the blood and gore would gush from his ruined face and cover her knuckles. He had to be punished before they could move to the next step. He had to *understand* how much he'd wronged her lady. She really wanted him dead, and it took all her restraint not to grasp his mangled face in both hands and twist until he faced the concrete underneath him.

But even with her blood scorching and his dripping from her fists, she knew what Emily wanted, and it was information more than anything. Two more hits, she swore, unsure if she said it out loud or not. Just two more punches, and they would pull him up to the street and steal him away to talk.

She drew back her right arm to swing it one last time, and somehow, he was beyond her reach. Her body flew backward up the steps, just as it had come down seconds before. Something hard and cold gripped her wrists.

Lindsey kicked at the steps with her heels as she rose, struggling for purchase, before she was lifted into the air, and something else grabbed her ankles.

"No!" she howled, bucking against the Feral arms and hands holding her a few feet above the ground. "Let go of me!"

The plaguers, half a dozen of them, loomed around her, saliva dripping from their gray fangs. They pulled her back into the first-floor parking area, making room for another group to climb the steps, half dragging Lars by his hands and feet. The two groups of captors threw the pair of them to the ground hard, jarring her head forward and rattling Lindsey's teeth. Then her wrists and ankles were each covered by the foot of a different Feral. Another stood near her head, leaving no mistake as to his purpose if she didn't behave and play along.

From the corner of her eye, she found Lars subdued in the same way. She screamed and swallowed bitter, metallic blood.

"Your friend was right, Lindsey," Kallus mocked as he climbed the last step to reach the first floor.

His face put itself back together quicker than she would have expected. Still mostly a collection of swollen, blood-stained knots, his eyes had cleared, and she could see the smirk in them. Her blood boiled, and she pulled at her arms and legs, trying to free them.

"Now, now. None of that." His voice was muffled, thick, as if he spoke through a mouthful of marbles. "I don't want to have to order my pet there to start kicking. You played a good game and almost got me, but it's over now. I knew it would be a risk, letting you trap me alone before I could get my fetches into position, but they promised me you'd want to teach me a lesson before either killing me or dragging me off." He worked his jaw open and closed. "I'm glad you did not disappoint. And now," he added as his face coalesced back to its normal, odious shape, "it's time to go see my lord."

CHAPTER 23

T HE WALK TO WHERE COLIN had instructed Ana
to search for Lindsey was six or eight blocks, and Ana
took them at a leisurely pace, going over everything
that had just happened. The night air was heavy, which
matched her frame of mind, and humid enough that her
shirt should be clinging to her. Of course, sweat was a
human function and not something she needed to worry
about anymore.

As she approached the bridge at the end of the road,
she stopped. A pair of Feral marched back and forth
across the street in a macabre approximation of security
guards. She shook her head with a mix of wonder and
revulsion. If someone had told her plaguers could be used
as sentries, she never would have believed it. At least not
without their handler standing over them. Yet someone
had set them in place to watch the bridge entrance and
had left them to continue the task indefinitely. That suggested an impressive level of control. Someone had put
a lot of time and effort into learning how, and it almost
made her want to ask Colin about it. *Almost.*

He'd been specific that she should cross into Cincinnati using that bridge exactly, though she wasn't certain

why, and he hadn't elaborated. She would have to get used to being left in the dark, apparently. Colin was much too smart to give her more information than the minimum needed to accomplish her assigned tasks. Getting even with him would be a good deal more difficult without his trust, but she would figure something out eventually.

She approached the Feral guard with care, not sure what to expect. She curled her fists, expecting to have to put the plaguer down. She had to cross the bridge behind them, and they were almost certainly programmed not to let anyone by.

She coughed and tensed, ready to rush them.

The pair, one in a polo shirt and the other in a band T-shirt of some kind, stopped and looked at her, growling. Neither approached her, though. Instead, each grunted and resumed marching across the streets, ignoring her.

Curious. She would have to get to the bottom of that somehow.

With slow, deliberate steps, she approached them, still not trusting them to let her be. They glanced at her as she got closer but maintained their constant pace, never altering their path. Constant, but not matching, she noticed. The male one in the polo shirt shambled a step faster than the other. Something to keep in mind for later.

After they passed each other in opposite directions, she stepped between them. She turned to walk backward toward the bridge, not wanting to be surprised if they suddenly remembered they should stop her. On the contrary, they didn't even look her way when they spun to face each other, continuing their shuffled march, back and forth.

Ana reached the bridge and chose the walkway on the

right side, along its east face. She'd crossed it a few times last year when she'd been hunting for Tom and hadn't liked the steel grating in the center of the deck. It had small gaps to allow for expansion but also let her see the river below. The walkways were concrete, solid, and felt much more trustworthy. It was a silly thing for her to consider, honestly, being mostly immortal. How many years, or decades, would it take to shed her human concern?

The trek across the river was pleasant, and a somewhat cool breeze blew at that height over the river. The sky hinted at a shade of rose on the eastern horizon, though. She couldn't linger more than a moment to appreciate the view at what she took as the midpoint of her crossing.

She expected to find more Feral either along the bridge somewhere or at the end of it and was surprised when she reached the start of regular asphalt without a matching pair of guards at the exit. Maybe the coming morning had flushed them to cover. The smell of ash hanging in the air caught her attention, though, and a quick inspection of the ground found two charred spots on either side of the street.

Two Feral had been present at some point recently, and they'd met the daylight. Killed the night before, maybe, with the bodies left to burn at morning? Had Lindsey come this way?

Ana glanced toward the east again. The rosy band at the horizon thickened, turning orange. Daybreak couldn't be far off. She needed to find cover if she didn't want to end up a third spot of ash in the street.

A small glass-and-brick structure stood about a block away, and she remembered that nearly the entire riverfront area had a huge parking structure beneath it. It wouldn't be quite as useful as brewery tunnels or the unused subway, but it would keep her alive until nightfall.

The glass door to the tiny building was unlocked. Inside, she found a pair of powerless elevators and a flight of steps descending below ground. Ana followed them into a parking garage, just as expected. Rows and rows of mostly empty parking spots ran into the murky distance for as far as she could see in any direction. Abandoned cars and trucks dotted the space here and there, left by long-dead owners who'd undoubtedly expected to return in a day or so to collect them.

She knew she should settle onto the ground and Rest for the day, but Ana didn't manage that well even in places she knew and trusted. She would never find the calm needed to accomplish it there.

Out of either boredom or idle curiosity, Ana moved away from the steps and headed north, the direction she would most likely follow come sunset. Whatever source was supposed to supply power to the garage had long since been cut off, and the farther she got from the stairwell, the blacker the darkness around her became. Her eyes adjusted well enough to see in a twenty-foot radius or so, but the lack of light lent the emptiness a feeling of mammoth vastness. Water dripped slowly somewhere off to her left, likely from a water pipe inching closer to rupturing completely. Rats or mice—she could never tell the difference by sound—skittered about constantly, but the echoes of their claws bounced around the concrete structure like they were being swatted in a game of racquetball. They could be anywhere, or everywhere. It could be a handful of them, or a swarm.

At some point amid her aimless stroll, a grunt to her right split the emptiness. Not the usual growled grunt of a plaguer but something softer, almost tentative and vulnerable. And it was close—the sound didn't quite bounce like the rodents' skittering claws.

Ana hesitated. The dark likely held things that wouldn't be friendly. But she'd never heard a Feral make a sound like that, if it was a Feral. But what could it be besides that or some kind of animal? It certainly didn't sound like a dog or cat.

Giving in to her curiosity, she turned toward the sound. Concrete support pillars were spaced evenly throughout the parking structure, so she moved from one to the next, peeking out from behind each to keep from running into the unexpected.

Then the grunt came again, plaintive but a little louder, too, as if whatever was making it knew she was out there. She crossed to another pillar, then another before it filled the air once more. The latest was more of a mournful whine than the previous grunts.

Reaching the next pillar, she could make out a hunched shape standing beside one of the structures not far away. It barely moved at all until Ana stepped away from the concrete column and into the open. Then the thing shifted its body toward her and whined again, louder than before.

Ana advanced toward it, walking free and in the open, wondering if that would draw the thing toward her. Still, it held its position. A few feet later, the horror of why became clear.

Her jaw dropped. The thing *was* a Feral, as she'd half expected, but that was the only thing about it she'd expected. It stood with its back to the pillar and both arms splayed outward, bound by shackles. The irons had then been bolted to the concrete behind it, making it impossible for the thing to move. Its head hung against its chest, not quite limp, but as she got close enough to make out more details, it lunged toward her and let loose a miserable howl.

It was a pitiful, diminished thing. The skin of its neck and chest was nearly translucent, and it had only a few strings of hair hanging limply from the nearly white crown of its head. It opened its mouth, barking softly at her and revealing that the fangs usually giving the monsters such terrifying form were gone. Was it just the front teeth and fangs or was the whole mouth empty? Best not to get close enough to find out.

The sad thing was almost skeletal, too, its ribs standing out in sharp detail. What had happened?

It sang another mournful whine, and she shook her head in disbelief. For the first time since her very first experience with a Feral, she felt pity. Whatever had been done to the creature had been cruel, and leaving it bound down there in the dark was even crueler. She moved to her right, around the pillar where it was bound to come up behind it, curious how it would react. It strained first to the left then right, struggling to track her movement while offering a few sad barks.

Continuing to slide to her right and intending to

come back around to its front, Ana kicked something in the dark that rolled away with a clatter. She spun, eyes wide, struck with a jolt of panic that something might have heard her.

Her breath caught in her throat.

The bones of dozens of creatures lay scattered around her, all in piles beside the concrete columns. The skull of the plaguer she'd accidently kicked had rolled a few feet away and had come to rest with empty eye sockets glaring at her. It struck her how they looked human again, when stripped of everything that made them monsters.

She frowned. What had been going on down here? And who was responsible? Alexander? Colin? She didn't want to admit what she suspected.

"Someone has to stop this," she murmured. "Someone has to fix things."

The lone surviving plaguer groaned, and Ana sighed.

"What am I supposed to do with you? I can't fix you here."

It whined again, hollow, bitter.

"I can fix things. I have to. I have to fix it, somehow."

A single bolt driven into the concrete held the Feral's shackle. She gripped it and tried to twist it out of the column. It refused to budge.

She would start fixing things beginning with that pitiable chained beast, undoing the work of whoever had left him there, forgotten. Then she would find a way to undo the rest of it, one perverted thing at a time.

She took the bolt with both hands. With a crack, she snapped it in half and let it drop.

The Feral squealed. It leapt away from the column until the chain still holding its other side pulled taut, yanking it backward. It growled at the shackle still holding it then looked at Ana with wild eyes.

"Calm," she whispered. Then she grasped the other bolt and pulled hard. It snapped in half, and before she could let it go, the Feral jumped away, pulling it from her hands. It stopped after a few feet, glaring at her as if unsure what to do next. The look lasted only a moment, though, before it turned and flew into the dark. The sound of its bare feet slapping against the garage floor soon trailed off far ahead of her, and she was once again alone with nothing but questions.

Questions and a vow to put things right.

CHAPTER 24

A JARRING STOP FLUNG TOM AGAINST his safety belt, forcing him awake. The sun, still hanging above them, shone into his eyes as he blinked the sleep away and looked westward at the mostly empty expressway. "What happened? Where are we?"

"Shit, T, I screwed up." Shan unbuckled her own belt and opened the driver's-side door. "I think we ran out of gas."

"You think?" Tom stretched to get a better look at the dashboard from the passenger seat. The gas gauge's needle stubbornly pointed at the E mark.

"Okay, smartass. No, I don't think. I know." She slipped out of the Lexus SUV onto the searing I-70 asphalt. "Mother, it's hot."

Tom rubbed his eyes once more and unfastened his seat belt. He glanced at the clock embedded in the SUV's dash and noted they'd been on the road for a little over twelve hours. From Cincinnati, he'd driven them south through Louisville and topped off the gas. They'd turned west from there, aiming for Saint Louis while Shan mostly slept in the passenger seat. The plan had been to trade cars after they passed the Gateway Arch and crossed the

Mississippi River, but they'd beat the sun by a couple of hours. Neither of them much liked the idea of car shopping at night and risking an encounter with either vampires or Feral. The memory of their frenzied escape from Alexander was still too fresh.

They'd switched drivers after Saint Louis, and after another hour of watching the broken highway stripes pass by, Tom had fallen asleep just as a sliver of the horizon behind them had turned pink.

Lady licked the side of his face from the back seat. "Good morning, girl. Or afternoon, I guess."

He opened his door and slid off the seat then looked both ahead and back the way they'd come as Lady slipped out beside him. A seemingly endless expressway ran off in both directions, flanked by overgrown weeds. "Okay, so, where are we?"

Shan shaded her eyes and stared ahead, to the west. "We passed through Topeka maybe fifteen miles back. I'm not sure if anything's ahead of us or not. I haven't seen a sign for miles."

Tom did some quick math. "We should probably head back toward Topeka. We're looking at a three- or four-hour-long walk if it's really that far behind us. Hopefully, we'll find a gas station before we get there."

"Well, I really fucked this up." Shan slung her bag over her shoulder and stepped to the rear bumper. "Sorry, I got into my head and didn't think about the gas. I haven't had to worry about a car in a long time."

Reaching back into the Lexus, Tom grabbed the baseball bat from the footwell and his revolver from the center console. He slid the gun into the shoulder holster he could wear easily since Shan's paste had healed his wounded neck. Tom wanted to be mad at her for not thinking about needing gas in Topeka, but then, he'd slept right through it. Beyond that, and being grateful for how she'd healed him, he couldn't summon the anger. At least, not anytime in the near future. She was human, like he was, not a vampire who wanted to either consume or use him, and not one of the mindless plague-ridden Feral who either wandered aimlessly in search of food or became a brainless watchdog for its Maker. Twenty-four hours before, he'd been sure he was the only human left in the world. She proved that anything was possible.

"Don't sweat it. I didn't have anything else planned for today anyway. We're alive, and the sun is shining. How bad could a three-hour stroll to Topeka really be?"

She eyed him suspiciously. "Don't try sweet-talking me, dude. If I say I fucked up, I expect you to agree with me, or I'll make your life a pain in the ass."

With a chuckle, Tom nodded. "I got it, I got it. You're right, I'm sorry. Make sure you do better next time."

Shan dug through her bag and retrieved a bottle of sunscreen. "Watch your tone, T. You're not the boss of me. You want some SPF?" She slathered the cream over her arms and face.

"I'll take my chances with the sun."

She dropped the tube of sunscreen back into the bag that held what Tom imagined to be a full apothecary shop of witchcrafting supplies, and not for the first time, he wondered if she could actually turn him into a toad. That probably wasn't a real thing any more than killing a vampire with a stake to the heart was a genuine thing, but every day since Ana had woken him from his coma seemed to bring some unlikely surprise. So, he wouldn't rule it out.

With a smirk, he started toward Topeka, and Shan fell in stride beside him.

The afternoon strayed into early evening before they reached the outskirts of the city. Tom couldn't remember ever seeing such a stretch of empty expressway as the one they crossed back over. He'd hoped to find a gas station or hotel in five miles, give or take, but they came across nothing but weeds and overgrowth. Not so much as another abandoned car or truck. It very much felt like the middle of nowhere.

They had another hour or two of daylight, he reckoned, by the time they reached an off-ramp leading to a plaza with a strip mall. A Phillips 66 station sat beside a tiny used-car lot, Otto's Autos. The car place was a lucky find, but after several hours of walking across asphalt, without water, under the Kansas sun, getting a new car was a distant second to what they needed.

Shan wiped the back of her hand across her forehead. "Thank Mother. I thought I was going to die of thirst."

Tom half wanted to run to the gas station for a bottle of water but didn't have the energy. The best he could do was a quick step down the exit ramp and across the parking lot. Lady strolled between them, tongue hanging from the side of her mouth. The poor girl. He didn't envy her thick, dark coat.

The Phillips's convenience store wasn't locked, and the glass wasn't broken—all good signs. Lady dashed inside after he cracked the front door and returned a minute later without raising the alarm.

"Race you." Stepping inside, Shan came just short of running to the bottled water case in the back of the small store.

Tom was only a few seconds behind, and they emptied half a bottle each in two or three gulps. Then he opened a third one and poured it slowly as the shepherd lapped at the stream.

Shan finished hers and crushed the plastic in her hand before reaching for a nearby bowl of discounted Snickers bars. She dumped the candy and offered him the bowl. "Here."

He poured the rest of Lady's water into it and set it on the ground, then squatted beside her as she drank. He patted her flanks, once again feeling pangs of guilt about how warm her coat was to the touch. "I don't ever want to have to do that again, and I bet she'd rather not either."

"Same here. Maybe we should take a couple of gas cans with us so this doesn't happen again." Shan pulled two more bottles from the case, twisted one open, and offered Tom the other.

He cracked the cap and took another drink, finally relieved of the urge to gulp. "Not a bad idea."

"I think I saw a couple by the front. I'll grab them."

Lady finished drinking and raised her head.

He scratched between her ears. "Sorry, girl. I know that was hot. I'm thinking maybe we should find some-place cool to live. How do you feel about Seattle?"

She swiped her tongue across his cheek in reply.

Tom stood and checked the beer case inventory. A red

twelve-pack of Bud sat on the shelf, a tempting reward after such a long, hot hike. "Hey, Shan, do you drink beer?"

"Not since I was a dumb kid. How do you feel about hotels?"

He snapped his head around to where she stood by the doors. "What?"

"There's a Comfort Suites down the street. Imagine sleeping in a clean bed. And I don't know about you, but I'm a sticky, sweaty mess. I could go for a shower even if it is room temperature."

"I don't know, Shan." He met her by the doors and looked at the tan building across the street, weighing the risks in his head.

"What are you worried about? Nobody knows where we are, and we don't even know where we're going. Was your plan to just drive until we got to the ocean?"

"I… Maybe?" He scratched his beard.

"We've got a couple of hours of daylight. We can pick out a new car, make sure it's gassed up, and load some supplies from here. I bet they've got some delicious canned meat that hasn't gone bad yet."

"If you think Spam is going to sell me, you might want to reconsider your argument."

"Shut up, T. You know what I'm saying. We don't want to be out there at night anyway, especially when our big plan right now is to boost a used car from what could totally be Otto's house of lemons. So, why not check ourselves into the lovely Comfort Suites of West Topeka, get a little sleep in relative comfort, and try our new ride in the daylight tomorrow, after we've stocked up on water, food, and extra gas? If it goes to shit, at least we're not in the middle of the open highway at night."

"Fine." Tom stepped away from her and headed back toward the drinks. He opened the beer case and pulled out a red twelve-pack of Budweiser. "But we're keeping this too. I haven't seen any real Bud in almost two months."

Shan rolled her eyes but didn't argue. She set down the gas cans and grabbed a couple of plastic bags from behind the counter then proceeded down the first aisle, picking items from the shelves. "We oughta find a grocery, too, if we have time. I'll get what I can from here. Why don't you pick a car and get the gas?"

"You're with me, then." Tom looked down at Lady.

She cocked her head back at him and shook herself out.

"I'll be right back."

The German shepherd led him from the store back into the sun. They crossed a side street to the used-car lot, and Tom took stock of their meager options. Otto didn't have even a dozen choices to pick from, and Tom dismissed the two late-model pickups right away. Sure, the utility might be nice, but they would need a lot more gas and one already sported a decent patch of rust over the rear quarter panel.

Half the remaining cars looked like they'd been built when he'd just gotten his driver's license. It came down to a gray four-door Accord, a white Toyota Highlander, and a blue Ford Explorer. Deep down, he wanted the Explorer, but it looked older than the other two, and he didn't want to risk it. Either that, or Ana's constant complaints that he chose cars stupidly for living in a postapocalyptic waste-land had finally sunk in.

Thankfully, Otto's office was little more than a shack with a single door and a window, which provided a view of the entire room. The key box was mounted to the wall just behind the one desk. The door was locked, but apparently, no one had expected it to actually keep people out. One swing of Tom's Louisville Slugger, and the knob fell to the ground at his feet. The air inside the shack was musty, as expected, always a good sign that plaguers weren't wandering around. Lady confirmed that, needing only a few seconds to make sure the space was clear.

Tom grabbed the key fobs for the Highlander, pocketed them, and headed back to the lot. He opened the driver's-side door and let Lady jump up, then climbed in behind her and hit the power button beside the steering column. The engine didn't quite leap to life with the throaty roar of his Mustang, but it started faster than he'd expected, given the circumstances, and it hummed steadily.

"Well, girl"—he rubbed the side of Lady's face—"she isn't flashy, but she'll probably do. I guess we're better off with a family car now anyway."

He dropped the shifter into drive and headed across the street to retrieve Shan.

CHAPTER 25

MORE THAN AN HOUR HAD passed before they finally pulled into the parking lot of the Comfort Suites that stood a block or so down the avenue from the Phillips station. Shan had convinced Tom to find a real grocery store. The best they could do in the area was a Walmart Superstore, but from Shan's grin when she saw it, he would have bet it made her happier.

They left the store with a cart laden with more supplies than he ever imagined needing, but he had to remind himself that Ana, Emily, or Lindsey had been taking care of most of his needs basically since he'd woken from his coma. He and Lady might go out on the occasional beer run, but food and shelter had always been a given.

Shan knew much better than he did what they would need to survive on the road, avoiding anything and anyone that might want to consider them dinner. They loaded a cart with dried pasta and beans, rice, and canned goods, especially vegetables and meat as well as soups and tomato sauce. She wouldn't be satisfied with one twenty-four pack of water bottles, so he rolled out of the store with two on the bottom of the cart. He found an absolute jackpot of Budweiser twelve-packs, but she wrinkled her nose when he tried to take more than two. He already had one from the Phillips station, she reminded him, and they could always find more as they traveled.

"It'd also be better if you weren't getting shithammered, T. I left Cincinnati with you because I was tired of being alone. But if you're gonna act like Nickie, my worthless high school boyfriend, I'll be gone one morning, and you'll never see me again. I learned years ago that I don't need boys making more work for me." She turned away without waiting for a reply and pushed her cart across the store's center aisle, toward misses' fashions.

They picked out a few fresh outfits to replace the bloody, grimy, sweat-stained clothes they'd both slept in back in the auto service garage in Covington. Tom also loaded up on ammunition for his revolver and added a pump-action shotgun and shells from the hunting case. By the time he slipped out of the Highlander at the Comfort Suites, he felt about as well supplied as he had been since waking up to the end of the world.

The hotel's automatic doors didn't open when he stepped onto the pressure pad, but they slid apart easily enough when Shan pressed her fingers between them. Lady, following protocol, slipped inside and made a quick circuit around the check-in lobby. She padded back to the doors and sat down, then sneezed.

"Mind the…"

But before he could get the rest out, Shan entered the hotel, where her hands flew up to cover her nose and mouth. "Oh, Mother, it reeks. I forgot how bad it can get."

Tom stepped inside, expecting to want to retch, and

was surprised to find he only needed to wrinkle his nose. A few of the places he'd been through since waking up had made his eyes water with the stench of death and decay. The hotel wasn't great, but it didn't make him want to throw up uncontrollably. "Oh, this isn't too bad. If we leave the doors open for a little bit, I think it'll air out."

"Not too bad? What the hell else have you been smelling, T?"

"Try a hospital. I'm sure this place has a few bodies somewhere, but in hospitals, people died everywhere, and most were left lying where they passed."

"Gods," she muttered. "I never thought of that. Janine always led us away from places with a lot of people, once the world started dying."

"Still want to spend the night here?"

Shan eyed the lobby then nodded. "Nothing that burning some incense won't fix. Maybe a little sage, too, for good measure."

They crossed the lobby to the front desk directly opposite the entrance doors. To their left stood a medium-sized room arrayed with a dozen or so tables and chairs. A raised counter stood at the back, likely where the complimentary breakfast of rubbery eggs and undercooked bacon would have been served. Tom tried not to think about bacon, undercooked or not, knowing he was about to have a supper of canned ham.

The electricity situation was better than their meal options were likely to be, though, as nearly every room they checked on the first floor had power. Most of the desk systems seemed to work as well, including the magnetic key card machine that made keys for the guest rooms.

But what were the odds the hot water heaters had been running continuously for three years? A hot shower was almost too much to hope for.

"Do you know how the key machine works, T?" Shan gave it an uncertain glare, as if suspicious of it.

"Yeah," Tom replied. "I used to travel a lot for work, and one night, I was having a drink in some hotel bar in San Antonio, I think. Anyway, it was a quiet night. I was the only one at the bar, and the clerk was also the bartender. The place had some conference coming in the next day, so he had to make dozens of keys for their welcome packets. He showed me how it worked, and I helped him make a few. He also had a couple of beers I'm pretty sure he wasn't supposed to have, so he probably got fired the next week. Who knows?"

"The Universe has weird energy."

Tom cocked his head as he opened and closed drawers below the desk, searching for blank key cards. "What do you mean?"

"You had to have that experience in San Antonio years ago so we could have rooms now. Things happen for a reason."

"I don't know about all that." He found the blanks and pulled a pair out of a box. "Seems like, if the Universe really had a plan, it might have avoided the whole fucked-up global pandemic apocalypse thing."

She shrugged. "Think whatcha want. But tell me, what did Charon really cost the Universe, except for a load of people who never showed it much respect anyway? I'll take room one thirteen, please."

Tom stopped, and his face went cold. He met her

eyes, knowing his were harder than he wanted them to be, but he was helpless to prevent the look, stirred by the storm of emotion. "It cost me my wife and any chance of reconciling with her after my coma. It cost me everything that ever mattered."

Shan held his eyes with her own, never flinching. "I'm sorry, Tom. I didn't know. But you aren't alone. I never said it didn't cost us anything. It cost me everything too. But maybe everything isn't always about us, and that's the point everybody missed."

With his mouth half-open, Tom blinked back at her, grasping for some reply that would make sense. After a few seconds, he gave up with a grunt. "Whatever. What about something on the second or third floor? I'll feel better knowing some plaguer won't randomly wander past and glare into my window in the middle of the night."

After a little back-and-forth, they agreed to adjoining rooms on the third floor, at the end of the hallway, right beside the stairs down to the emergency exit. They crept, step by agonizing step, up that same flight, with Lady leading them. The small group reached their floor without incident, and their guardian shepherd checked, and approved, the whole floor before either of them pushed past the exit door and off the stairwell.

Shan took the room closest to the end of the hall, 326, because despite not wanting an even-numbered room, she allowed that at least it was a multiple of thirteen. She pressed her card against the lock. Tom stood behind her on her left, shotgun half-raised.

The magnetic lock clicked green, and she threw the door open hard. Lady rushed in, and Shan caught the door with her right hand as it swung back toward them. Tom slid past her and turned to his left, into the bathroom. Nothing moved. He sighed in relief and pointed the gun to the floor, releasing the tension in his shoulders as he stepped into the room.

A pair of queen beds stood against the left wall, facing a flat-screen TV. Someone had made them up as neat and tidy as he'd ever seen, as if housekeeping had cleaned the room earlier in the morning. The door set in the wall beside the TV stand had no knob but a single dead bolt at eye level. He twisted the bolt and pulled it toward him, revealing a nearly matching door behind it. It was smooth, though, lacking the lock.

Tom rapped on the opposing door with a knuckle. Shan scowled and opened her mouth, no doubt to ask him what the hell he was up to. He put a hand out instead to stall her and listened for a response from the other side.

He turned away. "Good."

"What the hell?" she asked.

"If something—a vamp or, what do you call them, blood zombie?—had been on the other side, the knock would have set them off. Nothing lost its mind and started trying to chew through the door, so pretty likely nothing's in the room next door."

Nothing wanting to feed on them, at least.

"You could have warned me." Shan dropped her new travel bag on the bathroom floor as well as the shoulder bag with her supplies then turned the faucet handle. The water ran for ten seconds as she sat on the edge of the tub, then she crossed her fingers while giving him a hopeful face. She slid her other hand under the running water, and her eyes doubled in size. "Oh, Mother, T, it's fucking hot. Can you believe it?"

As Shan stood, she pulled the elastic band from her hair. She started to pull her shirt up but paused, thinking better of it. She shot him a glance that made it very clear he should be somewhere else.

"I'll be next door, if you need anything. I'll leave Lady here with you." Through the open doorway to the hall, he turned and gave the dog a look.

He pointed to the ground outside the bathroom, and she padded to that spot. She cocked her head with a question in her eyes, as if not sure that was really what he wanted.

"Stay," he replied.

Lady dropped to her belly and crossed her forepaws, panting contentedly.

Tom let Shan's door close then stood in front of his own room. With his key card in his left hand and his right prepared to raise and fire the shotgun, he pressed his card to the lock. The light went green, and he turned the handle with a surgeon's touch. It clicked, and he pushed it away from him, jamming his foot at the base to wedge it open. He swept his eyes across the sleeping area first and, finding nothing, moved into the bathroom. Both spaces were empty.

Setting the gun on the TV stand, he unbolted the door between the rooms and set his travel bag against it so it wouldn't swing open by accident. If Shan or Lady needed to get to him, they could, but a little privacy would be nice.

Entering the bathroom, he did the same thing Shan

had and marveled at the hot water flowing along his wrist and the back of his hand. He hadn't felt warm water since leaving the Chalet, and his skin prickled with anticipation of a hot shower. He grabbed the paper-wrapped bar of soap from the sink, unwrapped it, and inhaled deeply. The clean, floral scent that hotel soap makers used in the waxy bars triggered memories of traveling for work long before the plague began.

Smiling, he dared to hope that maybe he and Shan could find some way to live normal lives together, hidden away from the others and their miserable conflict.

CHAPTER 26

WITH ONE LAST GRUNT OF effort, Lindsey hung her head and sighed in frustration. She'd tried to break free of the shackles binding her hands behind her back at least a dozen times and had nothing but aching wrists and blood-slick fingers to show for it. Kneeling on a dirt floor, a matching set bound her ankles to steel chains, all of which were linked through an iron hoop on the stone wall behind her. With little to no slack in the chains connecting everything, she couldn't get any measurable leverage. Certainly not enough to have any hope of breaking free.

Lars knelt to her left, hog-tied the same as she was. He'd been fuming to himself since they'd been brought down and left in Colin's dungeon, wherever the place happened to be. The room looked a lot like the cellars below the old brewery that Alexander had used for his Family last year. The stonework making up the walls kind of seemed about the same, but Lindsey wasn't a masonry expert. They all looked like the same dusty old bricks to her.

She was, however, considerably skilled in sizing up her enemies, which made her think there was no way they were being held in the same place as before. Colin was too smart to have remained in Alexander's old hideout, especially after being humiliated by Emily's intervention. He wouldn't want her to have such easy access to him any more than he would want Alexander to have the advantage of knowing the building better if the former Master of the area brought some kind of attack. The cell they were in had to be somewhere completely different, then.

Which also explained being hooded before they'd brought them in—Colin was protecting his location. And that meant she couldn't tell Emily where to come rescue them. They would have to get out of their predicament on their own, somehow.

The room was nearly black, but there was no telling whether Colin either hadn't had time to run lights through the place or simply hadn't bothered. They were all vampires, after all, a species that was arguably the peak predator ever to stalk the Earth under moonlight. Her night vision was better than her daytime vision had ever been in her first life as a poor human. The narrowest of slots in their cell door let in just enough ambient light that Lindsey could see everything almost as well as if they were out in the light of a full moon.

She and Lars were not alone in the cell. Across from her, another vampire lay on his side, breathing slowly. She presumed he was unconscious but couldn't tell if he was asleep or out of it for some other reason. His hands were also pulled behind him, and his legs were bent as if he'd been kneeling and had just fallen over. Likely, he was bound to the opposite wall the same as they were.

How long until she got so tired that she fell into the same position?

"Can you get any kind of leverage?" Lars broke the silence, surprising her with the question.

"Do I strike you as having gotten anywhere yet?" she shot back. "I don't reckon I've felt this useless since before I was Made."

"I've been in worse positions before, I think, but not much. What do you think about Sleeping Beauty over there?"

"Can't say as I think anything. If he's Resting, they must have worked him over good. Can't see anybody choosing to Rest in a bind like this. Do you know him? Could he be one of Alexander's?"

Lars shook his head. "I can't get a good enough look at his face to tell. Did you let Emily know?"

"You're being thick, darlin'. I messaged her before we even got here. By now, she's rounded up her war party and is aboard the Dragon, headed north."

"It's got to be daylight."

"The Dragon steams in daylight too. She's got blackout covers for all the windows and such."

"Then she should have all night to track us by the time they get here. Hopefully, it doesn't take too long to find us through your bond. The less time Colin has to get ready for her, the better."

"She'll let me know. Best we can do is be ready to get into it as soon as we're free. I reckon we're looking at a proper fight this time, not like that little skirmish back in—" She broke off at the sound of keys jiggling at the door.

It slid open, and two Feral entered first with that strange bob-step so many of the plaguers had developed. Behind them came three other vampires. The only one she recognized was Kallus, still as wide across at the shoulders as a billboard. The guy next to him was unremarkable in comparison—lighter hair, slighter build. The only feature Lindsey registered as something of interest was the arrogant smirk on his otherwise-forgettable face.

She flexed her wrists against the steel shackles one more time for good measure. She would happily have traded away her grandmomma's pimento cheese recipe for a chance to wipe it off his face.

The last vampire inside was tall and oddly put together. His torso was longer than his legs, and his spindly arms matched his upper body. He half reminded Lindsey of the wooden puppets with all the strings she used to see at street shows as a kid. Wearing an ill-fitting white lab coat that didn't quite reach his hips and carrying a small black bag, he had to be another one of Colin's science types. Lindsey hissed almost without thinking.

"Patience, sister." Lab Coat gave a sinister grin. "You'll have your turn, I promise. But I haven't got much time today, so you will have to wait." He nodded in her direction and said to the other two vampires, "Put them over there for now. I want to speak to him without them looming."

The Feral each silently took a position to one side of her and Lars, no doubt at the direction of Kallus, who, along with Forgettable, moved to the far back of the room, away from the door.

Lab Coat went to one knee beside the unconscious prisoner and dug something out of his bag—a vial, by the size of it. He unscrewed the top, placed the vial against the resting vampire's mouth, and tilted his head back.

The prisoner instinctively swallowed whatever was inside. A second later, he groaned. He murmured something she couldn't make out then, "Drake? Not again, Drake. It's not time yet. Please, no."

Science Guy pulled a syringe from his bag. "I'm afraid so, Rafe. You're correct that I'm a little ahead of schedule today, but it can't be helped. I do not always make the schedule. One more time, though, then we'll be done."

The prisoner—Rafe—shuddered then wailed, "Nooo, Drake! No more. Please." The poor fella bucked and twisted on the floor, trying to get loose.

He sounded halfway to hysterical. Hard not to feel a little sorry for him.

"What are you doing to him?" Lindsey asked. "Let the man be."

Drake shot her a sympathetic look. "Please do not interfere. I need to concentrate and would hate to have you silenced."

The plaguer closest to her looked down and made some unholy growling coo that was half-threat, half-anticipation. A drop of saliva slipped from its partially opened jaw and splattered next to her. She curled her lips in disgust and burned every face around her into her mind. They would all have a reckoning when she was free.

She seethed while Drake went back to his work, inserting the needle into Rafe's arm, then swapping out a vial from the syringe for another. He wasn't dosing him with anything but instead taking blood. She'd never seen a vampire take blood from anyone, vampire or otherwise, and not consume it on the spot. Shame Ana wasn't there to figure out what he was up to.

Finished, Drake capped the needle and dropped it back into his bag. He pulled out another one filled with a much lighter fluid. "Tell me how you feel, Rafe."

"Who… who are they?" the prisoner replied as if seeing Lindsey and Lars for the first time. "What are they doing here?"

"They are none of your concern, brother. Now, if you don't mind, how do you feel?"

"I'm… tired, Drake. Always tired. And so thirsty. You've never given me anything more than a vial of blood. If I could find a rat or something, I'd never complain about having to feed on the filthy things again."

"That's all you feel? Tired and needing to feed? Nothing else?" As he spoke, Drake lifted Rafe's eyelids, one after the other, and scrutinized something in his eyes. Satisfied with whatever he saw, he then pulled the cap off the new syringe and jabbed it into the vampire's neck.

Rafe cried out as whatever the syringe held flooded into his bloodstream. He whimpered like a beaten dog for a few moments then muttered a string of unintelligible noises into the floor before finally falling silent.

As calm as if sipping tea on a Sunday, the monster in the lab coat looked at his watch then capped the syringe and placed it in his bag. He stood, unfolding his lanky frame to its full height. After picking up the bag, he moved to the doorway, where he stood and waited, checking his watch again.

"What the hell did you give him?" Lars growled.

"It's of no concern to you, brother. At least, not yet."

"I'm not your brother, pencil neck. You call me that again, you'll regret it."

Drake flashed his soft, sinister grin. "I very much doubt that." He glanced down at his watch again. "But we can discuss improving your attitude another time. It's almost time to see how we've done."

Like he'd been waiting for permission, Rafe moaned then shifted in the dirt. He grunted twice, sounding like a gorilla Lindsey once saw at a zoo. He moaned again, louder and more intensity. Soon it became an angry growl, and he bucked and thrashed, trying to right himself.

"What is this?" he barked, looking around as well as possible from his position. "Who are you? You've come to kill me, haven't you? Well, you won't. You can't! Why am I bound like this? Let me out. Let me go! I'll kill you all!" The muscles in his arms pulled tight as he fought to break the shackles, and veins appeared in his neck as he strained against the metal. He bucked and thrashed, twisting himself around as well as he could until reaching a position that brought Drake into his view.

"*You!*" He cursed. "You did this! I hate you! I'll tear you apart. Into pieces! Tear and rend! Rip and pull! And drink. Yes, drink so much! Every drop from you! You. Will. Pay!"

Lindsey watched in horror as Rafe mutilated his wrists to fight against his bindings. Moments before, he'd been a pathetic excuse for a vampire, weak and mewling for pity. But then, as if a switch had been flipped, he'd become something almost animal. For the first time, she understood why the room was littered with chains bound to the walls. Glancing at Lars, she guessed from his wide-eyed expression that he was thinking the same thing.

Rafe found a way to slither along the floor by pushing himself with his legs, inching his way toward the mad scientist, his face twisted in hatred and rage. His shouted threats alternated with screams of agony and frustration. Finally, he stopped, squeezed his eyes shut, and ground his teeth. A gut-churning series of cracks and pops echoed off the walls, and he threw one hand into the air, cheering himself. The thing was mangled and bloody, his thumb hanging the wrong way and wrist flopping wildly. The fool must have broken it in several places just to slip it from the steel cuff.

Grinning at Drake, he pushed himself into a seated position with his other hand. Turning his back to the door, he faced the chain connecting the shackles on his feet to the wall. He waved the ruined hand back and forth in the air a few times, as if he'd simply burned it on a hot stove. Lindsey gasped, and her mouth fell open as the drooping, bloody mass at the end of his arm firmed back into the correct position. Rafe flexed it several times, opening and closing the fingers to be sure they worked once again. Even the thumb somehow functioned the way it should.

She looked at Drake, half expecting him to back out of the room or ready something to contain Rafe. Instead, he looked on with curiosity, raising a hand toward the other two vampires at the far end of the cell. He didn't want them to interfere.

Chuckling to himself, Rafe grabbed the irons clasped around his ankles and pulled against them with the same grimace of exertion as before. The chuckle became a maniacal giggle then a bloodcurdling scream as he focused all his energy on the effort.

A loud metallic crack rang out, followed by the clang of steel hitting the floor. "Drink so much!" Rafe shouted, enraged as he turned to, once again, face his tormentor.

Drake still showed no outward sign of concern. He checked his watch then cocked his head.

Rafe stood, but hunched slightly, and began panting like a dog. "All. Blood!" he shouted with murderous glee.

Drake never uttered a word, but the Feral converged on the berserk vampire quicker than Lindsey had ever seen plaguers move. Before Rafe could take another step toward his quarry, they had slashed him open across the neck and abdomen. Blood sprayed the walls, and the vampire's insides spilled onto the floor. The acrid tang of blood and meat filled Lindsey's nose, and for a moment, she was racked with a twinge of longing, hunger. She pushed the urge away as quickly as it filled her. No use getting twisted into a blood frenzy when bound to a wall.

The Feral stepped back, grunting and snuffling, and Rafe fell to his knees with the once-ruined hand pressed against a gaping gash across the front of his neck. A bewildered look settled on his face as he investigated the grotesque mass spilling out of his abdomen. It seemed almost as if he couldn't figure out where all of it had come from.

After a few seconds, though, he shot Drake another sneer filled with hate. "All your blood. All of it."

Drake tsk-tsked and shook his head. "He's yours. Leave the others untouched."

With that, Kallus and Forgettable flashed across the

room and latched onto Rafe. Bloodred mouths worked at opposite sides of his already-crimson neck. They drained him quickly then let him fall back to the ground. When they'd finished, they looked at each other and laughed.

Drake was already gone.

"That was fucking amazing," Kallus grinned.

Forgettable patted him on the back. "Damn right. Haven't eaten that good in almost a year." He turned a lustful gaze on Lindsey. Her skin instantly felt like she was covered in spiders. "I wonder how long until he'll be done with these two."

"I wouldn't be counting those chickens just yet, if I were you," Lindsey replied a little faster than she would have liked.

Kallus cut in before Forgettable could say anything else. "Cut it out. No telling what that weirdo is planning to do with them. Just remember that we have to keep all this to ourselves for the time being. Not a word to anyone. Now, let's have the dogs clean up, and we'll get out of here."

The plaguers picked up what was left of poor Rafe by his shoulders and feet. They carried him out the door in tandem, shuffling awkwardly. Not a single drop of his blood hit the floor. Drake's lackeys followed them out and sealed the door behind them.

"Christ, Lindsey," Lars said, the strain of his shock still noticeable in his voice. "What the hell was all that? And then they just drained him. Right in front of us! What are we gonna do?"

She shook her head. "I don't got the first clue what they're up to, darlin'. But whatever all that was, it for sure ain't good." Lindsey did know what she would do first, though.

"Lady Emily, we have to talk," she thought.

"I hear you, Child," came Emily's reply directly into Lindsey's mind.

"Lady, I have the evidence you asked for, but me and Lars are being held. I don't know what Colin's up to, but something wronger than a five-legged cat is going on here." She forced the last few minutes of her memory to stream across their bond.

Emily somehow tsk-tsked disapprovingly by thought. *"I'm coming. And when I arrive, there will be a reckoning."*

CHAPTER 27

A NA CREPT ALONG THE PATH she imagined the newly freed Feral had taken, despite not really knowing for sure. Before long, the darkness in front of her changed from black to charcoal with a faint diffusion of daylight, and after that, a pinpoint of bright light appeared on the horizon. Hard to fathom a parking garage that sprawled beneath a city until its exits were so far away that it had a horizon. The garage ranged for blocks and blocks. No wonder they'd chosen it for whatever horrible project they'd been working on.

Assuming she might still come across Feral roaming the city uncontrolled, or worse, controlled by Alexander, Ana resumed the cautious dance from column to column, pausing at each to get a good sense of the surrounding area. She found nothing but emptiness. That was, until she reached the exit.

She crouched behind the last support before the ground of the parking garage ramped upward toward the machines that had once let cars out, one at a time, using a lightweight, hinged horizontal pole. The swinging barriers had long since been busted into pieces, though, and the garage was open to anyone willing to test the shadows inside.

In front of the gate machines, a pair of Feral stood by the large opening leading outdoors. Neither was the one she'd released, and both looked much healthier insofar as plaguers could look healthy. They were as pale and disheveled as their kind always were, and they stood with arms drooping at their respective sides, heads lowered, chin to chest. They swayed in time together to some song only they could hear, with a long, narrow shipping crate between them that looked about the right size to hold a coffee table, or maybe a rack of rifles.

She couldn't recall ever seeing one at Rest like that, even during the day. Usually, when they were indoors, hiding from daylight, they spent their time rummaging for whatever they could find that might be edible. Watching the pair just wait with an almost patient calm for night to fall made her skin crawl.

So much of what she'd seen since returning from Atlanta was just wrong. She had to assume it was mostly Colin's doing, but whoever it was, they'd been quite busy. The question was, to what end?

Ana couldn't see the actual horizon from the garage exit—she guessed it was facing west—but the quality of light changed quickly. A few minutes prior, it had been orange with threads of shadow, but it became a mix of purple and gray. The sun had to be setting.

As if in response to that thought, the Feral came to life. Both their heads snapped up in unison, and they bent to lift the crate between them. Each shouldered one side of it, holding it steady with their other hand, then they turned toward the exit. They remained standing like that for a minute, almost like robots, until, with no other warning, the pair stepped into the outside air.

Intrigued, Ana followed.

They trekked out into the street and headed north before turning left at the end of the block, as if following some kind of preset path. As if following a pair of plaguers carrying a wooden box like beasts of burden wasn't strange enough, they lumbered on as if specifically trained, or even bound to a pattern, like Feral-on-rails.

Reaching another cross street, one running north to south, they turned again in unison, heading north.

Even as she followed, she frowned, wondering how long Colin would allow her to keep it up. He'd told her to find Lindsey, and instead, she'd decided to tail the two Feral on a whim.

Was it a whim, though, or was it more her need to understand what was happening around her? To uncover whatever plot Colin had schemed up for them.

With a start, Ana stopped and put a hand to her mouth. Everything about their trip north after the attack on Tom had been part of the scheme. Colin's plan wasn't just about driving Alexander out of the region he'd once controlled. Somehow, it was every bit as much about *them*. Tom and Lindsey, herself, and Lars. Possibly, almost certainly, even Emily. But Lars had been the trigger. Lars had arrived perfectly in time with the attack to prod Emily into sending them back to Cincinnati. That couldn't be a coincidence.

Had Colin somehow turned him against Alexander? He wasn't Descended from Alexander, so she had assumed their relationship was one of mutual agreement. She didn't really know Lars, though. Who was *his* Maker? Did they have ties with Alexander, maybe, making it more than a connection of convenience, or was he truly just a free agent, joining that Master sometime in the early days after Charon because he knew he had to side with someone?

Ana eyed the Feral as they crossed another street ahead of her. Maybe she shouldn't be following them, not when Colin had tasked her with finding Lindsey, but somehow, she had a feeling the beasts would lead her right where he wanted her to be anyway. She started forward again, tracing the path left by the Feral toward downtown, picking at the cuticle of her thumb as well as the threads of evidence in her mind.

They plodded north a few more blocks until they arrived at the crossing of Fifth and Vine and the city's Fountain Square along with its famous fountain, "The Genius of Water." She couldn't help but frown knowing it would likely never sing with water again.

The Feral, of course, paid it no mind but went straight for the entrance to the underground parking garage.

Her frown deepened at the sight of the entrance. She'd had her fill of dark, empty garage space. Having no obvious alternative, though, she proceeded behind them, even as they started down the stairs, one in front of the other with their freight slung between them.

Giving them some leeway, she let them reach the first floor before she started down. When she reached the turn of the steps at the first floor, she was struck by the unmistakable scent of fresh blood. She quickly found the source: a dark stain on the wall opposite her, halfway to the second floor. It was almost black and dried but not crumbling or flaking. Likely not more than a day or so old. For the first time, she felt relieved that Tom was gone. At least she didn't have to worry that it was his. Ana could only hope it wasn't Lindsey's.

Her Feral escorts had left the stairway at the second floor below, and she hurried to catch up. They continued to shuffle along their predetermined path in the darkness, soon coming to a large metal panel open slightly to allow access to something beyond. Sliding through, she found a tiled hallway with an opening at its end to the right, where the plaguers turned the corner.

As she rounded it, she gasped softly. Not that she was surprised to find a full subway platform—she knew the subway existed and that the passage would lead to either that or more beer storage, since the city was rotten with tunnels to both effects—but because eight Feral milled around in the trench where the trains would drive.

The pair she'd tracked to the tunnel handed their crate down to another pair, who moved to add it to a stack of matching ones against the far wall. Two others stared down the dark subway tunnels as if watching for someone, and the last pair climbed onto a manually cranked railway cart with a pair of crates stacked on its back. The courier pair that had carried the crate across the city and into the garage turned and bob-stepped past her, back the way they'd come, paying her no mind whatsoever.

The manual cart's crank groaned, and the wheels squealed as it started forward.

Ana didn't hesitate. She stepped out onto the platform, making sure her steps were loud enough to draw attention, should the Feral be interested.

The workers ignored her, but the guards each glanced at her for half a moment before resuming their respective duties. None of them cared about her at all. It confirmed that the entire operation—whatever it was supposed to accomplish—belonged to Colin.

Dropping from the platform into the train well, Ana entered the darkness of the western end of the subway and jogged after the train cart.

CHAPTER 28

T HE SQUEAL OF THE UNSEEN railroad cart's wheels grated in Ana's ears, and combined with the rhythmic thump of the crank mechanism sliding up and down in the darkness pressing around her, she began to wonder if it might be some kind of punishment Colin had concocted for her. She almost wished she were one of the Feral on the cart, freed of any independent thought or feeling, incapable of being annoyed by the chafe of metal wheels rolling on a nearly hundred-year-old steel track.

They had traveled in the inky black for miles, either west or curving north. The tunnel was on the opposite side of the city from the one Lars had used last year to bring her and Tom to Alexander, and she had no idea where they would end up. Was it the same subway line, even? Perhaps it was linked to that one somewhere to make a massive loop.

Before she was forced to consider the likelihood of traversing the perimeter of the city of Cincinnati on foot, she realized that for the first time since leaving the subway station, she could just make out the shadow of the cart twenty feet or so ahead of her. Not long after, she found a point of dim light some distance away, growing with every footstep. They exited the tunnel beneath a clear summer sky filled with stars, entering the not-quite-cool night air plump with the breath of growing things.

The rail cart came to a stop with an earsplitting screech, an exclamation point in the assault on Ana's ears. The Feral hobbled down and moved to the back of the cart, where they lifted the first of the two crates off. They shambled in unison over to another stack of boxes lining the outside of the subway wall and set it on the top. They did the same with the second crate then clambered with all the grace of a landlocked penguin back up on their little freight cart. Then, as they gave a few alternating pushes of the hand crank, its wheels sang their woeful lament back into the tunnel.

The crates were piled eight high, with four stacks in total. Ana had thought they were devoid of any writing or markings, but up close, she saw all the crates had been stamped with a number, one through four, on the front right-hand corner with the number matching their stack from left to right.

She needed to get into one of them and see what was worth the effort of taming dozens of Feral and training them, apparently, to ferry goods across the city. She pulled a crate down from the first stack and set it on the ground in front of her. The wood making up the box was old and worn smooth. Had Colin made those, too, or found a collection of them somewhere and commandeered them?

A crowbar would have been perfect, or even maybe a multi-tool, but Ana was without either. The best she could do was hope to pry the top off by hand. She ran a finger around the outside of the top and found a spot where the wood was warped slightly, creating a slight gap. She wedged the index and middle fingers of her right hand into the space and pulled upward with a grimace. The nails holding the cover down gave way to the pressure, and it pulled back from the box with a crackling moan before the entire thing came away in her hands.

Ana set the crate's top aside and cocked her head. Inside, dozens of small glass vials of clear liquid were nested in straw and packing materials. She reached in and took one, raising it to eye level.

She squinted then scowled. "Why in the hell are you moving epinephrine?"

She set the vial back into its place and checked the others in the crate. All of them matched, dozens and dozens of little vials of adrenaline. Leaving the crate on the ground, she grabbed a box from the second stack and popped it open the same way to find vials of pseudoephedrine. Crates from the third and fourth stacks contained blood pressure and erectile dysfunction medications, respectively.

Ana leaned against the wall beside the crates and scowled. What was he doing? What purpose could Colin possibly have for stockpiling such a strange array of drugs?

Movement from the corner of her eye broke her chain of thought. Another pair of Feral workers, from what she was starting to think might be an endless supply, shambled across the street in front of her. Each took one of the crates from the stacks, ignoring the opened ones on the ground. Those must not be part of their training. With the containers hoisted on their shoulders, they turned around and headed back the way they'd come.

The path they followed led straight to a huge art deco building several blocks in the distance with a familiar semicircle façade, Cincinnati's Union Terminal. Icy dread knifed across her stomach. She may not know exactly what use he had for those drugs, but the fact that they were being delivered to the city's famous train depot that shared common real estate with the tracks that Emily's train had arrived on last year could not be a coincidence.

As if the tingling fear spreading through her wasn't bad enough, a glance to the south showed a line of gray smoke rising into the sky some distance off. That could only mean one thing, Emily's Dragon was approaching. As if thunderstruck, the pieces Ana couldn't make fit together slammed into place. The complete details escaped her, but whatever had happened to Lindsey—and Ana desperately hoped it had nothing to do with that blood stain in the garage—had prompted Lady Emily to make a trip to the city. Unlike last fall, though, Colin expected her. He had something planned.

She and the others had been tricked into serving as bait, and her Maker was about to spring a trap.

Ana dashed away from the tunnel wall, racing toward the railroad yard to the west. Halfway there, a familiar voice sliced through her consciousness.

"Daughter." His presence across their link was somehow *more* than usual. Heavier, more powerful. She skidded to a stop and dared not reply.

"You will bear witness, but you will not interfere."

Then he was gone, leaving her with nothing but dread.

CHAPTER 29

A STREAM OF BLACK SMOKE SLID from the train's stack while the chug of the steam engine shattered the peaceful calm of the night. Ana spied a few fireflies dancing around the abandoned train cars, and she envied their simplicity, their ignorance. None of it meant anything to them. If only things could be that simple for her kind. Instead, the belching smoke and the hiss of steam pulled her attention back to the Dragon's arrival, back to the horrors of her second life.

She squatted behind the half-open door of an old cargo car that was part of a set of three left to rot in the train yard. It was the same place where Emily and her Family had arrived with Tom last year when they'd come to deal with Colin and save her. It was the same place where she'd boarded for the trip back to Atlanta.

Her observation spot was about fifty yards from where the Dragon had come to rest back then, and at the rate the steam locomotive was slowing, it seemed likely to end up in just about the same place again. She should be able to watch whatever was about to happen without giving herself away beforehand, as commanded.

Ana mostly wanted to vomit.

She looked over her shoulder for the eighth time to make sure the door on the other side of the car—the one leading away from the trains—was still open and that no one approached. She half expected to see Lars and Lindsey come into view from the east, but it could just as easily by a slobbering gang of trained Feral. At the moment, nothing and no one was out there.

"Why do you need me here?" she muttered to herself.

Ana folded her legs beneath her and scratched at the side of her thumb as the Dragon slid to a stop at the exact location she expected it to. The Captain—an old vampire she'd met once in her months at the Chalet—was apparently as skilled a train engineer as he was salty. In their one meeting, he'd barely done more than grunt, cuss, and eye Tom as if the man carried some kind of curse.

If only she could think of a way to send Emily some signal, anything to tip her off about the danger she was walking into. Unfortunately, nothing even half clever enough to get around Colin's order not to interfere came to mind.

Vampires began to stream out of the passenger cars behind the engine. By her count, thirty set up a circle around the front of the Dragon before Emily stepped down. Her face was set hard, almost a scowl. It showed none of the kindness or the twinkle of jest she often showed at the Chalet. Ana had only seen her like that once, last year, when she'd found out that one of her brothers in the Family, Ash, had killed and fed on vampires in Emily's region. Since Charon, feeding on their own kind was forbidden. It was the only law they had. Killing another lord's Family wasn't often done, either, as it tended to start wars, and Ash had done both.

Colin had claimed that Ash had acted alone and without consent, which was the only thing that had kept Emily from ending the rival lord then and there.

Hard not to wonder if she had come to regret that decision in the months since.

"Such a large party," Ana whispered. It gave her some tiny sliver of hope. Maybe the lady had brought enough support that Colin's trap wouldn't work.

Emily, wearing pressed khaki slacks and a light blouse with a shawl, strode purposefully to the front of the locomotive. The vampires arrayed in a half circle began to move forward, and she settled into the middle of them. The ones on the edges of the circle came together, closing it. Emily said something, and they marched ahead—the general at the center of her soldiers.

The formation came to an abrupt halt. From the gate where Emily was headed, another group of vampires appeared. It was a larger one, maybe twice the size of Emily's, with nearly as many Feral alongside. Colin, a head taller than all of them, entered the train yard behind what had to be his own war party. At his side, another pair of vampires—one short and wide with muscles and a shaggy, stringy, salt-and-pepper mess of hair who she knew from before, and another she didn't know but who held all the distinctiveness of a discount store manager—held chains connected to two prisoners shuffling along in manacles behind them.

Lars and Lindsey held their heads high, but the tightness on their faces spoke volumes.

"Oh, shit," she murmured.

Her jaw tightened. The tension pressed against her.

"Lord Colin," Emily boomed from fifty yards away, "while it is typically a delight to see you and your fine Family, I fear a misunderstanding must be remedied to restore the goodwill!"

"Indeed, lady? Do proceed."

"If it isn't too much to ask, I would enjoy an explanation of exactly why you have had one of my Children and another of my oldest friends brought out to me, bound in chains?"

Colin raised his eyebrows, feigning shock. "Surely you cannot be surprised, Emily, that we were forced to take precautions to protect ourselves from your agents. I thought they might be here merely to spy at first, but within the hour of their arrival, they had killed members of my own Family. On my land, even."

"That's a lie," Lindsey spat. "We didn't cross the river until later, and we didn't actually kill anyone. *Unfortunately.*"

Colin shot a vicious scowl over his shoulder at her. "Every last Feral you killed these past days are of my Family! Do you deny leaving a path of the poor things dead as you rampaged your way to me? Do you deny attempting to kill Kallus, here, who is my Child?"

Lindsey glared daggers into the back of her captor, who Colin had just called Kallus. Ana frowned. He'd gone by Gordon when she'd left California to hunt down Tom, and she couldn't remember him being all that remarkable.

"I only wish I *had* killed him. Let me free, and I'll do it right."

Turning back toward Emily, Colin went on, raising his voice. "Do you hear? By her own admission, she has violated our one law. I do hope it was not by your order, Emily."

"No!" Lindsey shouted, before Gordon—or Kallus?—slapped her across the face.

"The prisoners will remain quiet," Colin stated, "until an agreement between lords has been made. It is my right."

Closing her eyes and clenching her fists, Emily took a deep breath. Releasing it, she relaxed her hands as well. "What are you about, Colin? What will you have from this charade?"

"Call it a charade if you wish, ma'am, but I am within my rights, and you know there are only two ways to satisfy the charges. If you demand a trial, we can wait to convene the tribunal at the Conclave. Or you can agree that as punishment for their crimes, they meet the coming morning."

Emily's soldiers gasped.

Lindsey, though, was not having it. "Your claims are bullshit, you jumped-up old goat."

Colin didn't even look at her but smirked at the toothless insult.

"My daughter speaks out of turn," Emily allowed, "but she has a point. I have neither seen nor heard real evidence of any crime. I will certainly not consent to leaving them for the dawn."

"The tribunal it shall be, then," the lord replied. "I'll ask you, in that case, to leave my territory before any further misunderstandings lead to a break in the peace."

Emily's face became stone once again. "I will not leave here without my daughter, Colin. If you aren't spoiling for a fight, then you had best reconsider your actions."

"Are you threatening me? Here, in the open?"

Lindsey's Maker, growing angrier by the moment, stepped forward with her fangs on full display. Witnessing a vampire of her age exerting the full force of her will gave Ana goose bumps.

"Son, I will not give a second thought to standing up to anyone, anywhere, who is putting my Family in jeopardy, and I should think you would understand that very well by now. Now then, are you going to release her, or will I have to come take her? Before you answer, I'd think on what passes through your lips next."

After stroking his neatly trimmed beard for several of the tensest heartbeats Ana could remember from either of her lives, Colin finally said, "Perhaps we can resolve this unfortunate matter without bloodshed. I should say I do not want to be the focus of our peers at the Conclave. That might be… counterproductive."

Emily narrowed her eyes. "Go on."

"Well, madam, it seems that I have someone of yours, a daughter, and you have a daughter of mine. Perhaps we could allow each to return to their proper home and Master—a trade, if you will—then go our separate ways with no hard feelings."

Crossing her arms, Emily glared at the other Master. "I see your game now, Colin. It's a shame that I can't rightly say where your daughter happens to be. She left with those two, and I have not seen or heard from her. But surely you know that I'll honor my word. Return

Lindsey to me and free Lars, and I swear none of mine will interfere with you calling Ana back home."

"Have no fear." He sneered. "The prodigal daughter is close, and I believe she is coming to meet us. I fear I feel somewhat compelled to hold on to your child for the time being, though, just until mine appears. As a token of generosity, though, I will release Lars to you."

When he finished speaking, his expression drained.

Ana went stiff, paralyzed by the force of her lord.

"You will not move."

His presence came and went in the blink of an eye, and his face brightened. If Ana hadn't been the target of his attention, she doubted she would have noticed.

Lars was led outside the line of Colin's vampires by the store-manager-looking vampire, and they made slow, shuffling progress to the midway point between the two groups. There, his captor pulled Lars to a stop, took a key from one of his pockets, and unclasped both of his ankle and wrist shackles. Rubbing his wrists, Lars growled and flexed his fangs at the shorter vampire, who took a quick step back toward Colin, half-dragging the chains to a chorus of laughter from Emily's entourage. Colin himself twitched a half smile.

Lars met Emily in the center of her circle, and she took his hands. He whispered something, but she shook her head and waved him off. Ana managed to read the words, "Stand ready," from her lips.

"If we are to do this without violence, which surely would be everyone's hope," Emily called, "let's do it and be done. I'd like to get back to my home before sunrise, and we all know just how little night there is in the middle of the summer. Is your child close, then? Let's go our separate ways and move on to our own affairs."

With a smug grin, Colin raised an arm and snapped his fingers. Emily's people tensed at the motion, but no attack followed. Instead, a smaller group entered the train yard from the gate behind Ana's lord. Five vampires, a mix of male and female, rolled what looked like an animal cage with wheels—the kind from pictures of an old circus show—alongside his line of guards. Inside, a hooded body in a dress lay crumpled in a ball at the center.

"Before we get to that, lady, I have one more surprise for you."

Colin nodded, and Store Manager again took out a key and opened the cage.

"What is the meaning of this?" Emily's voice was tight.

Ana tried to force herself to cry out in warning but could not. Danger hung thick in the air, and the soldiers surrounding Emily and Lars closed ranks.

"I have a surprise for you, Emily. A gift in your honor. Something I've been planning for quite some time."

A pair of guards surrounding the cage reached in and dragged out whoever was inside. They pulled her onto her feet not far beyond Colin's protective line. The woman, whoever she was, was also bound at the hands and feet, as Lars had been, but with double the chains. She stumbled at first but succeeded in keeping her balance. She snarled under the hood and shook to free herself, but the keepers at her sides held her tightly.

Ana frowned. Something was off about her. She seemed familiar, but nothing Ana could put a finger on.

She didn't quite stand up straight and continued to buck and twist in the hands of her captors, trying to pull away. She snarled again then grunted.

Realization slammed into Ana with the force of Emily's locomotive. "Christ, that's a plaguer." The word dropped from her lips like a stone.

"Damn you to hell," Lars shouted, "you didn't!" He turned away from Colin, a mask of panic covering his face.

Ana couldn't believe her eyes. She'd seen Lars fight nearly every kind of anything a person could imagine, and he'd never shown even the smallest hint of fear. She believed there was no contest, no challenge that he would shrink from. Yet he was about to flee from whatever—whoever—Colin had trapped under that hood.

In that same moment, one of the guards lifted that covering, revealing a pair of coal black eyes and a mouth full of deadly pointed teeth set in a gray face.

"Genevieve!" Lars cried.

The Feral screeched at the top of its lungs and lashed out with what had to be more than twice the force it had before. One of the guards holding it lost her grip on the berserk plaguer and was underneath the monster before she could recover. Colin's vampires surged forward, racing past the angry animal and slamming into the soldiers surrounding Emily.

Even in the chaos, with vampires streaking from place to place and striking each other, Lars caught Ana's attention. His eyes had turned to that unseeing black that took over her kind when they reached a blood frenzy. His face was the picture of ravenous menace with fangs on full display. He screeched his own spine-chilling battle cry, an imitation of the Feral's, but a fuller, stronger blast.

Then, to her horror, he slashed at Emily from behind.

246

CHAPTER 30

T HE BATTLE RAGED FOR WHAT felt to Ana like an eternity but couldn't have been more than thirty gut-wrenching seconds. With the raging Lars catching Emily unaware and from behind, she had little choice but to focus on fighting him while he attacked her with a ferocity Ana had never seen. With their lady's unwavering attention on him, her soldiers fought hard but were outnumbered and quickly overwhelmed by Colin's onslaught.

For his part, the tall lord hung back, watching with satisfaction, one hand on Lindsey's shoulder and the other keeping an iron hold on her chains. Her face alternated between shades of horrified disbelief and barely contained rage.

At last, Emily got the upper hand on Lars, and she twisted his right arm, spinning him around. He ended up standing with his back to her, and she wrenched his arm into an angle not found in nature. The sickening cracks Ana heard even from inside the train car confirmed the bone had broken. Emily threw him outside what re-mained of her circle, and he landed in a heap beside the now-dead female plaguer, whose head faced the wrong direction. The one guard who had been attacked by the Feral was red in the face with a mask of her own blood, and she writhed on the ground, moaning.

"Enough, Emily!" Colin called. "Submit unless you wish to see your Family killed."

More than half her soldiers were bloodied from their wounds, and all were being held by one or two of Colin's soldiers, with razor-sharp claws poised at their necks. Emily snarled back and took a step forward.

Colin tsked. "I daresay I hoped you understood me better. Cadence, demonstrate."

Without hesitation, a brunette woman in a flannel shirt twisted the head of the prisoner she'd been holding then raked her claw across his throat. She quickly lapped at the wound as she lowered the unmoving body to the ground.

"I will kill each of them if you force me to, madam. And all at once if you take even a single step toward me. Submit."

"You haven't the right, Colin, and the Conclave will be fixing to take your head for this atrocity."

"I wouldn't bet on them so fully if I were you, Lady Emily." A man's deep voice came from the entry gate.

Ana gasped as Alexander strode into the train yard alone.

"You might find you don't have the friends among them you once thought you had. Or the pull."

That voice still made Ana shiver.

"My lord," Lars groaned, coming back to himself to find his shackles had been reattached. "What happened? What's going on?"

"Alexander." Emily tried to hide the mixture of surprise and dismay in her tone. "How convenient."

"As convenient as your visit last fall," he replied. "A shame you chose not to stay a little while longer then. I could have used an ally."

"You should have tried to contact me. Sent Lars to meet with me. We might have worked something out. We could have been tremendous allies." She paused. "You seem to have found a less advantageous match in the time between." The comment dripped with disgust.

He shrugged. "Misery makes for strange bedmates, lady. And we'll see who has the advantage in the end. As it happened, I eventually came to realize that Colin and I had more ideas in common than I'd first imagined. So here we are."

"Quite so, Alexander," Colin chimed in, giving Lindsey's chain a jerk for effect. "Now then, where were we? Indeed, discussing your submission, lady. I will be taking your lands—"

Alexander cut him off. "Not so fast. Your scheme may have gone off better than I'd imagined, but you still have a problem."

"Is that so? I fail to see what it might be."

Nodding toward Emily, the gruff-looking Master simply said, "Whether you want to admit it or not, she's right."

"I daresay—"

Alexander raised a hand. "The Conclave won't let you get away with simply declaring yourself lord of the South, whether she agrees to submit or not. Things like this are expected to be handled in a certain way since the pact.

This is not that way, and you know it. They might believe you'll scheme to overthrow one of them next, especially if you've already taken down the oldest of us. If you proceed with trying to take over by force, you're damn sure to make enemies. More than you can manage on your own."

Hearing Alexander take her side, Emily crossed her arms and offered a smug grin.

"But I'm not on my own, my lord partner," Colin said.

"I may have helped you in this case, but my aims go only as far as getting you off my land, Colin." He took out a crumpled pack of cigarettes and lit one, blowing smoke above his head. "I won't fight the Conclave for you."

"You're putting me in a difficult position, Alexander."

Another cloud of smoke filled the air. "Not at all. In fact, I have a suggestion."

"Please, do go on."

"You want her lands and people? Follow the pact's rules."

Emily laughed. "Why, shoot, yes, Lord Colin, by all means, challenge me to single combat if it means so much to you to be named Master of the South."

Ana narrowed her eyes. Everyone knew Emily would have the upper hand in direct combat. She was older than anyone knew and had killed more humans and vampires in combat than anyone could fathom. Colin—a relatively younger lord—couldn't hope to compete.

Ana's mouth dropped open, then, when Colin replied without hesitating, "You will accept my challenge?"

What could he possibly be thinking?

Then she remembered the crates of drugs, and apprehension washed through her. They had to be related. She wasn't sure if the drugs were for training Feral or for something about the fight, but she suspected both.

"Oh, son," Emily returned coolly, "as surely as the moon will fall in the morning, I accept. If this was your game, you should have just come out and asked without all this nonsense. Let's finish this, just you and me." She moved a few steps forward and took up a fighter's stance, her right foot ahead of her left and her body slightly turned. She raised her arms to bring her hands closer to her face, brandishing talon-like claws. She gave him a wide, wolfish smile, showing gleaming canine fangs.

Colin shoved Lindsey in the back hard, forcing her face down into the dirt. Grinning, he handed the chains to one of his Family and moved toward Alexander, who had advanced to meet him. The lord of the West removed his blazer and handed it over, followed by the three-button vest he always seemed to wear. He then unbuttoned his shirt sleeves and rolled the cuffs to his elbows. The accomplice lord handed something back to him, but with the distance, Ana couldn't make it out.

"If you're quite through undressing, son, I have a train to catch," Emily taunted.

If it got to him, Colin gave no sign. Instead, he raised his head to the sky and closed his eyes. Odd to see an almost-reverent display from him, like a prayer. But that couldn't be. He was surely not religious. Or was the look more one of relief and satisfaction? Ana couldn't quite tell. Whatever it was, she didn't like it. Her frown deepened.

After handing back whatever Alexander had given him, Colin shook his head twice, as if trying to clear his vision. He turned to face Emily, the whites of his eyes becoming red with trails of swelling veins. He grunted hard then again more loudly.

Ana bowed her head and brought her hands to her temples. He was there with her again but stronger, much stronger, almost wild. He sent nothing to her, no words, no orders, but she was filled with the overwhelming urge to charge out of the car, to tear into the throng of vampires indiscriminately, slashing until either she or they were all dead.

"Something… is wrong," she whispered. She closed her fists and forced herself to take several deep breaths, concentrating as she pushed the air from her lungs. She imagined the strange animal sensation leaving her and, after a few moments, felt like herself again.

"Emily!" Ana's Maker bellowed. "Bitch! I will tear you to pieces and drain you to the last drop."

His opponent smirked, and her eyes twinkled. "I'm right pleased to see you finally drop that stuffy facade, Colin. We should have done this months ago." With that, she launched forward, moving so fast Ana had to squint to follow the action. In a blink, she was face-to-face with Colin, raining a barrage of claws toward him.

Surprised for a moment with the speed and brutality of her strike, he was forced to step back to avoid getting raked across the eyes with her first swing, which sailed past his nose. He got a hand up in time to block her second swing and the third and fourth as well. She pressed her advantage with more jabs and crosses and the occasional knee blow, keeping him off balance. He defended himself well, though, meeting each of her assaults before it reached him to do any significant damage.

With each block and parry, the twinkle in Emily's eyes faded. The mirth was soon replaced by the strain of effort, followed by irritation, then the barest hint of concern. She moved like a hummingbird, darting all around him, but still, each attack was turned away. Finally, she floated backward and shifted her stance, inviting him to go on the offensive.

He gave her a mocking laugh that filled the train yard with menace. "Tired already, old girl?" He laughed again, the sound trailing into a low growl.

"Plenty left for you, son. How 'bout you show me what you've got?"

The growl grew fiercer, louder, and Ana gulped at seeing the change in him. The lord's eyes went from deep bloodshot to coal black, and his mouth opened wide, showing his ferocious fangs. He charged, swinging wide with a battle cry that would have made a bear cringe.

Emily danced to the side, easily missing his first barrage, and ducked under the cross that followed. He anticipated her movement, and as she came back up to his eye level, he drove his forehead down into the bridge of her nose. It exploded with a sickening crunch, and a cloud of bloody mist filled the small space between their two faces.

Dazed, Emily stumbled backward, and with another animal shout, Colin came at her again. His face a mask of her gore, he swung with a series of devastating fists, and she couldn't avoid them. The first caught her in the left jaw and the second in the right temple. Her eyes rolled up into her head, and she crumpled to the dusty ground in a heap.

A round of cheers went up from Colin's soldiers.

Her gut twisting around a tempest of fear and horror, Ana just made out a scream that sounded like Lindsey but was quickly cut short. She tried to turn her head, to locate Lindsey in the crowd, but she couldn't take her eyes off the fight.

Except it wasn't a fight any longer. Colin stormed forward and stood over Emily, who still bled on the dirt. He threw two fists in the air and called out with another ferocious battle cry tinged with a hint of victory and loud enough to ring in Ana's mind. Then, bending down, he pulled Emily's rag doll body up by the neck, holding her with one hand. Her head lolled in defeat. With an angry grunted, he shook her side to side and cursed, "Wake up, bitch. Wake. Up!"

At last, her eyes—red as well but from the damage his headbutt had visited on her face—fluttered open, and she clawed at the hand holding her. She gasped and croaked something, but Ana couldn't make out what she'd said. She doubted anyone could.

"Submit," the coal-eyed animal demanded.

Even with Lady Emily's face mutilated by the savage force of his blows, Ana could read the disdain on it. The lady narrowed her eyes, gave the best sneer she could muster, and spat dark, vampiric blood in his face.

Colin cried out in rage. "I told you, bitch. Every. Drop." His hand closed around her neck, crushing her throat and windpipe and snapping her spine at the base of her skull. Her head sagged forward.

He threw her lifeless body to the ground.

Still face down in the dusty train yard, Lindsey screamed with the kind of blood-chilling terror Ana had only imagined in nightmares. Something in Ana's head cried for her to do something, to act however she could, but she was paralyzed, as much from her own horror as her lord's command.

"Ana, Daughter, come out. Come to me," he called as his eyes phased back to normal and his fangs receded. "Kallus, bring her chains to me."

She let out a breath, and her body went slack. It was hers again, but only so she could obey.

CHAPTER 31

ANA CLIMBED THE NARROW, CREAKING staircase from the brewery's main room to the floors above one more time, fighting to control the storm of dread swirling in her gut. The last time she'd gone up those stairs, it was for the same reason, to meet Colin. He'd known then that she had defied him by helping Tom escape, and it very nearly cost her everything. If not for Tom and Lindsey, she would have been turned to ash six months ago. As she awkwardly made her way to the third floor, this time in chains, it was difficult not to wonder if they had just delayed her fate. She figured she was about to find herself strapped to a support beam again, waiting for daylight. Morning had already come, though, while she sat brooding in a cell below the building. If Colin wanted her death to be as dramatic as possible, he would have to wait another day.

Kallus led her to the office where she'd first met Alexander. Alexander himself trailed a few feet behind them, still coming up the hallway. It spoke volumes that Colin occupied that office instead of Alexander.

"What's with everyone calling you 'Kallus,' Gordon?"

Alexander said. "I thought your old name was much more fitting."

"Lord Colin made me his gamekeeper," the stocky vampire shot back in a shrill whine. "I became a better man with new purpose. So, I got a new name, a stronger name."

He turned to knock on the door, but a voice inside boomed, "Come," before his knuckles touched the wood.

She was led through the doorway, still making the best of the awkward shuffle the leg irons demanded. It was far from the way she'd hoped or expected to reunite with her estranged Maker, but the best she could do was try to salvage as much dignity as she could. The weight of her failure hung on her, but she held her head high regardless. No reason to give him any more satisfaction.

He looked up from a note he was reading, and his pale sky-blue eyes met hers. They seemed to have aged some since the last time she was in the same room with him, but they were still clear and confident. Their apparent youth belied his white hair and finely wrinkled face. He held her gaze for a few moments, and she struggled not to look away. He could force her, she imagined, but instead, he shifted his attention to Kallus.

"Take those off her and leave us."

"My lord?"

"Son, I dispatched one of the three oldest and strongest of our kind last night without taking even a scratch of damage. I have nothing to fear from my own daughter."

"Sorry, Lord."

Kallus moved more quickly than Ana would have expected of someone his size and bulk as he set to removing her bindings. Once freed, she rubbed her wrists, glad to be rid of the heavy iron.

As Kallus turned to go, Colin added, "And, Son?"

"Lord?"

"I regret that the next time you question a command, I will be forced to turn you inside out. I Made you what you are. I can Make another just like you."

The bulky vampire stiffened and swallowed hard. "Yes, my lord. Forgive me."

"Go."

Alexander chuckled after the departure. "That boy doesn't have the sense God gave the common bull."

"In my experience," Colin returned, "cattle are exquisitely dumb animals. But he knows his job and manages it well enough."

"If you say so. The way he controls all those plaguers gives me the creeps. I'm going back to my storehouse while you spend some time with your daughter here. Is the timetable for everything else still on track?"

"The plan proceeds as devised, yes. A few days, and I'll be ready for the next step."

"We'll be ready, then. Send a messenger if you need me. And don't forget about that other nugget of information." With that, Alexander turned and left.

Colin rolled his eyes after the door closed. "The poor fool truly believes us partners."

"Below, I overheard Lars trying to warn Alexander that you'd double-cross him," Ana offered. "Difficult to tell from his reaction if he really understands what will happen."

"Do you know, Daughter?"

"No, Colin." She forced herself to say his name rather than giving him the deference of using lord. "But I suspect I know you well enough to understand you're taking advantage of him while he has value and you'll leave him behind the moment he ceases to be useful."

He motioned to a leather wingback chair behind her. "You may sit."

"I would prefer to stand."

"Always headstrong."

"Would you have me be meek in the face of my enemies?"

"Daughter, we do not have to be enemies. There's room for us to move forward together."

"Can we, my l… Colin? After what you did to me, with all that I blame you for, and what I've done in defiance?"

He steepled his slender fingers. "You're right about one thing…"

Her stomach clenched. She was destined for the daylight.

"I will use him until he is no longer useful. Indeed, I will use whatever resources I have to attain better ones, and in that regard, you are—can still be—quite useful. I would hate to throw that value away. But as I noted, always headstrong."

"Where does that leave us, then?"

"Come," he called toward the door.

It creaked open, and Drake scuttled inside wearing his usual lab coat and carrying a surgical tray covered by a blue cloth.

"Sister." He inclined his head toward Ana after setting the tray down on the desk in front of Colin.

"I wish I could say I was glad to see you, Drake. You've been busy."

"I hear the same of you, but perhaps not as much on the tasks our lord gave you."

Ignoring the jab, she inspected the tray. Not much to discern from a couple of odd shapes beneath a sheet. To Colin she said, "What is this, then? I assume this has something to do with what you were saying about us?"

"You and I both know that I can compel you to do what I want. But I suspect that will only redouble your commitment to seeing me to my end. So I'm going to give you a choice." He lifted the cloth from the tray to reveal what appeared to be an aging dagger set beside a surgical scalpel.

"What's this about?"

"Two knives. Two quite different purposes. Pick one."

She scratched at the skin beside her thumbnail and frowned.

"If you take the dagger," he continued, "I expect you to come at me with it. You know that will end in your final death, but if so, it will be your choice. Or you can choose the scalpel, a tool of your trade, and go back to work. Drake needs more reliable hands to finish the work he has begun for me. If you assist him and prove once again to be somewhat dependable, perhaps I will allow you to return, at some point, to the other work I set before you. Albeit, of course, with some added restrictions. This is your moment, Daughter. Choose."

Ana glared at the tray. She'd never known Colin to be so melodramatic, but it was fair to think perhaps she'd pushed him to it. After all, she'd never heard an account of Descended intentionally working against their Maker. But he had created her for a reason, and not many others could fulfill her role.

She scratched harder at her thumb, knowing it gave away her anxiety. But if she weren't working that old habit, she would likely be reaching for the dagger on instinct. Even with the knowledge that she could never succeed in attacking him, her Maker, the hatred she carried for him burned with such ferocity that she still desperately yearned to try.

And would it be so bad to be done with it all? Let him be someone else's problem. Ana was overwhelmed and exhausted. Emily's death meant that the one person most likely to keep Colin in some kind of check was gone. What could Ana hope to accomplish with the primary obstacle to his ambition removed? Especially with him co-ordinating with Alexander, the odds of stopping whatever power trip Colin was engaged in were long, at best.

With Lars and Lindsey also in chains below, surely Colin would be moving to assert control over Emily's land very soon. And with those resources combined with what he already controlled from the West, he would be in a position to challenge almost any one of the other lords across the country. Would they even see it coming?

At last, she slumped into the chair, prompting him to raise his eyebrows in surprise. "Have you decided?"

Lars. Lindsey. For that matter, Tom. What would

happen if Ana gave in, took the dagger, and forced Colin to end her? The first two would not likely survive the next few days, if they made it to nightfall. And Tom, wherever he'd skated off to, would likely stir up an even bigger mess very soon. Especially if he knew she'd been taken back to Colin. The fool man was twice as headstrong as Lindsey and half as reasonable.

What good would taking that weapon and dying in front of Colin do anyone? What harm, instead, could it bring? More importantly, what good might she do if she locked her burning rage away and picked up the scalpel instead? The sharpest edges were honed by fire. On top of that, surviving her decision meant having a chance to get to the bottom of what Drake and Colin were doing with the drugs.

Standing up again, she met Colin's pale-blue eyes. "I'll do it. What do you need from me?"

"Understand me, Daughter, I gave you this opportunity to choose because you mean something to me, and I want you to feel valued. You belong among us, and a time will come that you will be glad to be my Family. But if you do anything to challenge me again, I won't just kill you. I will find a way to make you suffer every single day for the rest of your miserable second life. But I very much would prefer not to be forced to do that, so be true to your Family and true to your word. Do we understand each other?"

"Yes, Lord, of course."

"*Very good, Daughter.*" His words boomed in her mind, taking her by surprise.

Drake moved to leave the room.

"Should I go with him, Lord?" Ana asked.

"Not yet, Daughter. First, you will tell me everything you know about this new woman with your boy Tom."

CHAPTER 32

Tom opened the bathroom door, letting the trapped steam escape into his room. He fastened his jeans with a new leather belt and shook himself into one of the two new T-shirts he'd picked out at Walmart. He froze midstep, though, seeing the door between their rooms partially open. His bag had been shoved aside, but the shotgun was right where he'd left it.

Peeking around the adjoining door, he found Shan's room empty. He frowned. "Hello? Shan? Lady, where are you, girl?"

He got no response.

Turning his attention back to his own room, he found a folded note on one of the beds. He picked it up and opened it. Shan had written, *Come to the lobby,* on the hotel stationary, in far neater cursive than he could have hoped to produce.

He ran his fingers through his still-damp hair, surprised by how long it was getting. Lindsey had been giving him haircuts at the Chalet to keep it neat, and he'd been needing one before he'd left Georgia. Tom needed to either learn to cut it himself or get used to it being longer.

Tom reached for the shotgun, but then stopped and

picked up the revolver instead. He slid his key card into his back pants pocket and opened the swing arm that served as a safety latch on his room door. He pulled open the door and stepped out into the hallway. The door came to rest on the latch arm, preventing it from closing all the way and locking. It was just the two of them and a dog, no reason to worry about locking the rooms yet.

Tom made his way down the two floors of steps with care, trying not to stomp and make unnecessary noise. Moving quietly had become a core part of his behavior after everything he'd been through. He could only imagine what Heather, his wife, would have said. Saying he had about as much grace as an angry bull was one of her favorite ways to tease him.

He noticed the stairwell exit on the first floor didn't have a latch. It sat flush against the doorframe and was adorned with a simple pull handle. He opened it a few inches and had to chuckle when he found Lady lying beside it. "I guess I can't surprise you, can I?"

The dog raised her eyebrows then stood. She padded beside him as he started down the west corridor to the lobby. The sun was sinking outside the hotel, leaving little light in the windowless hallway. At the end, where it emptied into the front lobby and common area, flickering orange light made shadows dance on the floor and walls.

The pair reached the opening to the lobby and turned the corner to find that Shan had laid out a surprise for them. On one of the tables in the dining area, a pair of short, squat jar candles sputtered with a trio of burning wicks each casting a warm glow over an arrangement of food Tom would never have expected. A large cutting board sat in the middle of the table, bearing canned tuna that had been emptied from its container and spread, well, as thoughtfully as anyone could spread canned tuna; slices of Spam; whole black olives; long, halved pickles; as well as some thinly sliced chips; and even a freshly sliced summer sausage. A couple of chocolate bars had been unwrapped as well, along with a few handfuls of M&M's. All of it was arrayed in neat groups, interspersed with three different varieties of crackers. A pair of ice buckets stood beside the board, one holding a green-glassed bottle of wine and the other bearing several cans of Budweiser.

Tom stood in the lobby, his mouth gaping.

"I really wanted some cheese, but I couldn't find any that wasn't fuzzy or green. And I know they say bleu cheese has mold in it already, so it probably would be okay, but I just couldn't do it."

"Shan…" he stammered.

"Now don't get it all twisted. This ain't like a romantic dinner or anything. I just wanted to have a meal like a civilized person, on an actual table for once, and I knew better than to turn the lights on. I thought maybe this'd be okay."

He blinked at the candles and fixed his eyes on the front windows, thinking of the plaguer he'd accidentally drawn to himself in Iowa last year with a little light and too much jukebox. "Actually, this is still probably too much."

Her face dropped. "Oh. Okay, sorry." She leaned forward to blow out the nearest candle.

"Wait, no." Tom crossed the room to the windows and drew the heavy taupe-colored curtains hanging beside each, one by one. "There. That's probably safe for long enough to have dinner. Ana would kick my ass, but I think we should be fine."

"Well, your vampire girl isn't here anymore, so I don't care what she'd think. And with some luck, we'll never see her again. Now let's eat. I'm starving."

Tom pulled a can of Budweiser from its bucket and cracked it, reveling as he took a measured drink. Shan poured herself a paper cupful of the wine and layered a cracker with a pickle slice and some tuna. Following her example, he forced himself to pick at pieces of the delicious spread a bite at a time, but he really wanted to shove half the olives and as much sausage as he could squeeze at once into his mouth.

"My god, this is good," he mumbled around a cracker of pickles and Spam. He never would have imagined Spam could be so wonderful. "It hadn't occurred to me to try the canned meat."

She laughed. "Then what have you been eating, you dolt?"

He finished his beer and opened another. "When I was by myself? Mostly stale snack chips, jerky, and breakfast bars. You, know the really hard ones."

"Yeah, those are pretty good. Not as good as Club crackers and cured meat." Her eyes, the color of pale topaz, twinkled as she crunched another bite. "And, man, how the hell have you survived this long on stale Doritos? You don't look like you've been undereating."

Instinctively, he tightened his stomach muscles, hoping to disguise the small beer belly he'd earned from all those nights drinking beer on the porch with Lady and, when she wasn't busy with Emily's work, Lindsey. Shan looked down at the table and pretended to rearrange the olives. Was she trying to hide a smirk? God, he was an idiot.

Another swallow of beer wouldn't make him feel any better about himself, so he set the can down and broke off a piece of dark chocolate. "You have to remember, I spent most of the last eight or nine months living with the others. Emily kept me pretty well-fed, considering."

"No shit, she did. Farmers always fatten up the live-stock." Shan chortled at her own jab and threw a pickle at him, hitting him in the chest.

It fell to the floor, where Lady snapped it up before Tom could move.

"Oh, sorry, girl." He dropped a piece of sausage, a slice of Spam, and a couple of crackers for her. "And it wasn't like that. She owed me one and was trying to take care of me." He smirked. "Besides, I'm not sure half-drunk fat guys are what a vampire considers prime grade, you know?"

"From what I've seen, T, they don't much seem to care, but whatever."

Tom frowned. What had this woman seen? He'd never really considered the horror of what it must have been like to survive the weeks and months after Charon wiped almost everyone else off the planet. And she'd said her mentor—Janine, maybe?—had been taken from her by one of them, hadn't she? Just standing next to Ana must have been incredibly painful.

"Yeah, you're mostly right," Tom agreed. "Anyway, the food where I stayed was pretty good. I don't know why, but Emily always had them growing crops and stuff. And even keeping some livestock. Real animals, I mean. We had bacon once. I helped them with the garden sometimes during the day, since I could."

"You helped them grow stuff?"

"Yeah, I didn't have much else to do anyway."

"Hot damn. We've gotta figure out how to make a garden somewhere. We can't live on tuna and Spam forever."

"You planning to hang around with me for a while, miss?"

"I'm planning to hang around with her." She nodded at Lady, who had left him to lie beside Shan's chair. "If I have to keep you around for her, I guess that's okay. At least until you piss me off."

"I'll be on my best behavior."

"Good. Remember, I'm a witch, T. I can put a curse on you so it burns like a thousand fire ant bites every time you have to pee."

Tom's face went slack. He swallowed his bite of sausage and took another long drink of beer.

She was kidding, right?

Right?

They made small talk while they continued picking at small bites and fed Lady. They spoke about their lives before the plague and where and how they grew up, filling in the conversation with anecdotes about what they stole from convenience stores as kids, what they hated about high school, and the stupid, risky things they'd done in their early twenties.

When they finished eating, as they talked about what it was like to become an actual adult with a job and responsibilities, Tom wrapped the remaining food into plastic zipper bags. Shan poured herself a second cup of wine and blew out one of the apple-scented candles. She carried the other to the small lounge just past the front desk and set it on an end table before curling into a heavily padded chair, pulling her legs up beneath her.

After sealing the last bag of food, he grabbed two more beers and settled onto a small couch next to her chair. Lady jumped up beside him and tucked herself into a snug, furry ball with a sigh of contentment.

"I almost got us a Monopoly board at Walmart," she said after a sip of wine, "but figured we'll piss each other off by nature soon enough. No reason to help that along."

He popped open one of the beers. "God, I haven't played a board game since before I got married."

"What's it like being married?" She held his eyes with the question, curious and waiting.

"Hard." He looked down at the can in his hand. "But worth it."

Silence lingered in the space between them for a minute or so until, at last, she asked, "Where you wanna go?"

He met her eyes again. Her look of fragile hope was something he'd never guessed he would see on someone's face again. "Someplace with good soil, I guess. And sunlight. Plenty of sunlight. And open space so we can see the fuckers coming."

Shan nodded. "I like it. Where's the good farming? Mother, I can't believe I just said that."

"They moved to California to farm in *The Grapes of Wrath*. Maybe we should do that too?"

The reference earned him a confused look. "The grapes of what now?"

"It's an old book."

"Oh. Well, whatever." She wrinkled her nose. "Anyways, California is probably off the list for growing stuff. They nuked LA, remember?"

"Oh, shit. I actually did forget that."

"I don't want corn that glows in the dark."

Tom chuckled. "I can't argue with that."

They sat together in the flickering light of the candle for an hour or so after, talking about where they could go and what they would need to do when they got there.

After Shan finished her cup of wine and hid her third yawn behind the back of her hand, she stood. "I'm heading up. Good night."

The second Budweiser beside him on the table was still half-full. "I'll finish this down here. It's kind of nice to sit in an actual lounge for once."

"It is, but it ain't half as nice as that bed is going to feel. Don't get shit-faced. I'll see you in the morning." She turned and headed for the west hallway.

Lady lifted her head and watched her go then turned her eyes to Tom.

"Go on, you traitor. I'll be fine. Make sure she makes it upstairs okay." With that, Lady hopped down and padded after the woman.

Tom lifted his beer and took another drink. Just a few more mouthfuls and he would go up to his room. God knew he was plenty worn out. The stress of the previous three days lingered in his bones. He crossed his arms and put his feet up on the tan coffee table in front of him. The near-permanent tension he carried drained away.

Just a few more sips, and he would go up, but no need to rush it. He was about as comfortable as he'd felt in the whole past year.

He yawned, then his chin fell to his chest. He blinked, but a little longer than a blink usually lasted. He shook his head to clear it. He wasn't ready to fall asleep yet. He blinked once more, but his eyes betrayed him, and his eyelids stayed closed.

They flew open again what felt like only seconds later. Icy panic shot through him as a cold iron hand covered his mouth. A face bearing a neatly trimmed beard and long fangs loomed just inches from his own, and arms that felt like steel wrapped around his chest from behind.

"Easy now," the bearded man hissed. "Let's not make this difficult."

"Is it him, sir?" someone whispered from behind his head.

"Yes. This is the one they're looking for."

CHAPTER 33

SOMETHING HARD POKED SHAN'S SHOULDER, ruining her dream of lounging beneath the warm sun in a low-slung beach chair beside an unspecified ocean. Her eyes shot open, and she tensed, ready to bolt from the bed. Lady whined above her and tapped her shoulder harder with a second paw.

"Ow, what the hell?"

The German shepherd hopped down from the bed and moved over to the doors between their two rooms. She sat between them and whined again. Somehow, Shan could tell the dog was unsettled.

She got up and met Lady, patting her side. "What's the prob…?"

The doors stood open, the way she'd left them after dropping the note on Tom's bed before dinner. He'd never come up to his room.

The digital clock beside her bed read 3:47. She'd slept for almost five hours already.

He must have just fallen asleep in the lobby. Mother knew she'd been bone-tired by the time she'd reached her room. So tired that she had almost forgotten to put on her nightly warding spray. So tired it hadn't even occurred to her to close the door to his room from her side.

Lady stood and entered his room, turning to sit and stare at the shotgun next to the doorframe. She whined once more but deeper, not quite a growl but creeping close to one. Her hackles were raised too. Shan didn't like it.

"You want me to take it?"

The shepherd looked back at her. Shan couldn't explain it, but her brown-and-black-furred face held a look of tense expectation.

Shan picked up the weapon. As soon as she gripped it and settled her index finger along the outside of the trigger well like Mack—one of her more regrettable ex-boyfriends—had taught her, Lady stood again and moved to the door leading into the hallway. Tom had left it unsecured, resting against the swing arm of the security latch.

She frowned even deeper. She should have checked that she was secure behind locked doors before she fell asleep. They hadn't cleared the whole building. A blood zombie could have been lurking anywhere in the hotel.

Thinking of those things—Tom had called them Feral—made her stop before going further. Anything might be out there. She wanted more ward spray.

Returning to her room, she set the gun down carefully and grabbed the perfume sprayer sitting on the TV stand next to her bag of supplies. She squeezed the button several times, creating a sizeable cloud that she immediately stepped into. The cold spray settled against the skin of her arms and neck, always sticky at first. It dried quickly, thank Mother, but left her thinking she smelled like stale air and the tang of rust. If a blood zombie was out there, though, the warding spray should keep it from detecting her unless she moved or made noise.

Armored as best she could be for whatever she might run into, she took the shotgun again and met Lady at the door to Tom's room. With the barrel of the gun, she pulled the door open a couple of inches, just enough to put an eye on the hallway. Seeing nothing right outside, she widened the gap enough to stick her head out.

Lady, seeming confident nothing was there, slid into the hallway and turned toward the exit stairs. Shan looked in both directions to satisfy herself then, barefoot, followed the dog. Janny always said there was no better shoe for sneaking than the one nature offered.

When Shan reached the exit, she pressed the latch and said a small blessing before pulling the fire door toward herself. Again, she started with just an inch or so to give them both a chance to make damn certain nothing waited below. The stairwell looked empty to her, and the dog didn't hesitate before padding down the steps. Shan followed, trying to ignore the sound of her heart thrumming too fast in her ears.

They reached the first floor, and Shan pulled the handle on the door to the west hallway, relieved it didn't have a latch. She and Lady stepped into the carpeted hallway beyond, and Shan pressed her palm against the door behind her as it inched shut. Ahead of her, the light from the one candle she'd left in the lobby still danced among the shadows.

Lady froze, head slung low in front of her, teeth bared.

Voices from down the hallway made Shan's stomach leap into her throat.

"Why can't we just drain him a little, sir?"

"Even suggesting that is insubordination, soldier. The Brigadier said they were to be brought to him unharmed. He made a deal with our new ally, not that it's any of our concern."

"Of course, sir. I beg your forgiveness."

"I'll expect you to report for additional work detail when we return. And you'll sacrifice half a blood ration."

"Yes, sir."

"Your orders, then, sir?"

"The intel said there should be two of them, and a flea-ridden mutt. We need to find the other one. A woman."

Someone with them muttered or growled, then Shan caught the unmistakable sound of a firm hand slapping a cheek.

"Stay quiet, animal."

Shan scowled hard. Vampires had Tom—the same kind that had killed Janny. The kind that had drained her mentor while she watched, unseen and undetected, from the gap in a closet door. Her face burned as the familiar rage spread through her. She wouldn't let it happen again. She wouldn't let it happen to *him*.

Carefully placing one foot in front of the other, Shan moved toward the lobby. Lady kept pace with her until they reached where the hallway wall ended. Shan pressed her back against the wall and hefted the shotgun. She just needed a plan. How could she put shells into both vampire heads at one time?

"He said I could share the dog with you if we caught

it. The ally has no use for it, so the Brigadier said it could be our reward. But only if we catch them all. Do you get me, soldier?"

"Of course, sir."

Could she separate them somehow? She had to think of something.

Lady seized the decision. Without warning, the shepherd sprang forward into the lobby, racing away from her.

Shan dared peek an eye around the corner. Tom still occupied the couch, but his hands were bound at the wrists by a zip tie, and his legs had been roped together. Duct tape covered his mouth. He met her eye but gave no sign of recognition. A pair of vampires in ragged army uniforms surrounded him, facing each other. One loomed over him from the front, and the other had a hand on his shoulder from behind the couch.

"Do you smell—" the one with his back to her began.

At the same time, the other shouted, "The mutt!" The second vampire's voice matched the one called "soldier." He turned left and raced to the right side of the lobby.

Lady charged right at him, barking wildly. He put his hands out in surprise, and she raced past him and through the front door.

"I'll get her!" The soldier shot after her into the night.

"No, you idiot!"

Shan's belly tightened with fear, but she forced it from her mind and raced out from behind the wall, shotgun raised to eye level. She crossed the lobby in three quick strides and shoved the barrel against the other vampire's head just as he began to turn.

She pulled the trigger. A tremendous *crack* split the

air, and his face erupted into a sickening red mist. The vampire crumpled to the floor in a heap of bloody flesh.

Before it had even settled, Shan raced to the front door, taking up a position a few steps to its right. As she expected, the automatic doors swished open, and the soldier stepped inside.

"Did I hear a—"

With a near-deafening boom, his head exploded just as the other one's had.

Wiping blood splatter from her face, she returned to Tom. She cleaned blood from his eyes then pulled the tape off his mouth. "Are you okay?"

"I'm fine. Are you?"

"So much for being clean." She shrugged. Shan retrieved a knife they'd used to slice the sausage at dinner and cut the zip tie binding Tom's hands. She nodded at the heap of vampires at her feet. "Do you think they'll be able to recover from that?"

"Doubtful." Tom pulled at the knot binding his legs. "If you screw up their brains or nervous systems, that usually does the trick." He looked back over his shoulder at the remains of the soldier by the door. "And these two don't look to have moderately functioning brains anymore."

Shan allowed herself a brief, satisfied smirk.

Tom stood and wiped his face. The automatic doors behind them whooshed open again, and panic leapt up Shan's throat. He turned with a grunt as she reached for the shotgun.

Lady trotted inside. She stopped to sniff at the remains by the door, tail wagging.

They both exhaled, then Tom started for the west hall-way. "If either of their Makers are still alive, they'll know what happened. We have to assume more will be coming. We need to get out of here."

CHAPTER 34

NOT FIVE MINUTES AFTER THEY'D raced up the stairs to their rooms, all three were back in the Highlander with most of their belongings. Shan wasn't sure she'd managed to grab everything she'd unpacked from her new travel bag during their short stay, but they could replace whatever she'd forgotten. She had her trusted supply bag, and that was much more important.

"I still can't believe that stuff you put on really keeps them from detecting you." Tom pushed the SUV's shifter into Drive and turned the wheel toward the main road as he pulled away from the hotel. "What did you call it?"

"Warding mist," Shan replied. "And it's saved my life more than a few times. It works as long as you aren't too near them, but they can hear you breathe up close. That's why he turned just before I shot him. He knew, but too late. If I'd had more time to be sneakier, he'd never have known why the front of his face turned to red jelly."

"How does it work?" Tom wiped at the spots of red spatter on his face with a wet wipe while directing the car back onto the expressway.

"I don't know, really. Janine taught me to make it.

She said it covers up whatever funk and hormones people make, and it somehow keeps vampires from sensing your heartbeat so easy too. I don't know if she knew how it worked either. But it works."

He gave her a sidelong look, and his eyes were harder than she liked. "Can I get a gallon?"

"Easy, greedy. It takes two days to make just a soda bottle's worth."

He grunted and focused on the road ahead of them.

Shan watched out the window as the city of Topeka streamed by on her right. She frowned. That wasn't right. "Why are you going east?"

"Listen, we need to talk."

"Don't start that shit with me, T."

"I'm sorry, and I would never try to make you do anything, but I think I have to go back. Before you came downstairs and kicked those two bloodsuckers' asses, they said they'd been told to watch out for us. Colin somehow killed Emily earlier tonight, and whoever this Brigadier guy is just started working with Colin in some kind of alliance."

Shan scowled. "So the fuck what?"

He faced her, and even in the blue glow of the dashboard lights, the concern was obvious in the tight lines around his eyes. "They said Colin had taken a lot of Emily's people prisoner. That probably means Lindsey. It also means that Ana doesn't have Emily's protection anymore."

Shan shook her head. "You don't know that, and what does it matter?" It came out harsher than she meant it to, but she wouldn't stop. "You're not one of them, Tom. You and me, we're the same. You don't have to go running back to them just because it's hitting the fan for your former bloodsucking ex-girlfriends. They can work it out on their own. They don't need you!" She flung the last sentence at him in a near shout, making him flinch.

"That's not…" he stammered. "It's not like that. And what… what if they do? I have to find out. I have to do this last thing, then I'll be done." He tightened his grip on the steering wheel. "But you don't have to go. Once the sun comes up, we'll stop and find you a car. You can take the extra gas and go west. We'll name a place to meet in a few days."

Shan huffed and glared out at the horizon. As they traveled eastward, the sun would be reaching out with its first threads of light in an hour or so to start the morning climb into the sky. She didn't want to be alone again so soon, didn't want him going back and almost surely getting himself killed. How the fool had lived so long, as brash and stubborn as he could be, made her scratch her head. But maybe she could ease his worry about Lindsey and Ana. "What if there was another way?"

That earned her a raised eyebrow. "Another way to what?"

"Another way to find out if they're in trouble."

"You got a crystal ball in that bag of yours?"

She shook her head. "No, but I do have a tarot deck. Let's stop somewhere after the sun comes up, eat a breakfast bar, and do a reading for each of them."

Tom narrowed his eyes. "A tarot reading? You're going to sit there and tell me that stuff's real?"

Anger bubbled up inside her, and she was glad it was still dark. Her chest, neck, and face would be splotched with fiery red. "Listen here, you…" Shan trailed off, forcing herself to calm down. Shouting wouldn't do anything but convince him to go. "Look, T, you gotta give me the benefit of the doubt. The healing stuff worked, didn't it? And the warding spray? Yeah, this stuff is real. It's all real, and it can help you if you'll let it."

"Tarot readings?"

She could still hear his skepticism, but he hadn't said no outright.

"It works. I swear by the Mother. It's not science, though, so sometimes it's less clear than others. We'll do a reading for each of them, and if they come out fuzzy, you can go on and I'll go the other way. We can meet in Denver or somewhere in a few days."

"Okay. I owe you that much. But I want you to do a reading for me first. We'll see how that goes."

Shan frowned again. She didn't like him thinking she could do parlor tricks on command. But Janny always said sometimes people had to do things they didn't like to get the best from the world. Doing the reading for him felt like one of those things.

"Fine. As soon as it starts getting light."

They drove east, first through Topeka then through more countryside as well as a three-exit town called Lawrence, which Shan knew nothing about. They reached Kansas City after about forty-five minutes, where Tom turned off the headlights.

She gasped. "What the fuck? Are you nuts?"

"They were looking for us back there. They could be looking for us here too. We don't want them to know we're coming back."

"We might not be going back," she mumbled.

Silence hung between them for the rest of the drive. She had nothing more to add, and Tom's haggard face looked even more grim than she'd expected, cast in the pale light of the dashboard instruments. After the longest hour and a half of her life, and with the sun just barely saying hello on the eastern horizon, Tom took his foot off the gas and let the Highlander glide to a stop on the side of I-70. An exit sign a few hundred feet ahead advertised a place called Oak Grove.

Shan pointed at the sign. "Let's get off there. It's too light out to run into Feral, and maybe we'll find a park bench or something. We can have a breakfast picnic and act like we're civilized."

With a grunt, Tom followed her plan and drove the SUV down the expressway off-ramp, pulling into a mostly empty truck stop.

Oak Grove didn't look like much more than an expressway exit with a couple of gas stations facing off across a four-lane highway, but signs farther south promised access to a McDonald's, a Walgreens, and maybe even a strip mall. The Petro they'd pulled into had a couple of picnic tables outside the main truck stop building, which boasted both a Taco Bell and a Dairy Queen. Those would suit her just fine.

She opened the glove box and took out a bag of plain jerky and what would undoubtedly prove to be stale pizzeria combos.

"Breakfast of champions." Tom smirked as he opened the car door.

The pair settled down opposite each other on the

sturdier-looking of the two aging tables with Tom's revolver resting close to his right hand. They swallowed a few bites of chewy, dried meat and pretzel tubes filled with that unnatural reddish paste. They didn't really taste like pizza at all but had, for some reason, always been Shan's favorite. They were only about half as stale as she'd expected, and somehow, incredibly, they weren't covered in fuzz and didn't smell like a wet locker room. Lady had eaten a handful as well, and dogs didn't eat stuff that had spoiled, did they?

After a few glugs from a bottle of water to clear away the overwhelming taste of salt in her mouth, she wiped her hands clean and took her favorite tarot deck from her bag. She slipped it from its worn cardboard box and shuffled it with the experience of someone whose hands had made the same motions thousands of times over. "Are you ready?"

"Sure. Let's see what you've got."

She set the deck face down between them. "Cut it, thinking about yourself, where you are in the moment, and—if you have any—what questions you need help answering."

Narrowing his eyes, he split the deck into two stacks before putting the bottom portion back on what had originally been the top.

Intentionally leaving the deck on the table so he couldn't complain that she was palming cards or cheating somehow, Shan lifted four cards from the top, one at a time, and set each face up in a single row between them.

She clucked her tongue. "The five of wands, the star, the devil, and the hanged man."

"What's that supposed to mean?" He scratched his beard. "I don't like the sound of the devil or the hanged man."

"It's not quite as dramatic as it sounds." She tapped the five of wands. "This one suggests conflict, and that can either be an external conflict or an internal one. As if you're not sure about what to do. The star suggests hope and healing. The devil, now, he's the opposite. That usually means self-sabotage, hopelessness. Maybe obsession. The hanged man means uncertainty or feeling trapped. Pretty much not being where you want in life."

He scoffed. "I don't need cards to tell me any of that. I've got a choice and don't know what to do, but one of the options is probably better for me than the other."

Plucking the cards off the table, she slid them back into the deck. "That's kinda the point, though, right? To prove to you it's not bullshit? You wanted to see what you already knew, and there you go." With the same practiced motion, she reshuffled seven or eight times.

"Huh." His eyes still held a good measure of skepticism but less than she'd found before.

She set the deck down again. "Lindsey or Ana this time?"

"Ana." Tom cut the deck again and restacked it.

Shan flipped four cards into a new row, showing the devil, death, the three of swords, and the nine of swords. "Mother," she muttered. Her skin prickled.

"I know the devil now. What about the others?"

"I… Shit, T, it's pretty dark. Death doesn't always mean real death, but it can. It also points to an end. The three of swords is betrayal, loneliness, psychological torture or trauma, and the nine of swords is about fear and anxiety, feeling persecuted. And something else about the devil is that it can refer to enslavement or bondage as well as obsession."

"Christ, Shan. So it's saying she's being tortured—at least psychologically if not physically—is afraid and enslaved. That's more than just dark." He stopped for a second, thinking. "But I guess if she's been forced back to Colin, that all makes a lot of sense."

Shan hesitated. Ana's reading was much worse than expected. Maybe trying the readings hadn't been a great idea to convince him to turn around and go west. She scooped the cards together. "Let's do another one for—"

"No. That told me what I needed. I kind of get this now and how this can be useful. Let's do Lindsey."

With a gulp, Shan reshuffled and presented the deck once again. Tom nodded to himself then cut and stacked it. Regretting that she'd suggested the readings, Shan revealed the top four cards. All the warmth drained from her face. The hanged man, the hermit, the tower, and the eight of wands lay staring up at her. The cards didn't really have energy themselves, but she was half convinced she could feel them radiating negativity and danger.

"Fuck me."

"What?"

She tapped the hanged man, the hermit, and the tower in succession. "She's alone, isolated, at the end, and destruction is looming. The tower signifies actual death more strongly than the death card." Shan paused and locked eyes with him before stabbing the eight of wands.

"And this one represents haste. Whatever the other three really represent, it's coming fast."

Tom stood and whistled. "I wasn't sure before, but now I am. I have to go back."

"I know it looks bad, T, but why? Why you? You aren't one of them." She stuffed the traitorous cards back into their box.

"Because they'd both do it for me."

"But, dude, what do you even think you can do? Just avoiding blood zombies is a big enough pain in the ass by itself, and you're somehow going to free those two vampires on your own?"

He flipped the cylinder of his gun to the side and nodded, then slid it into its holster. "I'll figure something out. Lady and I did this before." He turned toward the Highlander.

"Didn't you do it with the help of that Emily's whole damn—what do you call them—Family?"

Tom stopped and turned back to her, his face hard with resolve. His eyes gave him away, though, sagging at the corners with a soft hint of pleading. "I'm going back, but I'd never expect you to go too. Let's find me a new car, and you can keep the SUV."

Her tarot deck hit the bottom of her bag with a dull thud that matched her mood. The last thing she wanted was to go back to Cincinnati. Ignoring the bad memories, she'd barely had time to come to terms with the idea that she'd been living at ground zero of some kind of weird vampire civil war and, somehow, hadn't ended up dead. Going back felt like tempting fate. But the readings had been almost as bad as any she'd ever seen. Only the ones she and Janine had done back during Charon had been worse, and not by much. Whatever Tom's friends were dealing with, they really would be in deep shit soon, if they weren't already.

"Why does the Universe do this to me?" she mumbled.

"Probably because the Universe doesn't care about us," Tom shot back.

Janny had always said that once a person found their people, they stuck together through thin or thick. She wasn't sure exactly where that came from or even if their situation was a thin or a thick, but she knew what Janny had meant. He was going back to be with his people because they needed him. Only problem was, he had become part of her people in the couple of days since they met, and she knew deep down that he needed her to stick with him.

Shan stood from the table. "All right, T. I'll come with you. You'll need my ward spray and someone to put you back together afterward. But you better not get me drained or anything worse, or I swear I'll murder you."

CHAPTER 35

TEN HOURS LATER, TOM LET the Highlander slow to a stop in front of an old bar with a large front window clouded with soap. It had likely been closed since before the pandemic hit, an eyesore to people in the neighborhood going about their lives. Those lives had all ended three or so years ago, and almost all the buildings he looked at shared the same lonely, abandoned air worn by the little neighbor bar. Death really was the great equalizer.

It had taken him a good half an hour to find the place. Lindsey had driven them to the spot the year before, when the two had snuck into what had become Colin's lair after he'd run Alexander off. They'd come to rescue Ana from being put to death, from being chained to a post in the rising sunlight. He'd come back and hoped to sneak in the same way to rescue both Lindsey and Ana. He wanted to laugh at the coincidence, but with as fast as his heart was racing, if he started cackling, he likely wouldn't stop. He had to hold himself together.

Kneeling in front of Lady, he stroked the caramel-colored fur of her chest. "You remember how to get in? We have to find them."

She woofed softly then padded across the street to the east.

"Are you sure about this?" Shan had twisted her hair up into a bun and held the barrel of the shotgun in the crook of her left arm.

She'd sprayed them with so much of her ward spray that, at first, he'd worried his clothes would be damp for the rest of the day. Luckily, they had dried in just a few minutes.

They crossed the street, following the shepherd. "Yes and no. Yes, I'm sure this is the place I was looking for, but no, I don't know if this is actually the right place. Colin was using one of these buildings as his base—or I guess you could call it a lair—last year, but he might have moved."

After a few blocks, they came to a tall brick building with a board covering its front entrance. Tom pried the wooden panel forward, and a gust of warm, stale air hit his face. Lady darted through the opening and disappeared into the dark. She returned a few seconds later and woofed softly again.

He looked over his shoulder at Shan. "I'll go first, just in case."

She nodded. He squeezed the grip of the baseball bat in his right hand then slipped past the makeshift doorway.

The room inside was just as he remembered it, large and dusty, but otherwise empty. A series of footprints in the dust led from the entrance to an opening at the far end. The doorway led to a ramp, which led to a tunnel that would give them access to the lowest floors of the building he hoped Colin still used.

Lady led them toward the ramp, pausing to sniff the ground or air here and there. They slipped down the ramp with steady, careful steps and followed as it turned to the left, descending to a damp, musty tunnel. Built with old masonry stones, it formed an arch almost—but not quite—six feet above them. Tom had to hunch to stay a few inches beneath it.

Still following the German shepherd, they made their way through the dank channel, avoiding the crumbled stones that had fallen in the centuries since it had first been built. Tom silently urged it to hold together for a few more hours at least.

Ten feet before the tunnel ended, Tom stopped and waved for Shan to do the same. "Up there is another big room," he whispered. "In it, a hole leads right into Colin's building. Lady and I will make sure no one is there or on the other side first."

She smiled and offered him the shotgun. "You want to trade?"

"Nah." He hefted the bat in his right hand and nodded at the revolver in his left. "I'm good."

With a soft cluck of the tongue, he signaled Lady, who started again, crossing the few remaining feet of the tunnel, and they passed through the opening into the vast room beyond. After two cautious steps forward, Lady stopped. She put her nose to the air then gave a very low growl.

Tom tried to raise his revolver on instinct, but both it and his right arm were pinned down by what felt like steel. He was forcibly spun to his left, away from the opening to the tunnel, and shoved against one of the room's walls.

A heaviness pressed against his chest, and an iron grip squeezed his throat.

Strangely, Lady only growled. She didn't bark or launch herself into a frenzy of snapping jaws. The growl had become deeper and grew louder. It had become a serious warning, but nothing more, yet.

Then the tight grip on his throat loosened, allowing him to breathe. "Meat? I couldn't smell you."

Tom wanted to chuckle at the confusion in Lars's voice.

The shotgun's hammer being cocked clanked to Tom's left. "Well, I smell you, asshole. Now, let him go before I turn this side of your face into a modern art piece."

Lady stopped growling and sidled up next to Shan.

"Are you supposed to kill me, Lars?" Tom croaked.

Lars stepped back, releasing the pressure on Tom's body. "No."

"Then don't shoot him, Shan. He might be able to help."

She lowered the gun's barrel. "So, this is Lars, huh? If you're not going to drain us, it's nice to meet you, I guess."

Lars took a step back and raised his hands. "I won't drain you right now, at least. Who is this delightful morsel, Meat?"

"My name is Shan, and I ain't nobody's morsel," she barked.

"Oh, you found another feisty one. You definitely got a type, don't you, son?"

It was exactly the kind of joke Tom expected from him, but the vampire's voice held no mirth.

"More like, they usually find me. What happened?"

"Explain how I couldn't sense or smell you first." Lars spoke so quietly that Tom could barely hear him.

Tom nodded at Shan. "It's all her."

Lars turned his eyes to Shan, seeming to focus on her for the first time.

She glared back. "Do you trust him to know, T?"

"If he said he won't kill us, I believe him. But, Lars, you have to swear not to tell anyone."

"I have no one to tell. Cross my heart and hope to die. Again."

Tom cocked his head. What had happened in the last few days that could knock Lars down so hard?

Regardless, Shan seemed satisfied. "It's a concoction I make, like a potion. The spray masks us from your senses."

"Bullshit," Lars replied without hesitation.

"Believe what you want," she shot back. "But you can't sense our pulses right now, can you? If you weren't looking at us, our breaths would be all that gave us away, right?"

Lars crossed his arms. "Fine. Whatever. You have invisibility-from-vampires spray. I'm impressed. Now, why are you here? I heard you'd gotten away."

"We had," Tom whispered. "And Shan didn't want to come back at all. But we tangled with a pair of your type outside of Topeka who were on the lookout for us. They almost had me, but she and Lady saved my, well, my meat." He couldn't help but smirk. "They belonged to some guy called the Brigadier—"

"Oh, Jesus," Lars interrupted, nearly growling. "The last thing anyone needs is that idiot in the middle of this."

Tom shrugged. "I didn't pick up much more except they're apparently working with Colin somehow."

"Seems like Colin is working with lots of them. And he's up to something big."

"Anyway, they told me Emily was killed." Tom paused and caught Lars looking at his boots. "I was afraid that without her protection, Lindsey and Ana would be in trouble."

"Apparently, big trouble." Shan scratched between Lady's ears.

"Okay, yeah, Emily is dead. Colin killed her, and it's my fault. I might as well have done it myself."

"Come on, you couldn't have—" Tom began before Lars put his hand up to stop him.

"Alexander is working with Colin. They hatched a scheme to get Emily to come back here. He must've told that English git about my Maker, Genevieve, and went out and found her. She was Feral, and I didn't know it."

Shan gasped. "They made a blood zombie out of your Creator? Gods, even I think that's awful. I'm... I'm sorry." It was the first sign of tenderness she'd offered a vampire.

"No," Lars replied. "She was Feral already. I just hadn't seen or been in contact with her for years. But they dragged her back here and turned her loose fifty feet from me. And I don't know if you know, or if Meat told you, but we're psychically linked to our Makers. Genevieve went berserk like plaguers do, and somehow, she must have remembered me enough to push the madness through me too. I attacked the closest person to me, Emily."

Tom shook his head. "But you said Colin killed her."

"He did. Even though I was driven by a Feral berserker, Emily fought me off easily enough. But while she was dealing with me, his and Alexander's combined forces subdued the soldiers she brought with her. Colin challenged her to single combat, and he kicked her ass."

"How? I thought she was strong as hell from being so old."

Lars shrugged. "I don't know. I haven't been able to learn anything. They kept me bound for a while, locked down here with Lindsey, until Alexander finally came and set me free. He told me Colin wanted to put me out to daylight, but he'd convinced that asshole to let me live if I left for good. They wouldn't let me talk to anyone on the way out. I'm guessing Ana knows what went down, but I can't get near her. I've been hanging out in here, waiting for someone to come out of that tunnel so we can chat about what's really happening."

"Colin didn't chain her out for morning?" The words came out faster than Tom had intended.

"No."

Tom sighed in relief.

"I was surprised too," Lars continued. "But I guess he's got some project for her, and now she's got some pencil-necked lab coat watching her every move."

"They're both still alive, then?" Shan shouldered the shotgun. "Good. Let's do what we came for and get the hell out of here."

That made Lars cock his head. "And what exactly is it you two geniuses intend to do?"

Tom leveled a firm gaze at the vampire. "We're getting them out of here."

"Christ, Meat, that's ambitious even for you. You

think you'll waltz in there, grab Colin's two most valued prizes, then disappear?"

"They're probably in the cells down here, right?"

Lars shook his head. "Lindsey is. Ana is somewhere deeper with Pencil-Neck. And he for sure isn't gonna just let her go. By the way, where do you think you're going to take them, even if this harebrained scheme does pan out, against all odds? It's still daylight out there, Einstein, and will be for a few more hours."

Tom looked at his shoes. He'd hoped they could sneak in and out and free Lindsey and Ana unnoticed, or at least without much notice, then hang out in the tunnel or the first empty room until sundown. Hope wasn't really much of a plan, though. "We'll figure something out."

Shan groaned. "You might have mentioned the best plan you've got is flying by the seat of your pants."

"It's gotten me this far, hasn't it?"

"Mother, help me. Sounds like maybe your friends have gotten you this far."

Lars chuckled, losing the hint of sourness for the first time. "I like this one. She's definitely got you figured out already, Meat." He crossed his arms. "The good news is, I'll help you out again. I think I have an idea how to make this suicide mission work."

CHAPTER 36

NOT EVEN A FULL DAY into Drake lording over Ana with his pretentious self-satisfaction, and she already wondered if she wouldn't have preferred meeting the sunrise in the cupola at the top of the building. He'd made her put on the lab coat she'd left in the cramped room the previous fall, as if pretending they were actual colleagues and she wasn't being pressed to assist him against her will.

Then he would open his nauseating mouth and firmly remind her that he understood their relationship in exacting detail.

"Don't forget to double-check the enzyme inhibitor measurement before you heat the solution." He stood behind her in the makeshift lab, looking over her shoulder just as she was about to pour clear liquid solution into a graduated beaker. "Any miscalculation in this serum can have devastating effect. Nothing could be more important than precision. Our lord's life and many of our Family depend on it."

"You've said that seven times already, Drake. I understand. This is not my first time in a lab, and you know it. In fact, you know very well this was my lab last year."

He sniffed. "How can I trust anything about you

when, apparently, you spend so little of your time actually working toward the project you were tasked with? You were to be our savior when you found a human, and you wasted all of that potential on some pointless emotional conflict with Lord Colin. Well, we will have no repeat of that." He turned away from her, going back to his task at the microscope. "Finish making that batch of solution. Once I have verified its efficacy, you can draw the individual doses. His plan requires…" Drake trailed off, as if he just remembered he was supposed to guard their Maker's secret plan.

Ana couldn't yet be one hundred percent certain of that plan, but she'd pieced together a good portion of it. Unless she was totally off base, Colin fully intended to start a full-scale war with any vampire Family that chose to oppose him. And he had no intention of fighting that war fairly. She would also bet her freedom that it had something to do with the future Conclave meeting.

Satisfied with the proper measure of the inhibitor, she poured the contents into a larger beaker and set it on a burner. Not for the first time, she considered trying to over- or undercook the serum, which Drake had told her a dozen times would significantly impact how well it worked, but even if he didn't notice her tampering as she made it, he tested every batch.

She scowled as she watched the numbers on the beaker's thermometer rise and wondered how long she could continue. The work would help Colin in more ways than she could count, and she would never forgive herself if he achieved his actual goal. Carrying that guilt around for the rest of her immortality would surely drive her insane.

For as much as she hated helping Drake, spending the previous day with him in the lab had been more useful than she wanted to admit. In his quest to find a serum that could reproduce a Feral's increased strength and stamina, he'd stumbled across several breakthroughs that had eluded her since Colin had Made her. Drake had even solved the one problem that had most frustrated her in her search for her Holy Grail. And the previous night, he'd just blurted it while presenting the rest of the research he'd done over the previous two years, oblivious to what he'd given her.

All she needed was the right moment and enough time to herself, and she might really be able to fix it all.

Of course, that assumed Colin wouldn't have her killed as soon as she finished helping Drake produce the doses of serum the plan required. She figured they were long odds, at best.

The thermometer reported the solution had reached its target temperature, and she clicked a digital timer on the table beside the burner. It ticked down the seconds, at which point she turned the burner off and moved the beaker to a heatproof trivet. She then stirred it for a count of ten.

"The batch is done."

Drake didn't look up from his microscope. "Excellent. Take it down the hall to let it cool, and bring back the previous batch for testing."

Ana said nothing but picked up the hot glass beaker and crossed the room to the door, then reached for the handle.

"Are you forgetting something?" Drake whined.

She suppressed the urge to pour the solution down his back and smash the glass beaker into his pinched face. "Am I?" she grunted instead.

"I believe I instructed you to respond verbally in assent to all my orders before carrying them out. Did we not discuss that?"

Her jaw muscles ached from grinding her teeth, and she clenched her free hand into a fist but somehow managed to maintain control of herself. Barely. "My mistake," Ana muttered. "Of course we did. I will take this down the hall to chill and return with the previous batch."

"Very good, then." The words oozed across the room like a putrid jelly. "I appreciate your assistance. It's good to be working together."

"Yes. I'm so glad we have this opportunity." Not waiting for him to say anything else that might make her do something to end her second life, she left the room in a rush and pulled the door closed behind her faster than she'd intended. It banged against its frame. All she could do was hope it didn't provoke him when she came back.

She spun away from the door and pressed her back against the hard stone bricks that made up the walls. Air wasn't necessary for her at the moment, but she took several measured breaths, trying to calm herself. When she'd recovered her composure and was merely miserable rather than both that and filled with rage, she started down the hallway toward the storage room.

When she reached it, she peered through the small cutout in the wooden door to see if any of Gordon's plaguers were on guard. Finding it empty, she exhaled in relief. His mind-controlled Feral didn't worry her, per se, but the way they swayed in place when not moving around made her skin crawl. She needed a few minutes alone anyway.

She opened the door and entered the storage, which they kept cooler than the others on that floor—not quite cold enough to see her breath, but close.

After setting the beaker down on a worktable in the middle of the room, she ripped a piece of masking tape from the roll beside it, stuck it to the glass, and wrote the date and time with a Sharpie. The marker itself was attached to the table with a piece of string, as if the storage room were a bank and people came in just to steal pens. Not that there was much point in labeling it, as she wouldn't forget which batch she wanted when she came to get it for testing in an hour or so. But Drake had rules, and she was compelled to follow them to the letter.

Ana touched the glass holding the solution she'd left just over an hour ago and nodded, satisfied with its temperature. It was ready for testing.

"Don't turn around."

An electric jolt of panic shot up her spine, and she almost spun around to face the threat from instinct alone, but she recognized that voice, and something told her Colin didn't need to know about the conversation. "You startled me, Lars. You're lucky I hadn't picked up this beaker yet, because I might have dropped it, and that would have been problematic, to say the least. How long have you been lurking at the door?" She hadn't gotten even the slightest indication he was out there.

"Long enough to see you doing some pencil-neck's busywork. What are you doing?"

"The same thing as you. Trying to survive long enough to stop Colin."

"What is that stuff? I saw that lab coat guy—Drake, I think? He injected it into some poor bastard the other day, and the guy went nuts. He broke his own hand to get out of a shackle and had to be put down hard by a pair of Kallus's plaguers."

Ana stared at the tape on the glass cylinder in front of her and peeled it away a quarter of an inch at a time. She needed to look busy just in case Colin was paying attention. "What do you think it is?"

"I think it's what helped him kill Emily after I set him up."

She sighed. "Lars, that wasn't your fault. You couldn't have known or done anything differently."

"He set me up from the start, Ana. Alexander did. He sent me to Emily to tell her about the attack on Tom, all the while pretending we were still at odds with Colin. Hiding the truth from me because he wanted in on Colin's plan. I was a fool, and Alexander used me like a goddamn pawn in their game. And just like clockwork, Lindsey and I delivered her to him, perfectly in time to use his shiny new steroid injection." He paused, letting the silence between them grow heavy. "I'm going to kill him—Alexander, that betraying bastard. Right now. Can you give me any of that stuff? I'll kill Colin, too, if you do."

"I can't, Lars. I'm sorry. The doses are all back in my,

uh, Drake's lab. You know I would help you if I could." She pulled off a new piece of tape and began rewriting the date and time from the tape she'd removed. Halfway through, she stopped and cocked her head. "I'm surprised they let you walk around. You were in chains the last time I saw you."

"Alexander's one pathetic gift to me, born of his own guilty conscience. He talked Colin into letting me live, but I've been banished. I shouldn't be down here and definitely shouldn't be talking to you."

She allowed herself a wry smile, glad to know her intuition still served her well. "I'm glad I didn't turn around then. Do you realize how difficult that is when someone specifically tells you *not* to turn around and startles you in the process?"

"I'll keep that in mind," he said flatly. "Anyway, I won't tell you what's about to happen, but if I know you, you already have some scheme concocted and are just waiting for the right moment."

"Go on." She saw no point in giving him details if he wasn't sharing either.

"The moment is coming. Get ready. You don't have long."

"What does that mean? Do I have a day? Or an hour?"

Her questions went unanswered.

"Lars?"

Still, no response. At last, she spun around to face the door. He was gone.

Ana turned back to the table, picked up the older batch of serum, and smiled at no one. It was a genuine grin, the kind that she had very seldom allowed herself in the past three years. Drake would take the batch to test it and leave her in the lab to continue her work.

And that work—her work, not his—would give her the chance she needed.

CHAPTER 37

A S ANA HAD EXPECTED, DRAKE whisked the beaker away from her the moment she returned to the lab. He made a few backhanded comments about her taking too long as he drew up a few test doses, but she nodded as meekly as she could and began working on a new batch of solution. She wouldn't allow him to get under her skin. Wouldn't ever let that happen again. For maybe the first time since nursing Tom back to strength from his coma, she felt in complete control of herself. Her mind was hers again, as were her decisions. Drake could self-aggrandize all he wanted at her cost. She had more important things to do than worry about him trying to make her feel small.

He skittered out of the room a few moments later, and Ana went to work. She dumped the beaker and began work on a new solution, a different solution, one that she'd tried to make hundreds of times in the past year with no luck. But Drake had unwittingly given her the key that had eluded her all that time. Her next batch would be different.

Time was against her, though. He might be gone twenty minutes, or thirty, at most, unless he was summoned to Colin for some reason. She couldn't think about Colin, though. She had to focus on the task at hand. Ana had one chance to get it right, one chance to fix things.

She bounced around the small lab, grabbing the components she needed. Her hands flew over the various beakers, jars, and bottles of ingredients, slowing only as necessary to make sure her measurements were perfect. Finally, she gave her concoction a long, steady stir, counting the seconds to ensure a proper mix. Stepping back from it, she smiled again before grabbing a microscope slide and a pair of syringes.

The slide hit the table in front of her solution with a *plink*, and she rolled up one of her sleeves. Taking her own blood was second nature after all the work she'd done at the Chalet. She drew a small sample then applied a few drops to the slide. With a second syringe, she pulled a tiny amount of her solution from the beaker and added it to the blood, then smeared the mixture along the glass.

Ana's hands nearly shook. She picked up the slide with as much care as she could muster and swapped whatever Drake had been looking at on the microscope with her test. After expelling a long, deep breath to gain better control of herself, she peered into the eyepiece, welcoming the familiar process of adjusting the lens and focus until she saw what her work had—or hadn't—accomplished.

At long last, the image she had longed for came into clear view. She stepped back and covered her mouth, suddenly terrified she might cry.

Ten or fifteen minutes later, Drake returned in a frenzy. Ana nearly jumped out of her shoes as the lab door smacked against the wall behind it from the extra force he'd used to throw it open. She turned with a nervous start, and he rushed in, face pinched, lab coat flapping behind him.

"What have you been doing while I was gone?" The demand came out almost as a squeak, partially through his nose.

"I... I..." she stammered, caught off guard. For a split second, her mind conjured the worst, but then she reminded herself who was in control. *She* was in control. "I've been doing what you ordered, that is, asked me to do." Just in time, she remembered that Drake preferred to act like he was being generous and magnanimous in letting her assist his great work. She gestured to the glass jar on the burner on the table in front of her. "I've been working on the next solution. How did the tests go? Would you like me to dose that batch?"

Drake swept past her to his preferred station by the microscope. He snatched the batch he'd drawn up for testing and plunked it down next to her, almost hard enough to crack it. "Lord Colin spoke to me a few moments ago. He is uneasy."

She tried not to furrow her brow and forced her hands to remain still, in place. Colin might have seen what she'd been doing but could not have understood. It should have seemed like her normal routine to him. But he was suspicious by nature. What if he thought differently? "I am sorry to hear that. He did not share any concerns with me."

"You *are* the concern." Drake's nose wrinkled in a sneer.

Ana forced her voice to be steady, despite the storm of

ice swirling in her belly. "I have only done what he asked since our meeting upstairs. Did he share anything else?"

"Nothing about you, specifically. He said your friends were spotted in Kansas then disappeared. Colin is furious the Brigadier let them slip away after they'd finally been found. But our lord knows your human is a fool and is capable of incredibly stupid things. He wants to make sure that the man does not attempt to contact you."

"Well, surely he won't come here. That would be reckless, even for Tom. And I haven't left the lab since you went to do the testing."

Drake narrowed his eyes into an unsettling glare. She held the look, meeting it with as blank an expression as she could muster under the circumstances, especially knowing what she had secreted away in her lab coat pocket. "Did he say anything else? Or have specific instructions for me?"

At last, Drake broke eye contact and turned to his workstation. "Nothing else. Only that you are not to leave my side for any reason for the next few days. When it comes time to test the next batch, you will accompany me."

"Of course. Should I start making doses for this one, then?"

He rearranged his workstation, as he always compulsively did before starting to work on something. Over his shoulder, he said, "Yes, do that please. And make it quick."

"I will get started right away." Ana turned her attention back to her work area, intending to get started on the work he'd assigned her. She hesitated, though, and bit her bottom lip, uncertain. Lars had said soon, but how soon?

How long could she keep what she'd done a secret? She hoped it wouldn't be too much time before the chance arrived, but what if whatever he was planning interfered with what she needed to do? Could she risk waiting?

She set her left hand on the table in front of her and tapped her index finger. Her right hand found the pocket of her lab coat, seemingly of its own accord, and grasped one of the syringes she'd dropped in there. Ana needed to get started before Drake realized she hadn't, but something tugged at her memory—something important, some detail she'd overlooked.

Then her eyes went wide as the realization hit home. Out of instinct, she popped off one of the plastic syringe covers in her pocket.

"What is this?" Drake was bent over his microscope, peering through the eyepiece. "Did you do this? This isn't… this is impossible."

In her excitement, Ana had forgotten to replace her slide on the scope with his previous work. He could see exactly what she'd made.

She inhaled sharply. Her moment had come, and she could not miss it.

Whatever Lars intended to do, she would have to play it by ear. She spun to face Drake and shoved herself away from the worktable, then slammed her chest into his back, forcing him into the table in front of him. She pulled her serum from her lab coat pocket.

"What?" he squawked, half turning against her. His eyes went even wider in alarm as she jabbed the unprotected needle into his neck and smashed the plunger all the way down in one quick motion.

She staggered backward and pulled the second syringe from her coat.

Drake's face was a mask of confusion. "What have you done? What is that for?" Then, he lurched forward and vomited what looked like two pints of blood all over both of them.

"This is for me." She shoved the second needle into her chest just as Colin's thoughts flooded her mind at a shout.

"Daughter, what is this?"

The solution burned like nothing Ana had felt before as it filled her chest and spread through the rest of her body. A second later, her stomach churned in revolt against the solution. Like Drake, she folded partway at the waist, and an eruption of blood flowed from her mouth and nose. It was worse than her memory of throwing up a dinner of mashed potatoes, bile, and stomach acid as a kid, but she reveled in the sensation. It meant the drug was working.

Drake lay on the floor in the blood he'd puked up, hands and legs twitching.

She smiled even as her fingers began to tingle. "You can both go straight to hell." As she said it, her legs gave way beneath her, and she crumpled to the floor, barely catching herself with hands she couldn't quite feel.

Ana forced herself fully to the floor, lying on her right side, her right arm outstretched. She settled her head against it and watched Drake across the room. His body still twitching, his eyes shifted back and forth as if in REM sleep. His face was a mask of discomfort. She smiled again despite the excruciating pain radiating from her chest.

Ana groaned, and her vision turned black, yet she knew her eyes were still open.

Then, just as she felt her consciousness slipping away, she heard a single, weak heartbeat from somewhere in front of her. Her own heart fluttered in her chest then spasmed as a jolt of electric agony surged through her extremities.

Finally, with the room spinning around her, Ana shuddered and gasped for one last breath before her Second Life came to an end.

CHAPTER 38

FOOTPRINTS IN THE ROOM'S DIRT floor led to a small hole in the right-side wall that was just large enough for someone to squeeze through in a crouch. It was exactly as Tom remembered it, and he had a good idea of what to expect on the far side. Lars had passed through it almost ten minutes before, telling them to wait there and give him a head start.

"That's got to be about enough time, right?" Tom looked at Shan for reassurance.

She shrugged.

"Well, either way, I'm not waiting any longer."

Tom gave Lady a low whistle, and the German shepherd sniffed at the opening then slipped through. She returned a few seconds later and woofed, then disappeared again. Tom crouched low and stepped through after her. He stood once he reached the other side and gestured to Shan, who followed him in.

"This is the worst hike I've ever been on, T. I'm going to have dust in my nostrils for a week. What now?"

A heavy wood door was set into the aging brick-and-mortar wall on the far side of the musty but otherwise empty room. He nodded to it. "Through that door, we'll enter a hallway with several cell doors on each side. We'll need to find the one with Lindsey then wait until Lars does his thing."

Shan frowned. "Not a fan of the idea of waiting in the open. Why don't we wait here?"

"I'd prefer that, too, but if the cells have guards, we'll need to wait until they leave to try freeing her. It's the only way to get her out quietly."

"Okay, that makes sense." She cocked her head. "And if there aren't any guards?"

He smirked. "Then we do this the easy way."

Lady approached the door to the corridor. It looked heavier than he remembered, and he wished it had a small cutout or window so they could peek into the hall.

Tom rubbed the German shepherd between the ears. "Anything out there, girl?"

The dog pawed at the door in reply.

He pulled the door open an inch and peered out. The shadows beyond were silent and still. Tom stepped out with Lady at his heels. Shan came last, shotgun pointed at the matching door on the far side of the hallway.

Four cell doors lined the passage walls, two on each side facing the opposite one. Wooden doors matching the one they'd just gone through secured the left-hand cells. The ones on the right, though, had doors made from metal bars, like jail cells. Tom cocked an eyebrow. He didn't remember it being like that before.

He looked at Shan and put his index finger to his lips. She knew to be silent already, of course, but the open bars into the cells made him feel more exposed than he'd expected. She rolled her eyes then pointed the shotgun's barrel at the floor. With her free left hand, Shan reached into her supply bag and withdrew a small compact.

Tom shot her a bewildered look. What the hell did she need makeup for?

The expression quickly turned to understanding when she opened it and handed him a small mirror. He nodded back at her and mouthed the words, "Thank you." Then he pressed his back to the stone wall right beside the first of the barred cells.

Holding the mirror at shoulder height, Tom used its reflection to get a look at the cell beyond the bars. What he saw made no sense. A single Feral lay on the floor near the back of the room, appearing to be chained to the wall behind it.

Feral were usually used as guards in those cells, not held in restraints. And he'd never seen one look so lifeless. Was it dead, maybe?

"I think it's dead," Shan whispered not quite an inch from his ear.

Tom nodded then stepped to the side and turned to face the cell. It was a reckless move, and he knew it, but if the thing was alive and movement in the hall would make it take notice, they couldn't do much to sneak past anyway.

The concern was moot, it seemed. The plaguer showed no sign of activity when he stepped out and didn't so much as twitch when Lady did the same.

While he and Lady watched for the thing to come alive, Shan took the mirror from his hand and took position beside the bars of the next cell. She held the mirror up for a couple of seconds then dropped it and walked up to the metal bars.

Coming up next to her, Tom surveyed the second room, which looked almost exactly the same as the first. It was empty, though, and the shackles attached to the far wall lay on the floor near a large dark-red stain. What was going on down here?

Shan pointed at the wooden door opposite them, and Tom turned to look. It was the same cell Ana had been held in last year. It had a hole cut out in the door, but he didn't remember it being there before.

They both crossed the musty corridor, and Tom looked inside. The room was somewhat different, with multiple sets of shackles bolted to each side of the cell. Only one of them was in use, though. Lindsey sat with her back to the right-hand wall, head down, with her chin against her chest. Clumps of her usually wavy auburn hair stuck out in multiple directions, some of it colored with blood. She was covered in crimson stains that stood out on her clothes and formed crusted dried patches that masked parts of her face.

Lindsey was alone, though. There were no guards, either vampire or Feral. Tom couldn't help but smile at their luck.

He threw back the latch bolt to the door and twisted the knob. The door slid toward him, and Lindsey's head came up halfway. She crinkled her nose and raised an eyebrow, looking confused. Then her eyes lit with recognition as he crossed the room to her.

"Linds, are you okay?"

"Do I look okay, Tommy? And what the hell are you

doing here anyway? You have to get out of here." Her eyes fixed on Shan just behind him, and the look of confusion returned. "And who the fuck is that?"

"Nice to meet you too, honey," Shan replied. "I'm Shan. T and I have been working as a team for a few days."

Lindsey narrowed her eyes. "Are you… human? Why can't I smell either of you? The only thing I can smell in here is my own blood and dog."

Shan grinned. "Once we get out of here alive, I might explain it."

"It's a long story," Tom cut in. "And we don't have much time. We need to get out of here." He stood and holstered his revolver then held his hand out to Shan.

She plucked a small pair of bolt cutters from her bag and handed them to him.

Setting the cutting end against the bolt holding her shackles, he paused. "I'm sorry about Emily. I'm so sorry." With a squeeze of the cutter's arms, he snapped the bolt with its teeth, freeing her.

Lindsey shook off the chains and stood, rubbing her wrists. Then she flexed her hands into fists. "I don't know what to do with that, T, but I'm fucking furious about it, and I'm going to make that bastard pay." She gave Shan an appraising look then turned back to Tom. "I suppose you'd rather I didn't drain her? I need strength."

Shan raised the shotgun. "I sure as shit would rather you didn't."

"I'm sorry, Linds. But Shan's important to me, as much as Lady is." He pushed the barrel of the gun back down. "I promise she won't shoot you."

Lindsey grunted a curse. "Do you at least have a towel

or something? Wearing your own dried, caked-on blood isn't really a blast."

"T, can we go now?" Despite the concern in her voice, Shan pulled a pack of wet wipes from her bag and offered them to Lindsey.

"Bolt cutters, wet wipes?" Lindsey wiped flecks of brick red from her chin. "Where did you find a Mary Poppins?"

"A convenience store, believe it or not." Tom chuckled to himself.

After dropping a newly stained wipe to the floor, the vampire moved toward the door. "You two get out of here. I'm going to find Ana. If I can't feed, she might be able to help. And hopefully, I'll be able to settle at least one score right away."

"Lindsey, you can't rush up there. Lars has a plan—"

"Lars is here? They told me he was banished."

Tom nodded. "That's what he told us too. But you know Lars. He's gone up to kill Alexander."

Lindsey put a hand on the doorknob but glared back at them. "Tell me everything."

CHAPTER 39

L ARS SLOWLY CLIMBED THE STONEWORK ramp, one foot in front of the other, following the ghosts of dozens or even hundreds of his kind that had walked the same path over the past few years. A year ago, what they were doing there had made sense to him. Alexander had been in charge and had tried his level best to make sure the Family would survive on what they could find. Not many of them knew it, but they even built up a small reserve of Tom's blood. Alexander never would have been able to sustain the whole Family, but they had a stash for emergencies. As a lord, Alexander did a good job, too, of staying in touch with the other Families and managing their place in the fading world while hiding the knowledge that he'd come across a human survivor.

Since then, though, since Colin sent Ana and Ash out to meddle then eventually showed up himself, everything had gone to hell. As soon as they recaptured Tom, Alexander started acting like a fool, deciding to use him as a bleeding cow instead of trying to leverage more value out of him. Colin knew they had a human, and word was spreading to the other lords.

Alexander ran off to hide not once but twice after

that and had come back again only to prove he wasn't the leader Lars had believed. He sold himself and the whole Family to Colin, even letting that creepy bastard Kallus "retrain" most of the Family's Feral so Ana's Maker could put them to use.

Whichever of Alexander's clan hadn't sworn to follow Colin last year after their lord's first disappearing act might as well have gone ahead and done it. Alexander had never really tried to keep his people together after that. He abandoned them for whatever scraps he might be tossed after they finished enacting Colin's plan.

Even worse, he'd betrayed his right-hand man to accomplish it.

Lars would always carry the guilt of what he'd done in that train yard, would always believe he was at least partly responsible for Emily's death. But only partly. Colin would have to answer for what he'd done. He'd done it with Alexander's explicit help, though—Alexander, who'd betrayed Lars after years of working together. Alexander needed to answer for that first.

The white-hot fury bound in Lars's chest was like nothing he'd ever experienced before, and he was determined to harness it in the name of enacting revenge for himself, for Lindsey, and for Emily.

Reaching the top of the ramp, Lars stepped into the large room on the main floor of the building that had once been a brewery. He and Ash had fought in that very room not quite a year before. In hindsight, he should have killed Ash at that moment, when he'd had the chance. Though that probably wouldn't have changed anything in the long run.

No, the real mistake had been trusting Alexander after that moment.

Half a dozen plaguers stood on each side of the room, swaying in place with their arms hanging at their sides. They reminded Lars of a much creepier version of wallflower kids hugging the perimeter of the gym at a middle school dance.

"What are you doing here?" An Asian-looking man stepped from a doorway on one side of the room into the center of it. "Alexander said you weren't coming back."

"Nice to see you, too, Will." Lars tilted his head toward the other vampire. They'd known each other for years as part of Alexander's clan and had worked together often. Will had been the one who'd controlled the Feral that had captured Ana and Tom at the hospital back when things still made sense.

"I didn't expect you to come back either. Hell, I probably wouldn't have if I was allowed to leave. Things have gotten strange since Colin showed up. I don't even have my Feral anymore." He gave a weird look of longing at two of the plaguers in the corner.

"Right. Strange." Lars returned a dry, almost-somber chuckle. "And I wasn't *allowed* to leave. I was banished."

"Oh." Will gave him a confused look. "Then, why did you come back?"

"Where is he?"

"Where is who?"

"Alexander," Lars growled. "Where is that piece of shit?"

Will spread his hands in front of himself. "Look, Lars, maybe you shouldn't—"

"I thought we had an understanding," Alexander boomed from the landing of the staircase at the far end of the chamber.

Kallus stood behind him with a peevish grin.

"So did I, lord, one from a long way back." Lars's emphasis on "lord" dripped with bitterness.

Alexander lit a cigarette and crossed to the center of the room, coming up beside Will. "Tell me why I shouldn't have you taken apart this instant or captured and hung upstairs for tomorrow morning?"

Lars crossed his arms and set his feet, radiating inflexibility. He had come to satisfy his grudge and would not relent or be denied. "Because you were once a man of honor, a man of your word, and you will hear me out because of it."

After eyeing him for several tense moments, his once Master drew deeply from his cigarette then exhaled a mighty cloud of acrid smoke. Even across the room, the scent made Lars's eyes water. The man probably kept smoking after so many years solely to irritate the fine senses of the vampires around him.

"You've misjudged me, son. When it comes to deals with the devil, in for a penny, in for a pound. Kallus, you can let your—"

"I challenge you to single combat!" Lars shouted with a scowl. "Or are you so lost that you refuse to observe the most basic right of the pact?"

Alexander said nothing at first but took another puff while glaring at his former lieutenant. The air between them was so heavy with strain, Lars half expected the smoke he exhaled to fall to the ground from pressure rather than rise to the rafters. He flexed his right hand, balling and releasing a fist still tucked under his left bicep.

"Lord Alexander?" Kallus's question was almost a squeak.

"Shut up, you worm." Alexander scowled at Colin's Feral master, disdain apparent in the twisted wrinkles on his face. He turned back to Lars, dropped the cigarette to the ground, and crushed it with the toe of his boot. "Fuck it. You really want to challenge me for leadership of this Family?"

"For whatever Family you haven't already sold to Colin," Lars spat.

"Be careful what you wish for."

Kallus's eyes went wide, and his mouth dropped open. "Alexander, I think you should reconsider. I'll inform Lord Colin of what's going on here."

"Do whatever you like, maggot. But I'm going to honor this man's request." He rolled the cuffs of his plaid shirt and put his fists in front of his face, knuckles pointed at the ceiling like an old-time boxer.

With a squawk, Kallus fled up the stairs the way they'd come, no doubt to alert Colin to the impending fight.

Lars grinned and pushed his own sleeves up as he advanced to meet his former lord. He raised his hands to his face, setting his fists and feet in a more modern fighting stance. "I'm sorry it has come to this."

Alexander gave him a flat, rueful grin. "It probably always would have come to this, son."

The pair began circling each other, waiting for the other to throw the first punch, both with gleaming fangs revealed.

"I expect this will be a fair fight, though," Alexander said. "None of the bullshit with Colin's juice. You've come to this clean?"

Word had to be spreading fast. From the corner of his eye, Lars noticed other vampires, faces he knew and trusted, streaming into the room and lining up along the room's perimeter. He smiled, glad to see that the challenge was exactly the kind of spectacle he'd anticipated.

The kind of spectacle they needed.

"Yeah," Lars grunted. "With more respect for you than you deserve. Now, no more bullshit." He attacked first with a right jab, testing Alexander's reflexes.

Despite the older vampire's chain-smoking habit, he still had years on Lars, if not quite the strength. He deflected the jab with his right hand and swung a fast cross with his left, smashing a fist into Lars's chin and knocking him a few steps backward. The growing crowd cheered.

"This kind of reminds me of my youth, son. I'm going to have some fun with this."

Lars spit a tooth along with a glob of bright-red blood and reset his stance. "Bring it, old man. I'm sick and tired of you calling me son."

CHAPTER 40

THREE SHADOWY FORMS AND ONE German shepherd stole up the dark corridor with Lindsey leading, Lady following her, and Tom and Shan side by side at the rear. Lindsey tried to keep herself to a light jog to not outpace the others but forgot herself several times. Each time she accidentally pulled away, she turned back to them with a gloomy frown and waved at them to hurry along.

It didn't take long, though, to reach a three-way intersection in the hall, with the choice of a turn to the right or the left. Tom remembered it from before. A right turn would take them upstairs to the main chamber.

Lindsey didn't hesitate before turning left instead, and the group trotted down the next hall, passing several doors. Lindsey and Lady paused for a half second at each, with the former seeming to focus her attention beyond the entrance while the dog sniffed the ground.

Lady began softly growling a mere moment after Lindsey muttered, "Here." She narrowed her eyes. "At least I'm pretty sure. I definitely smell her, but something's tickling my senses. Something seems… off. Either way, I expect one of Colin's to be with her."

She whispered so quietly that Tom could only make out what she was saying by watching her lips move at the same time.

"Leave him to me."

He and Shan nodded, but both tightened their respective grips around their weapons. Tom looked up and down the corridor and furrowed his brow. Where were the vamps and Feral? The last time he'd been below the brewery, there were usually plenty of others moving through the halls in pursuit of some task he couldn't begin to understand. Especially near the cells—plaguers were always around the cells. They hadn't come across anyone, or anything. Could Lars's diversion be that effective? Even so, that wouldn't have drawn the blood zombies.

If Lindsey was concerned by the lack of Family, she gave no sign of it. She confidently set a hand on the door handle and put up three fingers. After ticking each one down, she threw the door open and barreled inside. Shan went before Tom, shotgun raised. As he stepped in behind her, she gasped.

Tom's mouth fell open.

The room looked like a scene from a particularly gory slasher movie. The floor was covered in blood, and the walls were splattered. On the far side of the lab, just in front of a workstation, someone in a lab coat that Tom didn't recognize, lay face down in a crimson pool. Ana lay on her side with her back to him.

"Jesus, Ana."

The man on the floor groaned then coughed several times, the raspy hack of a lifelong smoker. He lifted his head and blinked several times. "What… what have you done?"

Lindsey seemed speechless, something Tom couldn't recall ever seeing before.

She knelt beside Ana and pulled the hair back from her face. "Ana, honey, are you in there?"

A few heavy seconds later, Ana gulped in air then coughed it back out along with a spray of blood. "I did it," she murmured. "My god, I did it."

"What did you…?" As the words trailed off, Lindsey's jaw dropped open, and her eyes grew to the size of silver dollars. Then her head snapped around, looking toward the far side of the lab.

Across the room, the man in the lab coat clamored to his knees, looking every bit as graceless as a newborn colt. "You did this! You did this, you fucking cunt!" Finally getting to his feet, he searched the room wildly with his eyes for something. At last, he settled on the microscope behind him. He grabbed at it, yanking it hard from the table, but the power cord stubbornly held in the power strip where it was plugged in. He jerked at it a second time with both hands, and it finally came free.

With an animal cry, he raised it above his head and stepped toward Ana as she got to her knees.

Lady bounded past Tom just as Lindsey launched herself at the man in a blur of motion. She easily outpaced the shepherd and slammed into the man's chest while knocking the microscope to the floor with a tremendous crash. It burst into several pieces in a clinking symphony of broken glass.

Tom expected Lindsey to start pummeling the other

vampire, but to his surprise, she shoved aside the lab coat's collar and buried her face in the guy's neck. The thin, pale face above the coat twisted in abject horror then slowly went slack. His eyes melted shut, and the air of a child sleeping contentedly settled on his face.

Soft slurping sounds echoed off the room's walls, reminiscent of Lady lapping at a water dish. Lindsey was draining him, whoever he was.

"What the actual fuck?" Shan mumbled.

Tom had never actually seen Lindsey Feed before, and the vampire's rules against draining each other were very specific. Whatever he saw felt wrong. Even worse, he couldn't shake the sense that he was somehow intruding on Lindsey's intimate moment.

He looked away then knelt beside Ana, who had risen to a kneeling position with her legs tucked under her. Even covered in blood, she looked different.

"Are you okay?"

She sniffed once then again before tears began streaming down her face. She took his hand and raised it to her chest, setting his palm between her breasts.

The hollowness that often accompanied shock spread through him.

The hand holding his was *warm.*

Her chest was warm.

And beneath his palm, her heart pulsed against it.

"I'm…" she stammered.

Her eyes met his, shimmering like wet obsidian. "I'm cured, Tom. I'm cured." Then she began to sob.

CHAPTER 41

"WHAT DO YOU MEAN, *CURED*?" Lindsey faced them and let the drained, lifeless husk wearing the lab coat crash to the ground. She wiped the crimson stain from her chin and ran her tongue along her lips, then with a sigh, her fangs sank back into her mouth.

Ana composed herself and let go of Tom's hand, then pulled herself up with the aid of his shoulder and the worktable. She faltered halfway and, once standing, swayed unsteadily. Finally, though, she set her feet firmly under her, matching the width of her shoulders, and began scrubbing at the mess of drying blood and tear streaks that decorated her face.

"Exactly what I said. Cured. Vampirism is an infection, Lindsey—a disease. And I found a way to reverse it. I'm not one of you anymore."

Crossing her arms, Lindsey sniffed. "I can smell that, hon. Not sure I believe it, though."

"You didn't seem to question it much when it came to Drake." Ana gestured toward the body at the vampire's feet.

Lindsey shrugged. "Well, now, I gotta admit, that was

as much instinct as anything else, baby girl. With everything else going on in here"—she spread her arms wide to indicate the chaos all around them—"I didn't notice his heart beating right away. It hit me just as he started to come at you with that scope, and well, decades of being me took over." She wiped her mouth with the back of her hand again. "Sweet baby Jesus, that asshole was delicious. I feel like I could stop a train right now."

Shan offered Ana a wet wipe and a level glare. "This is all insane. You're saying you're not a Drac anymore?"

After scrubbing blood from her cheek, a rosy spot of color blossomed where Tom had never seen one before.

He shook his head, trying to work through all the implications. "You can really get rid of it? From all of them?"

"Hold on a sec now, Tommy." A hint of metal in Lindsey's voice made him look up.

"I don't know." It was Ana's turn to shrug. "Perhaps. Then again, I could also simply collapse in three hours from the shock or from some kind of delayed toxicity. What I did was extremely rash."

"Rash?" Lindsey raised an eyebrow. "Understatement of the decade right there, girl."

Ana faced her. "For what it's worth, I am sorry about Emily. She was a pretty decent person for being a centuries-old vampire."

"I appreciate that. We'll drink to her later. Right now, I got a more important appointment to keep."

Tom scowled. "What do you mean? You're both free, and we've got a clear path to daylight. We need to get out of here."

Lindsey clucked her tongue. "Daylight ain't much

used to me, Tommy boy. And if you think I'm leaving here without getting my pound of flesh out of Colin, you must not know me as well as you think."

"Mother above and dragons below, tell me she's not saying what I think?" Shan's eyes darted between Tom and Lindsey.

"She's going up there to fight." Tom sighed. "And there's not much we can do to stop her."

"See? You do get me." Lindsey favored him with a grin.

"I'm not letting you go alone."

"Oh, for fuck's sake." Shan groaned, exasperated. "Why didn't you tell me you had a death wish when we met and save me the trouble?"

At the same time, Ana muttered something to herself then, "Honestly, Tom?" She met Lindsey's eyes. "Can't you do something?"

Lindsey shrugged. "You know as well as I do he can't be Influenced for some reason."

"Ana, when we came down here to get you last year and you were already gone, Lindsey and Emily wanted me to leave. I wasn't about to do that, and I told Lindsey so. She defied Emily to help me get you. Besides, Lars is up there right now mostly because we needed a diversion, and it obviously worked. If he needs a hand, I intend to give it to him."

While Lindsey grinned, Ana rolled her eyes.

"They have several times the strength you do, are much faster, and have senses you can't possibly comprehend," Ana countered. "This is not the same. And Colin is using Feral in ways I've never seen before. He has one man controlling all of them, coordinating them. If he has some up there, they won't be rambling mindlessly."

Tom smiled and raised the baseball bat in his right hand. "That's okay. I've got this."

"Enough," Lindsey said. "Coming or going, it's the same to me. If you want to go up and see what you can do, you're a big boy and can make your own decisions. But before we get to all that, Ana and I need to talk about one more thing."

CHAPTER 42

T HE GROUP STOLE INTO THE hallway after Lindsey and Lady independently decided the space was empty of threats. They slunk to the three-way intersection leading back to the corridor of cells and the entrance. Once there, Lindsey crossed to the opposite tunnel while Ana and Shan turned right to head back.

"You're sure about this, T?" Shan asked. "I know I said the Universe doesn't care what happens, but I think maybe, in this case, it does."

Before he could reply, Ana gestured. "Look at his face. He won't be talked out of it. I've seen mules half as stubborn."

Tom gave them both a half grin. "She's not wrong."

Shan offered the shotgun she'd been carrying since they entered the building. "Take it. You'll probably need it more than we will. We'll take the handgun."

He pulled the revolver out and spun the cylinder out of habit, then offered it to her, handle first. He took the shotgun then frowned at the baseball bat in his other hand. "This won't work."

"Give me the stupid thing." The exasperation had

transferred from Shan to Ana, who despite becoming human again, had regained most of her cool demeanor.

"But I might run out of shells," he complained. "Then I'd need the bat."

Shan looked at him as if he were arguing that the sky was green. "If you run out of ammunition, get the hell out of there."

Ana nodded, and at last, Tom relented, letting go of his precious Louisville Slugger.

"Wrap it up," Lindsey urged from partway up the other corridor.

"I'll meet you both soon. I promised." With that, Tom turned to follow Lindsey.

Shan grabbed him by the sleeve. "Wait." She handed Ana the revolver and pulled a white square jewelry box from her bag. She lifted the top to reveal a bed of white cotton and several glittering crystal stones. From it, she plucked a smooth, dark, round stone and another, longer, slenderer, polished one with stripes he couldn't identify in the dark. "These are hematite and tigereye. The hematite will protect you, and the tigereye will give you courage. Good luck, T. You're an absolute buffoon most of the time, but I'm glad you found me bleeding to death in that store."

"I…" he stammered. "Thanks?"

"Are you coming or not?" Lindsey demanded.

Tom took one more look at each of the women and turned.

But before he could take a step, Ana grabbed his hand and squeezed. "Be careful, Thomas Woodford." Then she turned and strode away from him.

Lady gazed up at him with an expectant look.

"Why don't you go with them?" he asked.

She pawed his boot in reply.

"Have it your way."

Tom, with Lady on his heels, caught up with Lindsey, who didn't hesitate before starting up the hall.

"That was very touching," she teased. "I'm sure you'll all make a very happy family of cocktails."

"Shut up," he barked a little more forcefully than intended. "It's just nice not to be the only one anymore. To have people I belong with."

"Then why are you here with me?"

"Because you're my people, too, just different." He took off at a jog.

Lady trotted along as Lindsey stood for a second watching, shaking her head. She dashed ahead to rejoin them, and they hustled toward the end of the hall. They reached it and turned a corner to the right, coming to an open space. Dusty hunks of smashed wooden barrels lay scattered around the room. A door stood propped open on the far side, and beyond it, a crowd cheered.

They stepped through together. In front of them, a set of stone steps twisted up and to the right, where it ended in an archway. The sickening crunch of bones cracking filtered down from the arch, and the crowd called, "Ohhhh!"

"Halfway up the steps, we drop to our bellies and see what we can see." Lindsey gestured with a flat hand held at an angle.

She didn't wait for him but was up the steps in little more than a second. Tom followed, as quickly as he could, dropping at the turn then worm-crawling up to meet her. Lady sat at the landing, waiting.

Through the archway, Alexander and Lars sidestepped each other in a circle with their hands raised. Alexander had a cut above his right eye, but Lars was bleeding from the mouth, nose, and his left ear. He seemed to have taken the brunt of the violence from the fight.

Colin stood on the landing of the steps at the back of the room, his arms crossed over his vest, wearing a smug smile. A short, wide vampire stood next to him with a mix of fear and bloodlust in his eyes.

"Who's that?" Tom whispered close to Lindsey's ear.

"Kallus," she replied. "Greasy little scumbag. Seems he controls all the Feral."

"*All* of them? Ana was serious about that?"

She shrugged.

Alexander popped Lars in the jaw with a left then followed with a brutal right hook to the temple. Lars staggered sideways as the crowd cheered once more.

"He's getting his ass kicked." Tom shifted the shotgun in his grip. "Should we do something?"

Lindsey shook her head and put a hand on the barrel of the shotgun, keeping it down.

"Son," Alexander called out, "there's no shame in conceding. Well, no more shame than you're already carrying."

Lars, bent at the waist, spat blood at his own feet. "Not bad for an old man. Not bad at all. I guess maybe it's time to stop holding back."

With his back to Tom, Alexander chuckled. "You never did know when to shut up." The older vampire left his feet, flying forward, leading with his right elbow, intending to drop it on the back of Lars's head.

Lars instead launched himself at the lord in a half crouch, coming upward as the two met. He slammed into Alexander's chest, driving him backward to the floor. The room shook with impact tremors and rang with the crackle of what Tom guessed had to be multiple broken ribs.

Alexander groaned, and his eyes flew open in sudden terror. Lars, blood hanging in streams from his mouth, got to his knees, straddling the other man's chest, and began raining blows on his former Master's face.

Tom stole a peek at Colin's expression and found that same smug smile, as if he was indifferent to the entire conflict.

After a full minute of pummeling Alexander's face into something that resembled a misshapen fruit, Lars stopped. "There's no shame in conceding, old man. Well, no more shame than you're already carrying for becoming a betraying, bootlicking asshole."

Alexander's hands flailed, but he made no reply.

"Just what I wanted to hear." Lars stood then stepped up beside Alexander's distorted face. His expression embodied pure rage as he lifted his boot high over the lord's forehead.

Then it fell with as much force as Tom imagined Lars could muster. The crowd had gone utterly silent, and the repulsive crunch of Alexander's skull being viciously flattened reverberated through the chamber.

Clap, clap, clap.

Colin stepped down from the staircase, offering slow

applause as he moved toward Lars. "Good show. Good show, my boy." His clipped British accent always sounded mocking. "I needed to do that myself sooner or later. I appreciate you checking that off my schedule."

"I didn't do it for you."

"Of course not, but we can have a common purpose on occasion." Colin looked back over his shoulder. "Kallus, have him collected and chained. I want him upstairs tomorrow morning."

"Yes, lord."

The Feral on the right side of the room shuffled away from the wall, toward Lars.

"I challenge you, Colin, you usurping sack of shit. It is my right."

Beside Tom, Lindsey shifted and took something from her pocket.

Colin raised an eyebrow. "Is it now?"

"I challenged Alexander and won. I am lord and Master of this region now. And I want you gone."

"I fear I must decline your generous offer. You must have missed the announcement, but Alexander abdicated his power to me long before you turned his head into an unsightly mash. You have no rights here."

As he said it, a large number of Feral shambled in from the door on the side of the room.

Something to Tom's right clicked, and he glanced at Lindsey as she shoved a needle into her forearm and depressed the plunger.

"What…?" he muttered as she pulled the syringe out and tossed it aside.

Then she closed her eyes, and veins popped out on her temples as she clenched her jaw.

Lars stepped back toward Tom and Lindsey, spreading his arms. "That's too bad, really. I was hoping you'd fight me alone. Especially since you didn't happen to notice who came to watch our little boxing exhibition, did you?"

Lars paused as Colin cocked his head in confusion. Then, after the lord's eyes darted around the room, taking note of the faces surrounding him, they narrowed. "Kallus, call the beast you can bring in here."

Lars laughed darkly. "Nearly everyone here was sworn to Alexander, as was I before you twisted him. And I'm willing to bet my life they don't feel an ounce of loyalty to a weaselly turd like you, no matter what you say Alexander gave you." He turned to the vampires around him. "What do you say, Family? You ready to run this bastard off?"

All but a few of the crowd growled in agreement.

Next to Tom, Lindsey growled as well, a guttural, almost-animal sound he'd never heard her make before. Blood vessels in the whites of her eyes expanded, painting them an unnerving crimson. She flexed her hands and released them several times.

"I'm going to fucking kill him," she snarled. "Pull off his arms, rip his head from his neck, and drink from it. Drink from it!"

She shot forward from their place on the steps, storming toward Colin. She screamed his name, crossing the room in the blink of an eye.

Colin's head swung to face her, and he just got his hands up to deflect her first furious attack.

The room erupted. With clawlike fingers, the vampires

that had lined the walls during the first fight began swinging almost indiscriminately at Feral. More Feral streamed into the room in a steady rush, shuffling at a quick step to engage Lars's Family. A few vampires sided with Colin, attacking their own kind instead of the plaguers.

Lars alternated between cracking the heads of whichever Feral happened to lumber too close to him and taking shots at Colin when the lord's focus was fixed on Lindsey. The latter two moved almost too fast for Tom to track. The waltzing blur of fists and feet butted heads and nearly grappled each other, though neither seemed to land any serious blows or gain much advantage.

Tom frowned and tapped the shotgun with a finger. He hadn't come with Lindsey to what he'd known would be a fight only to hide on the stairs, but what could he do? He didn't have enough ammo for all the Feral, and he couldn't get a clean shot at Colin's head with Lindsey assaulting the vampire, keeping him in constant motion.

Tom wished he'd kept his bat. It might have been more useful.

Lindsey and Lars held their own, going toe-to-toe with Colin, and sooner or later, their numerical advantage would prove too much for the usurping lord. But the same was true for the Feral. They outnumbered Lars's Family heavily and were already gaining the advantage, despite being mostly mindless beasts.

Tom gasped. That was it. That was the key. The mindless beasts weren't actually mindless beasts in the fight. He glared across the room at Kallus, who still stood on the steps. His focus flickered around the room, taking in the details of each smaller engagement between his Feral to adjust their behaviors. His face was tight, strained from the effort.

With a snap of Tom's fingers, Lady padded up from the landing at the turn of the stairs below. He pointed at Kallus. "We're getting that guy. Go piss him off, and I'll meet you at the steps."

The dog woofed softly and sprang forward, dodging combatants as she crossed the room. Tom got to his feet and stepped through the arched opening, then slid to his right, pressing his back against the stone wall. He worked his way around the perimeter, keeping the shotgun pointed slightly upward as he went, in case anyone decided to take an interest in him.

Vampires and plaguers alike, fighting vicious, bloody individual battles just a few feet in front of him, either didn't notice or didn't care about him. He turned the first corner between the back and right-hand-side walls without incident. Every few seconds, he turned his attention to the steps at the front of the room to gauge Lady's work. She danced up and down the steps, nipping at Kallus without letting him get a good swing at her. His face had become a mix of stress and irritation. How long could he keep it up?

Halfway along the side wall, a vampire woman with brown hair and blood dripping from her clawed hands slammed into the stone beside him. She gave him a questioning look then turned her attention back to the plaguer that had tossed her backward. With a growled curse, she leapt away from Tom and back into the action.

Tom reached the second corner and turned ninety degrees to continue along the front wall. He couldn't see up the steps any longer, and Kallus was out of view. Lady hopped up out of sight then bounced back to the floor, twisting around to make another pass. Before she could move, though, a Feral smacked her across the ribs, knocking her sideways. The plaguer took a position between her and the stairs, blocking the dog.

She charged it and jumped up, slamming into its chest. The pale-gray monster lurched backward but somehow stayed on its feet. Lady's jaws clamped down hard on its neck, and a red cloud exploded around her.

The Feral grabbed the sides of her chest and pulled her away, trailing a ribbon of blood and viscera. Howling, the thing tossed her to its right, and she ricocheted off several other fighters before hitting the floor and returning to her feet. She shook herself out, seemingly uninjured.

Tom was done sneaking. He dashed forward with the barrel raised to match the back of the Feral's head. He pulled the trigger just inches away from it. With a deafening boom, the thing's brain became a mess of red and bone.

Without hesitating, Tom spun on his heel and sprinted forward toward Kallus, then mounted the steps, taking them two at a time. The vampire's mouth hung open, and terror shimmered in his eyes. The sheer panic in Kallus's face was more than Tom could have hoped for.

Kallus put his hands out in front of him, a weak effort to keep Tom at bay. For all his gifts with blood zombies, the henchman had apparently forgotten he was several times faster and stronger than the human coming at him.

Reaching him, Tom put the barrel of the gun against Kallus's forehead and drove him backward into the wall where the stairs turned right. He pulled the trigger, and blood and tissue exploded onto his face and chest.

Kallus slumped to the floor.

Howls of pain and confusion erupted behind Tom then became angry roars. Tom turned back to the room to find another plaguer climbing the steps toward him. He swung the gun upward, but the Feral batted it away and slashed at his neck where it met his shoulder. It exploded with pain he barely had time to register before another swing caught him in the temple.

Everything went black.

CHAPTER 43

"**H**E'S COMING AROUND."

The voice was familiar. Tom couldn't put a finger on it, mostly because his head radiated agony, and his shoulder—which Shan had just healed from the attack at Emily's barely a day or so before—wasn't much better. If he wanted to be honest with himself, everything hurt.

A rough, wet tongue painted the side of his face. He blinked a few times, and the world came into focus. He lay on a couch in a mostly dark room with heavy drapes and a single lamp. It, too, seemed familiar. Lady sat on the floor next to him, with her tongue half hanging from her mouth, seeming no worse for wear. Shan and Ana sat in wingback chairs opposite the couch. Lars and Lindsey sat across from each other at a desk on the far side of the room, clothes spotted with blood. They broke off whatever conversation they'd been having and turned to look at Tom.

"You all right, Meat? You took a beating there for a second before I got to you."

Tom tried to sit up, but a bolt of pain from using his left arm for support stopped him. He fell back on the couch with a grunt. His neck and shoulder were covered in a new wrapping. "I'm not dead, I guess."

"He'll be fine," Ana announced.

Even in the dim light, Tom thought she was almost glowing.

"Shan and I will have him as good as new in a day or two."

Beside her, Shan poured water from a kettle into a teacup and brought it to him. She set it on a side table and offered a hand. "Let's sit you up."

He gave her his right hand, and she pulled him upright on the antique couch beneath him. The burgundy color with paisley embroidered swirls was something he imagined his grandmother might have owned. Emily probably would have loved it.

A pang of regret-filled sadness washed over him. He had no real idea how much time and life she'd seen in her days, and she was gone because of him.

Shan offered him the cup, bringing his attention back to the room. "Drink this. It won't fix all the head pounding, but it'll take the edge off. And it's not the grossest thing I can make."

He took the tea and sipped. It was bitter but also piney with a touch of sweetness. "It's not awful." He smirked.

"You know, T, when I said I was coming along to put you back together, that was supposed to be a joke. Can you try not to get the shit kicked out of you all the time?"

He chuckled. "I'll do my best."

Lars's laughter boomed through the room. "Good luck with that, girl. Meat there seems to find trouble just about as often as he finds a sassy woman."

Tom was glad to hear Lars actually laugh. "Yeah, yeah. Laugh it up. Somebody had to save your new Family's asses. Team Feral was putting big points on the board."

"I guess I can't argue with that. You did do us a favor by turning that asshole's head to pulp."

"Yup, you sure did, Tommy boy." Lindsey's words seemed flatter than usual.

If he didn't know better, he would have guessed she had a hangover.

"But unfortunately, it let Colin get away."

Tom scowled. "Shit. How?"

"As soon as Kallus died, the Feral went nuttier than my grandmomma's pralines. They started attacking anything and everything that moved, including me, Lars, Colin, and even each other. Not that they were much of a threat, especially with Colin and me juiced on Drake's stuff, but you can't just ignore a roomful of frenzied plaguers. While Lars was getting you up here and I was fending off the animals, Colin somehow slipped out in the chaos."

The "up here" remark struck a chord in Tom's memory. "This is Alexander's office, isn't it?"

Lars nodded. "I wasn't sure if you'd remember. I guess it's mine now, if I want to keep it. But in the short term, it seemed like a good place to get you safe and stitched up."

"Thanks. And, Linds, I'm sorry I wasted your chance with that Hulk serum to get Colin back."

She gave him a mischievous smile. "Oh, don't worry your pretty head about that. I didn't waste anything. I'll have another chance at him."

Tom cocked his head then immediately regretted

it when pain sang through his shoulder. "What do you mean?"

Before Lindsey could reply, Ana cut in. "Drake's formula is not a one-time, short-term enhancement. From what they told me, Colin could fend off Lindsey because his own juice, as they're all calling it, kicked back in and allowed him to fight her like he had Emily."

Tom looked back at Lindsey. "So, you're a super vampire now?"

She shook her head. "I wouldn't say that, hon. In fact, right now I feel mostly like roadkill."

"Okay, so, what now?" Shan settled back into her chair beside Ana. "I would like to not hang out with vampires. No offense, but sitting here, knowing they're all over the place downstairs is giving me the creeps. I hold you all responsible for a lot of bad shit in my life."

"As do I," Ana added softly.

Lars started to speak, but Lindsey waved him off. "I reckon we can all agree that Tom living with us at the Chalet didn't really end well. I need to get back to Atlanta and rally the troops. I guess Lars will have to focus on putting Alexander's Family back together and ferreting that weasel Colin out of whatever hole he crawled into. We won't have time to babysit. Especially now that there's three of you."

Lars nodded. "Just what I was going to say. I don't want to be a bad host, but you'll have to fend for yourselves out there."

Tom started to reply, but Ana and Shan both beat him to it.

"Not a problem, buddy." Shan crossed her arms for effect.

"We've already made some plans." Ana's eyes fixed on Tom. "I assumed we'd stick together?"

Tom sipped the tea and considered. He and Ana had been through a lot in less than a year, not all of it pleasant. Hell, most of it hadn't been pleasant. They'd certainly butted heads several times and had experienced plenty of rough patches and hard feelings. But seeing the slight flush in her cheeks and her air of genuine happiness made him want to smile. As long as he'd known her, all she'd really wanted was to be free of Colin, and she'd found a way to make that happen. With her free of his influence, did Tom even really know her? He wanted to believe Ana might reveal more of her true human self in the future. And if that happened, he didn't want to miss it.

"Of course, we will." He gestured to Lars and Lindsey at Lars's desk. "They have their Families. And now we have one too. You're both stuck with me for good."

Shan and Ana smiled at him with bright twinkles in their eyes.

He wondered how many more they might add to their newly found family but didn't dare ask the question out loud. They would have that discussion when they were safe, somewhere far from anyone with fangs.

For the moment, though, they were alive and together, and for the first time, Tom knew where he belonged.

Thank you for reading *Fury*! Please consider leaving a star rating or review with your honest impression on Amazon, Goodreads, or whatever platform you prefer. Your feedback is always incredibly valuable.

Check out JR's blog and other work at jrandrewsbooks.com.

ABOUT THE AUTHOR

JR Andrews is the pen name for real life human Jason A. Rust. Born in Indianapolis, he has lived all but the first six months of life in Northern Kentucky, just across the Ohio River from Cincinnati, Ohio. JR has a wonderful and very tolerant wife, four very individual kids, two very lazy dogs, and a very active imagination. An avid reader and lifelong lover of Fantasy and Science Fiction, as JR Andrews he writes stories set in a world where the proverbial *&#% has already hit the fan or is just about to do so.

You can find him on Twitter: @AuthorJRAndrews
Facebook: AuthorJRAndrews
Instagram: AuthorJRAndrews